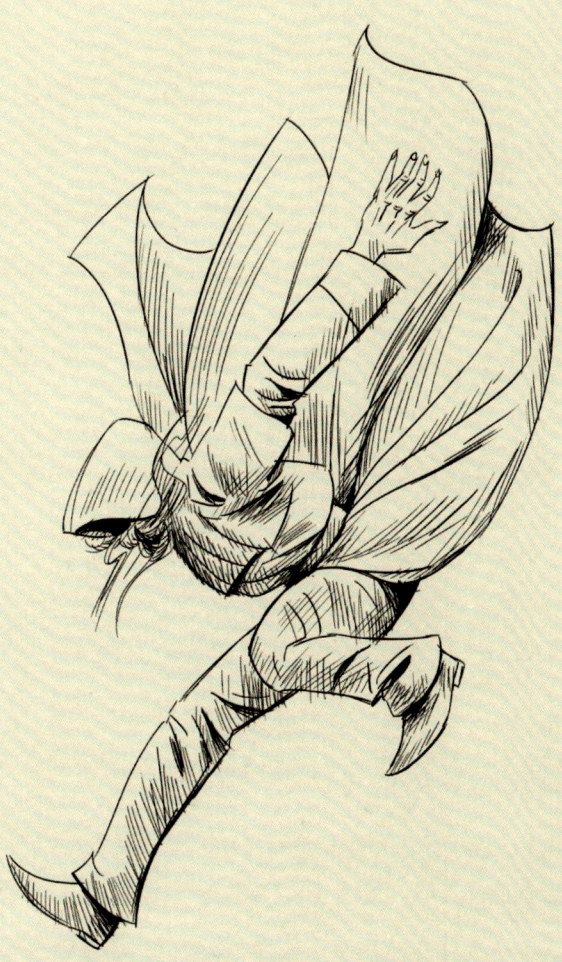

chapter Five

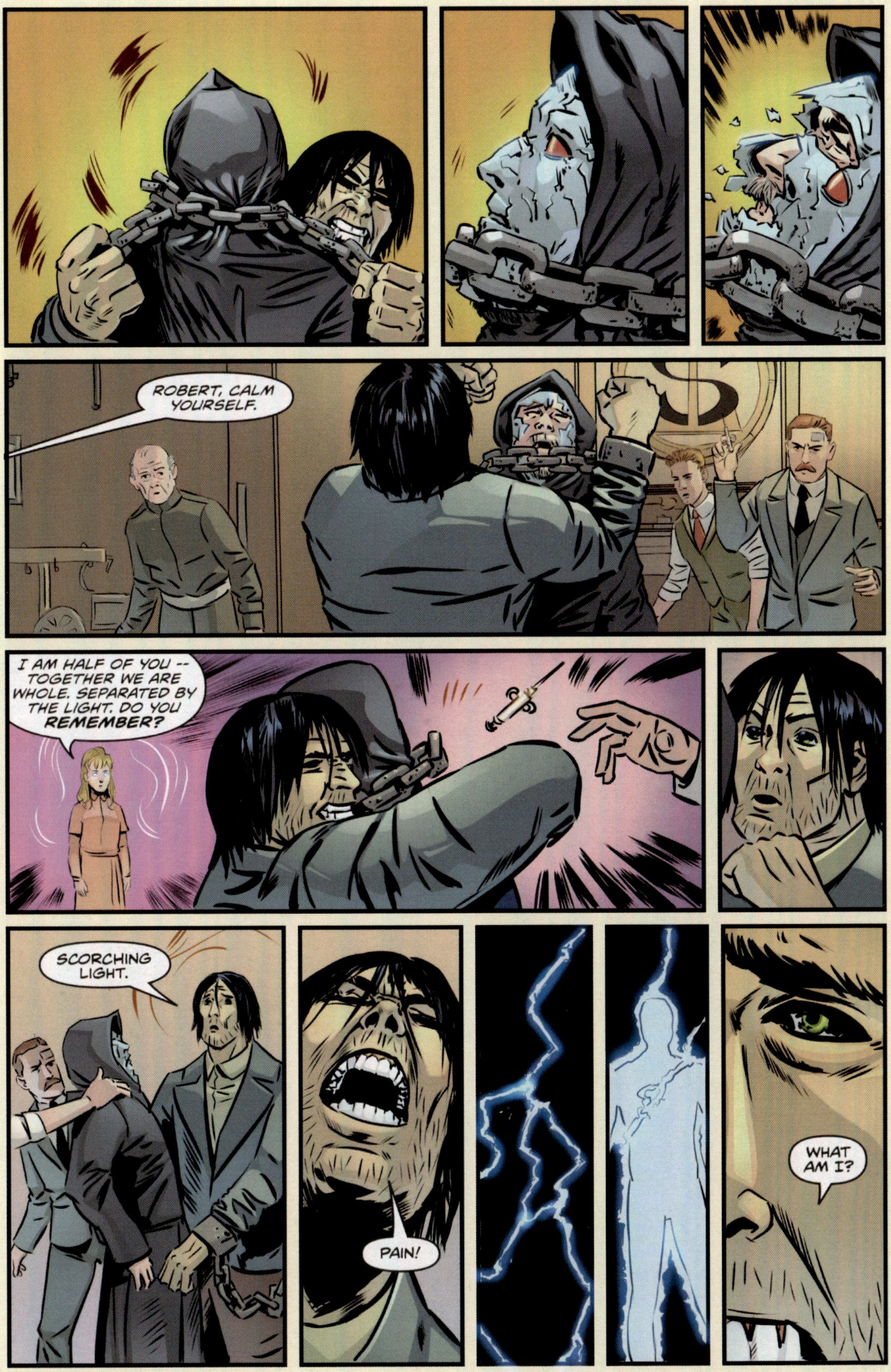
ROBERT, CALM YOURSELF.
I AM HALF OF YOU -- TOGETHER WE ARE WHOLE. SEPARATED BY THE LIGHT. DO YOU **REMEMBER?**
SCORCHING LIGHT.
PAIN!
WHAT AM I?

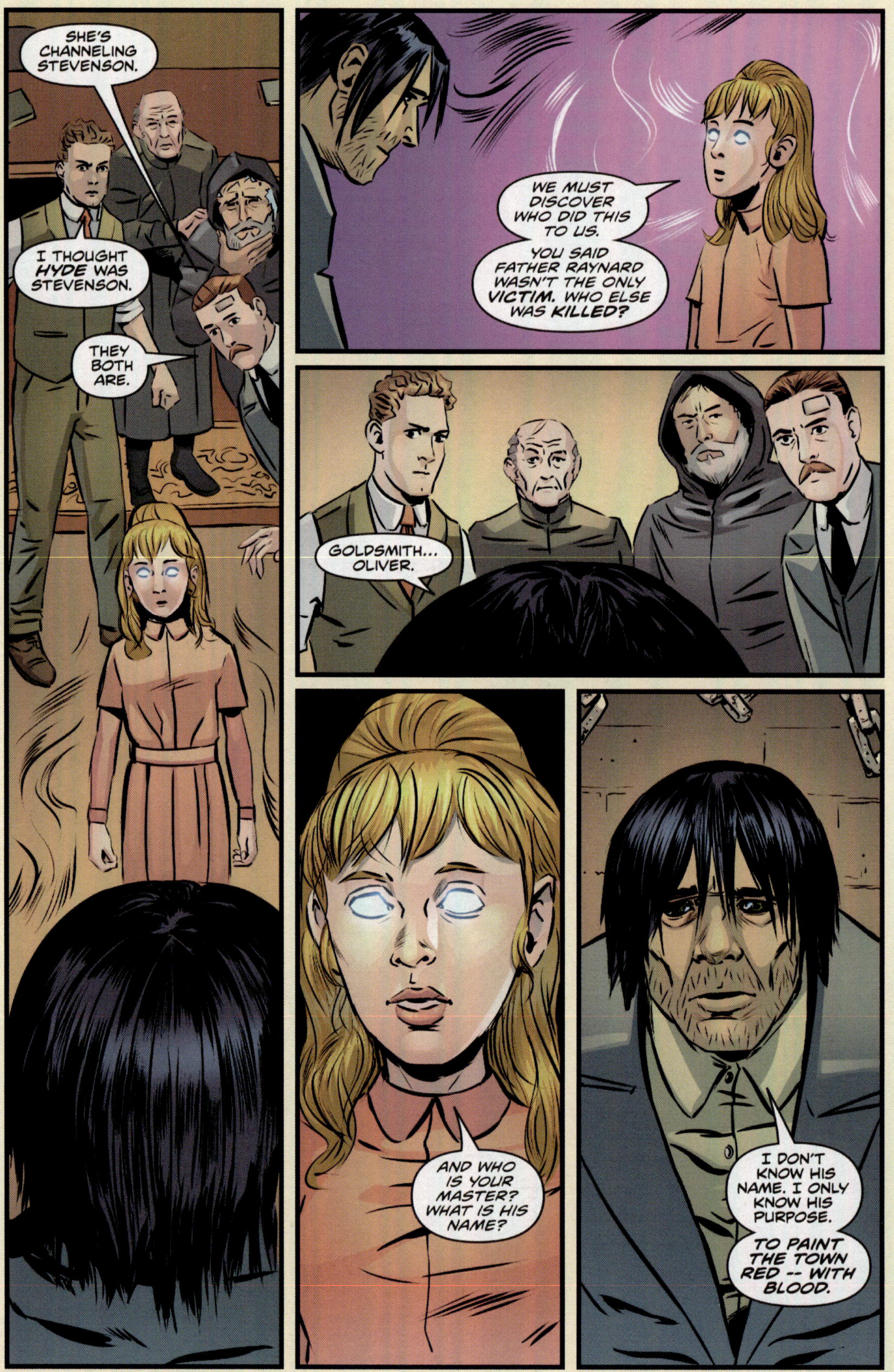
SHE'S CHANNELING STEVENSON.
I THOUGHT HYDE WAS STEVENSON.
THEY BOTH ARE.
WE MUST DISCOVER WHO DID THIS TO US.
YOU SAID FATHER RAYNARD WASN'T THE ONLY VICTIM. WHO ELSE WAS KILLED?
GOLDSMITH... OLIVER.
AND WHO IS YOUR MASTER? WHAT IS HIS NAME?
I DON'T KNOW HIS NAME. I ONLY KNOW HIS PURPOSE.
TO PAINT THE TOWN RED -- WITH BLOOD.

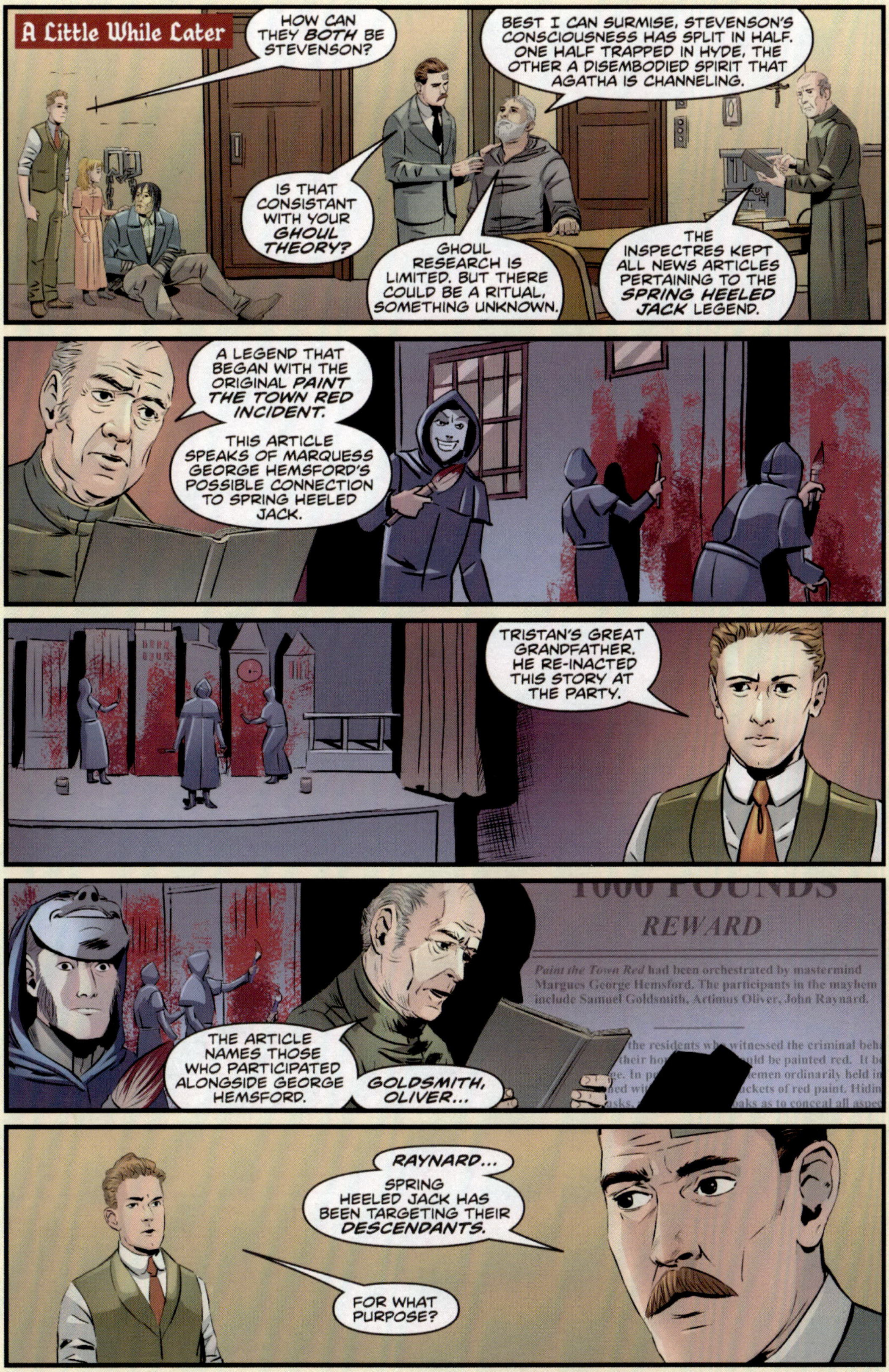

A Little While Later
HOW CAN THEY BOTH BE STEVENSON?
BEST I CAN SURMISE, STEVENSON'S CONSCIOUSNESS HAS SPLIT IN HALF. ONE HALF TRAPPED IN HYDE, THE OTHER A DISEMBODIED SPIRIT THAT AGATHA IS CHANNELING.
IS THAT CONSISTANT WITH YOUR GHOUL THEORY?
GHOUL RESEARCH IS LIMITED. BUT THERE COULD BE A RITUAL, SOMETHING UNKNOWN.
THE INSPECTRES KEPT ALL NEWS ARTICLES PERTAINING TO THE SPRING HEELED JACK LEGEND.
A LEGEND THAT BEGAN WITH THE ORIGINAL PAINT THE TOWN RED INCIDENT.
THIS ARTICLE SPEAKS OF MARQUESS GEORGE HEMSFORD'S POSSIBLE CONNECTION TO SPRING HEELED JACK.
TRISTAN'S GREAT GRANDFATHER. HE RE-INACTED THIS STORY AT THE PARTY.
REWARD
Paint the Town Red had been orchestrated by mastermind Marques George Hemsford. The participants in the mayhem include Samuel Goldsmith, Artimus Oliver, John Raynard.
THE ARTICLE NAMES THOSE WHO PARTICIPATED ALONGSIDE GEORGE HEMSFORD.
GOLDSMITH, OLIVER...
RAYNARD...
SPRING HEELED JACK HAS BEEN TARGETING THEIR DESCENDANTS.
FOR WHAT PURPOSE?

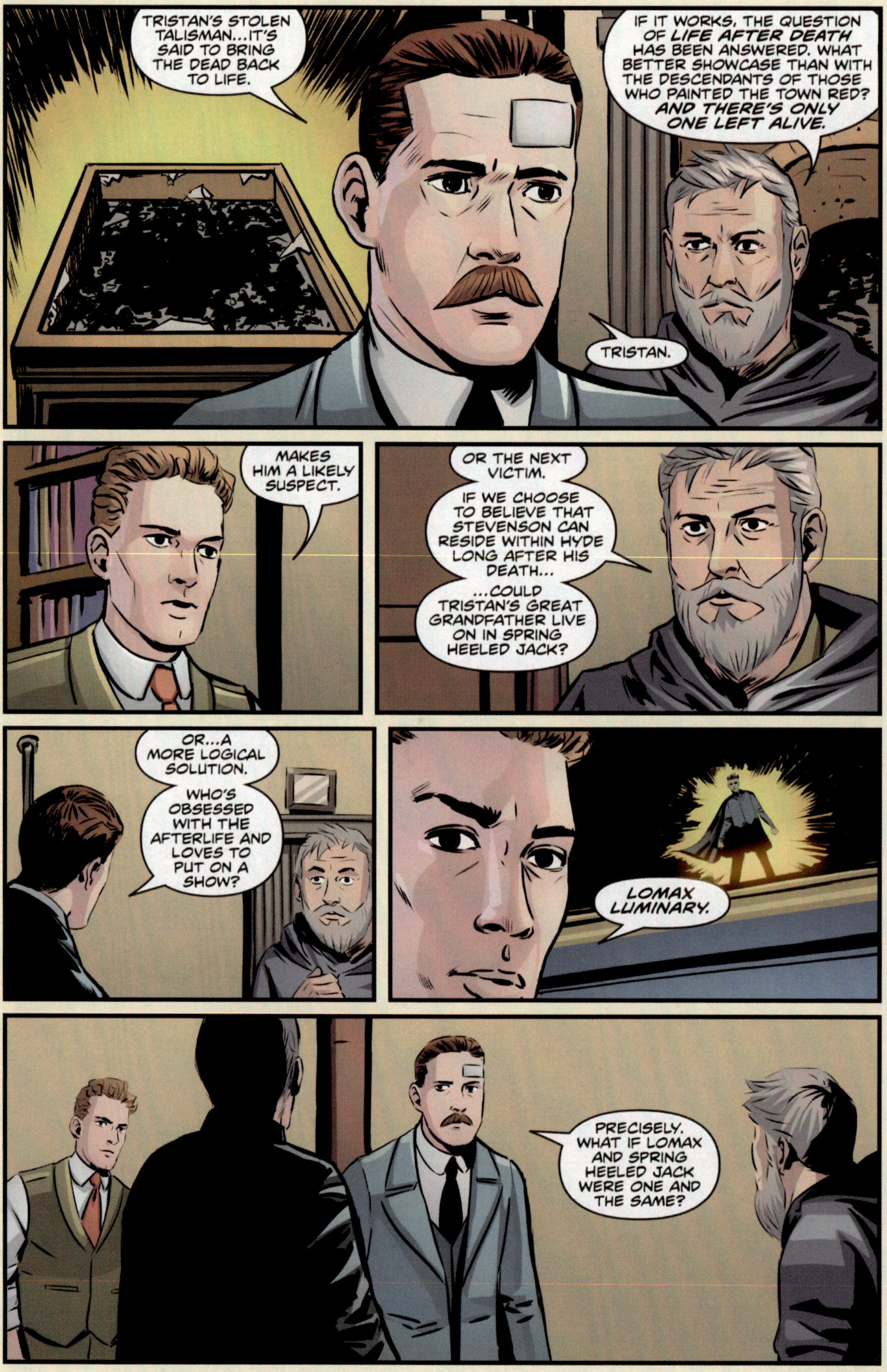
TRISTAN'S STOLEN TALISMAN...IT'S SAID TO BRING THE DEAD BACK TO LIFE.
IF IT WORKS, THE QUESTION OF *LIFE AFTER DEATH* HAS BEEN ANSWERED. WHAT BETTER SHOWCASE THAN WITH THE DESCENDANTS OF THOSE WHO PAINTED THE TOWN RED? ***AND THERE'S ONLY ONE LEFT ALIVE.***
TRISTAN.
MAKES HIM A LIKELY SUSPECT.
OR THE NEXT VICTIM.
IF WE CHOOSE TO BELIEVE THAT STEVENSON CAN RESIDE WITHIN HYDE LONG AFTER HIS DEATH...
...COULD TRISTAN'S GREAT GRANDFATHER LIVE ON IN SPRING HEELED JACK?
OR...A MORE LOGICAL SOLUTION.
WHO'S OBSESSED WITH THE AFTERLIFE AND LOVES TO PUT ON A SHOW?
LOMAX LUMINARY.
PRECISELY. WHAT IF LOMAX AND SPRING HEELED JACK WERE ONE AND THE SAME?

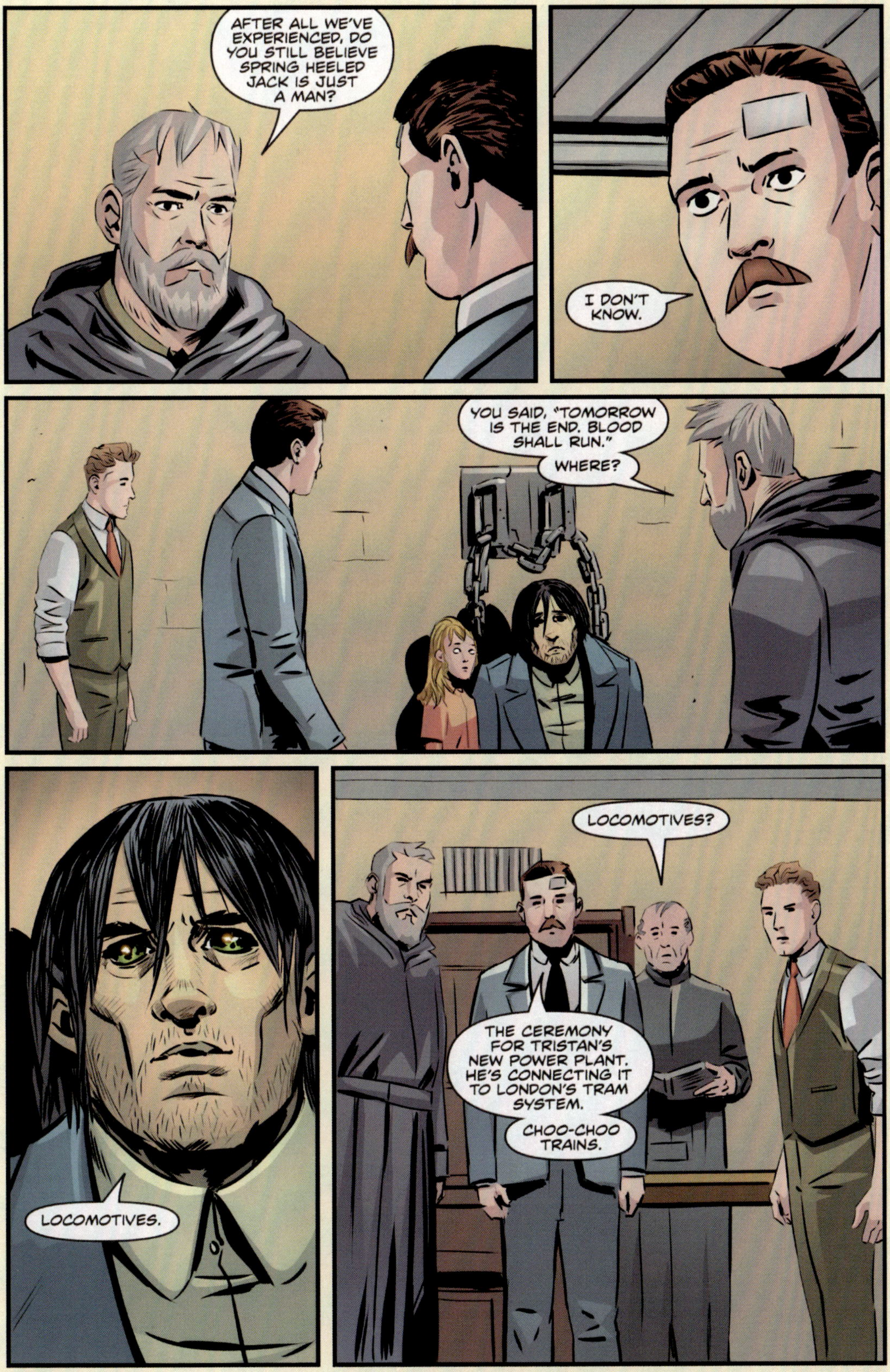
AFTER ALL WE'VE EXPERIENCED, DO YOU STILL BELIEVE SPRING HEELED JACK IS JUST A MAN?
I DON'T KNOW.
YOU SAID, "TOMORROW IS THE END. BLOOD SHALL RUN."
WHERE?
LOCOMOTIVES.
LOCOMOTIVES?
THE CEREMONY FOR TRISTAN'S NEW POWER PLANT. HE'S CONNECTING IT TO LONDON'S TRAM SYSTEM.
CHOO-CHOO TRAINS.

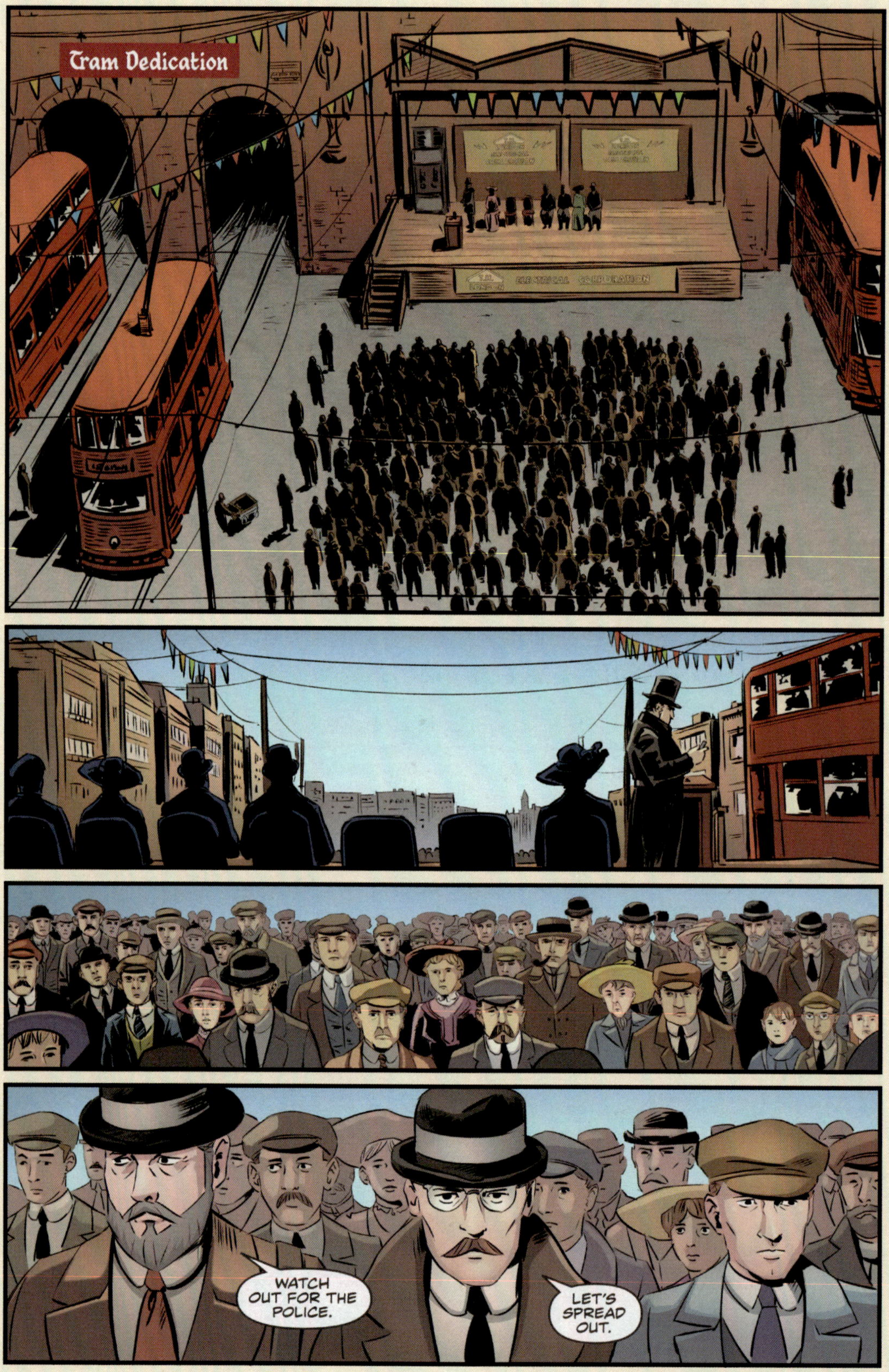
Tram Dedication
WATCH OUT FOR THE POLICE.
LET'S SPREAD OUT.

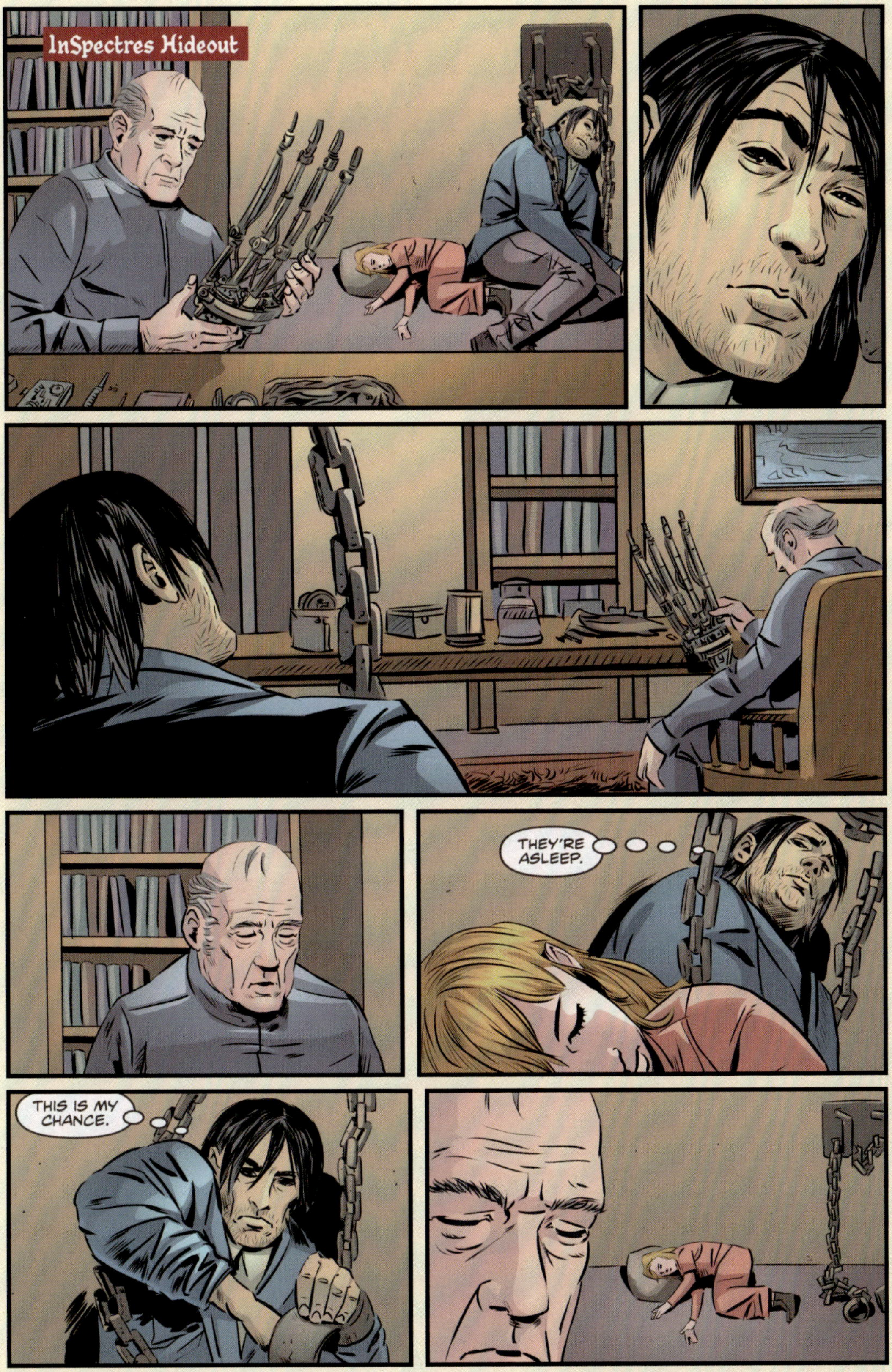
InSpectres Hideout
THEY'RE ASLEEP.
THIS IS MY CHANCE.

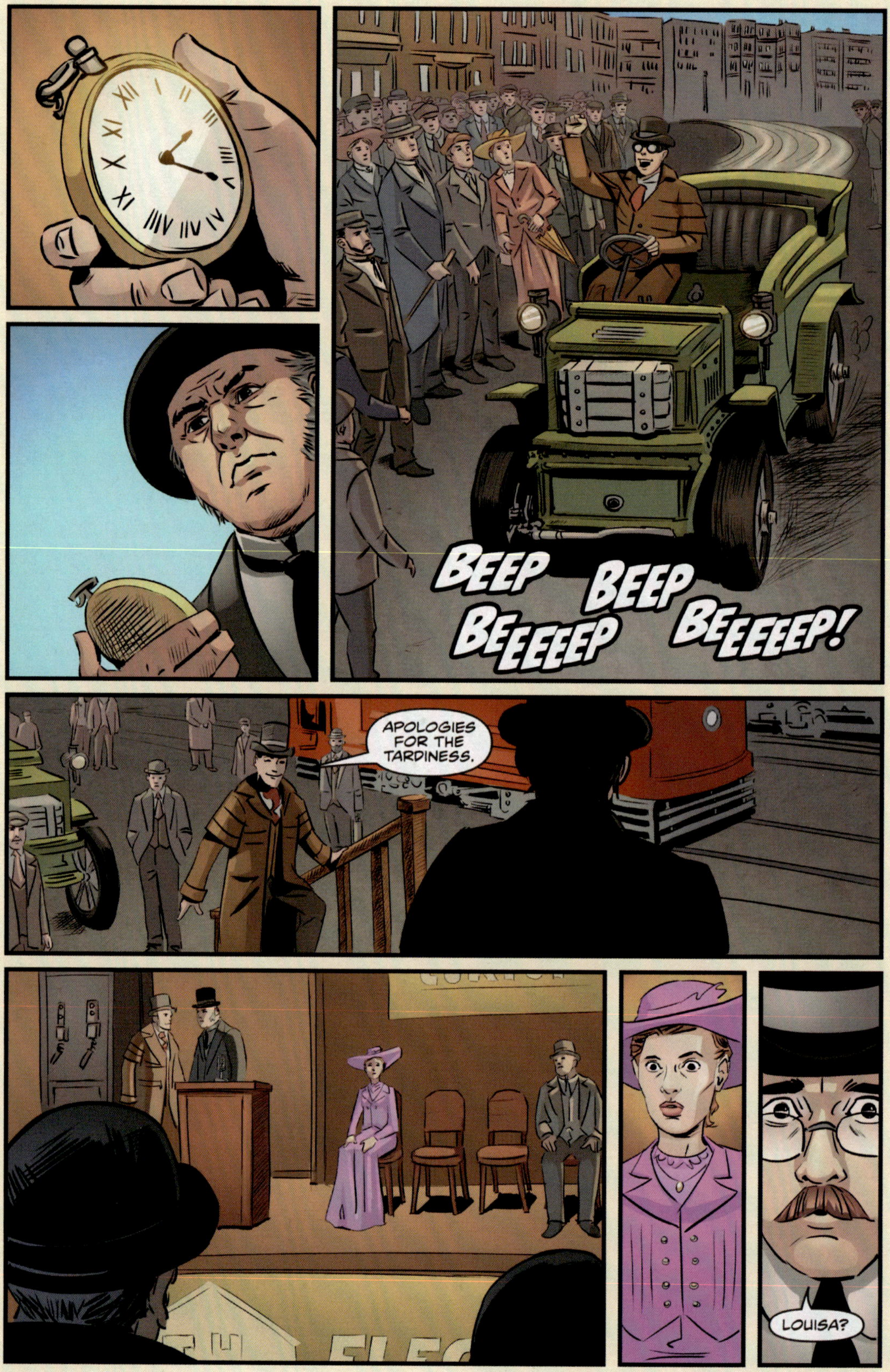
BEEP BEEEEEP BEEP BEEEEEP!
APOLOGIES FOR THE TARDINESS.
LOUISA?

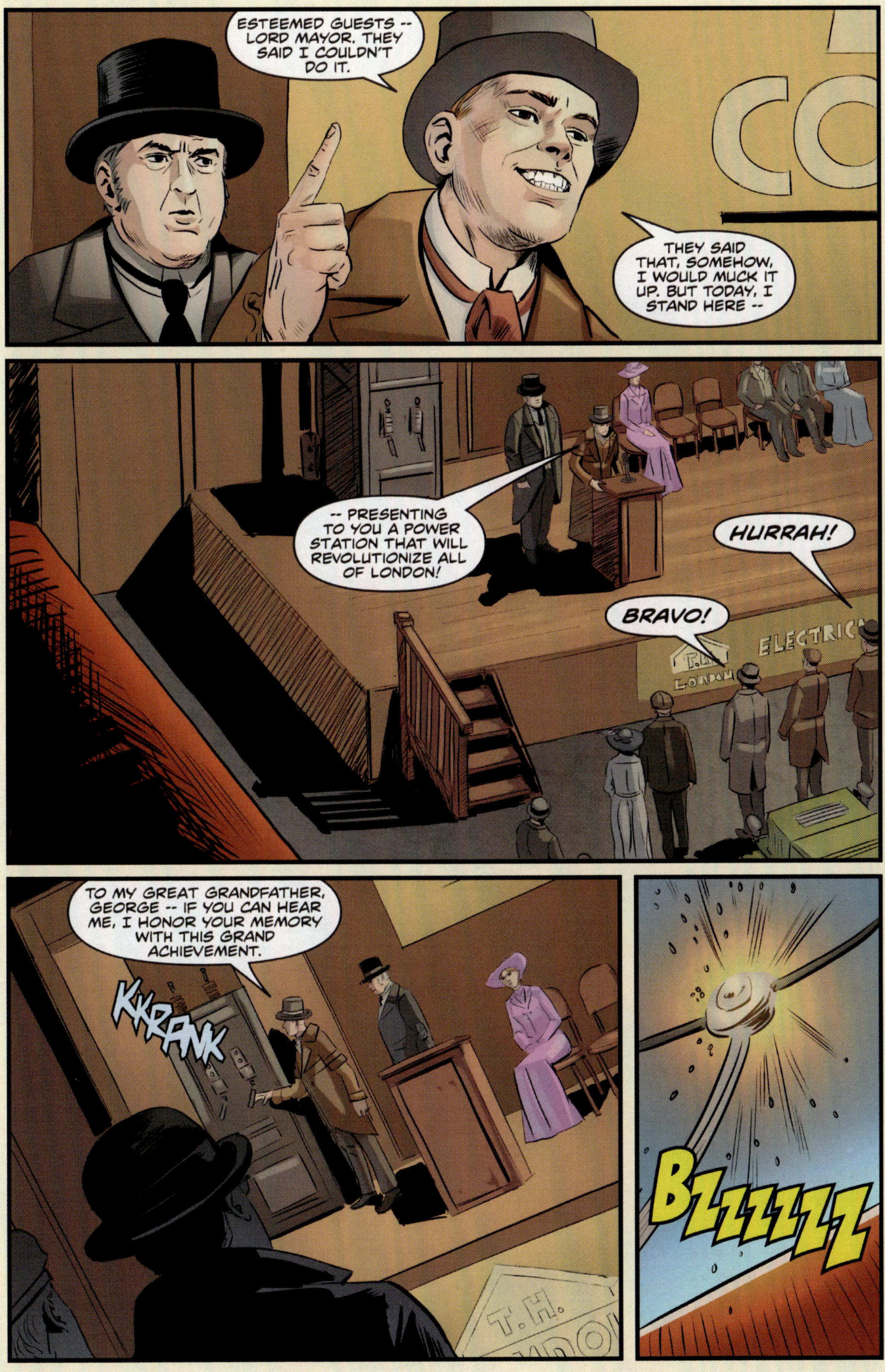
ESTEEMED GUESTS -- LORD MAYOR. THEY SAID I COULDN'T DO IT.
CO
THEY SAID THAT, SOMEHOW, I WOULD MUCK IT UP. BUT TODAY, I STAND HERE --
-- PRESENTING TO YOU A POWER STATION THAT WILL REVOLUTIONIZE ALL OF LONDON!
HURRAH!
BRAVO!
T.H. LONDON
ELECTRIC
TO MY GREAT GRANDFATHER, GEORGE -- IF YOU CAN HEAR ME, I HONOR YOUR MEMORY WITH THIS GRAND ACHIEVEMENT.
KKRANK
T.H.
BZZZZZZ

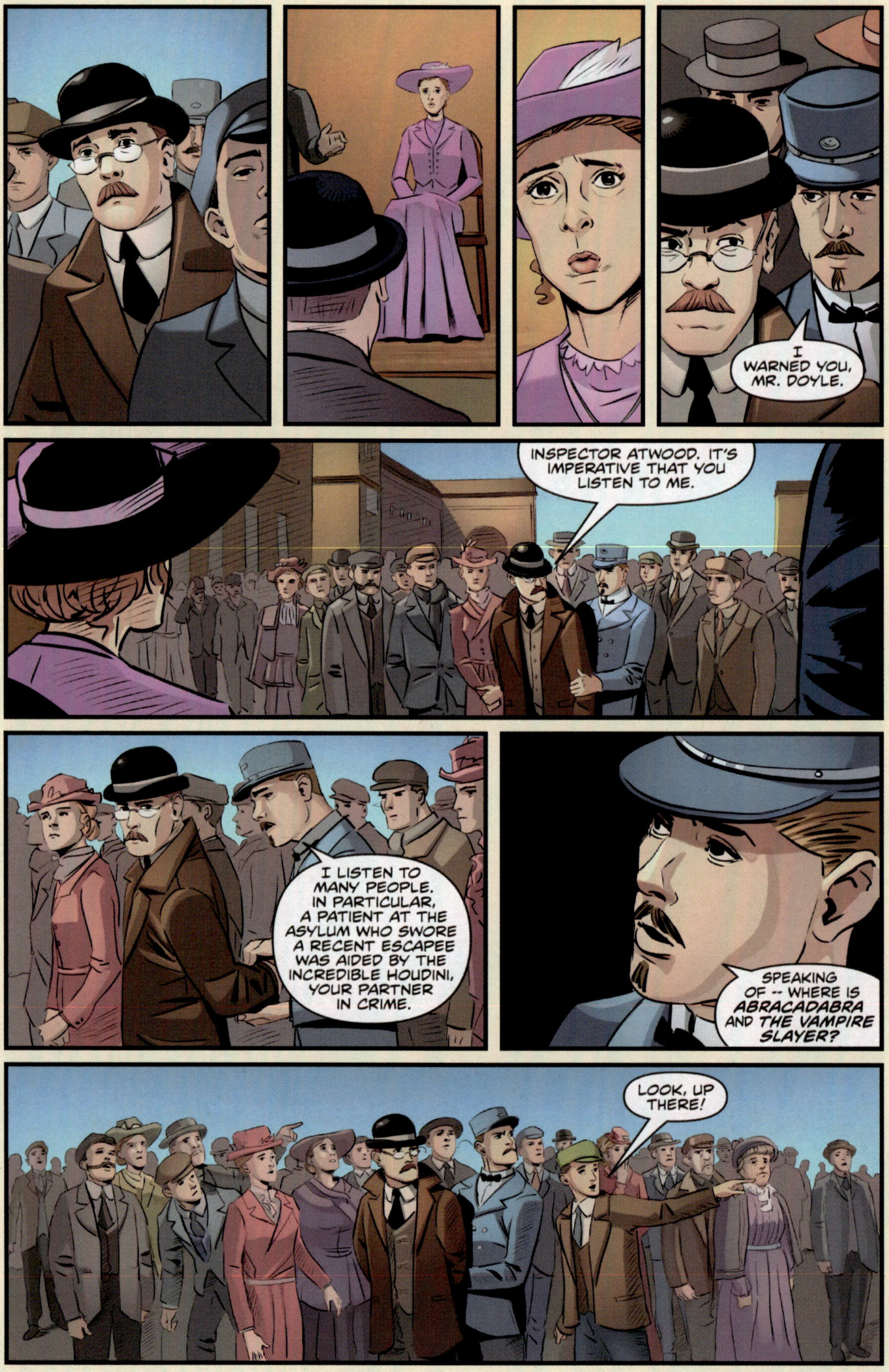
I WARNED YOU, MR. DOYLE.
INSPECTOR ATWOOD. IT'S IMPERATIVE THAT YOU LISTEN TO ME.
I LISTEN TO MANY PEOPLE. IN PARTICULAR, A PATIENT AT THE ASYLUM WHO SWORE A RECENT ESCAPEE WAS AIDED BY THE INCREDIBLE HOUDINI, YOUR PARTNER IN CRIME.
SPEAKING OF -- WHERE IS *ABRACADABRA* AND *THE VAMPIRE SLAYER?*
LOOK, UP THERE!

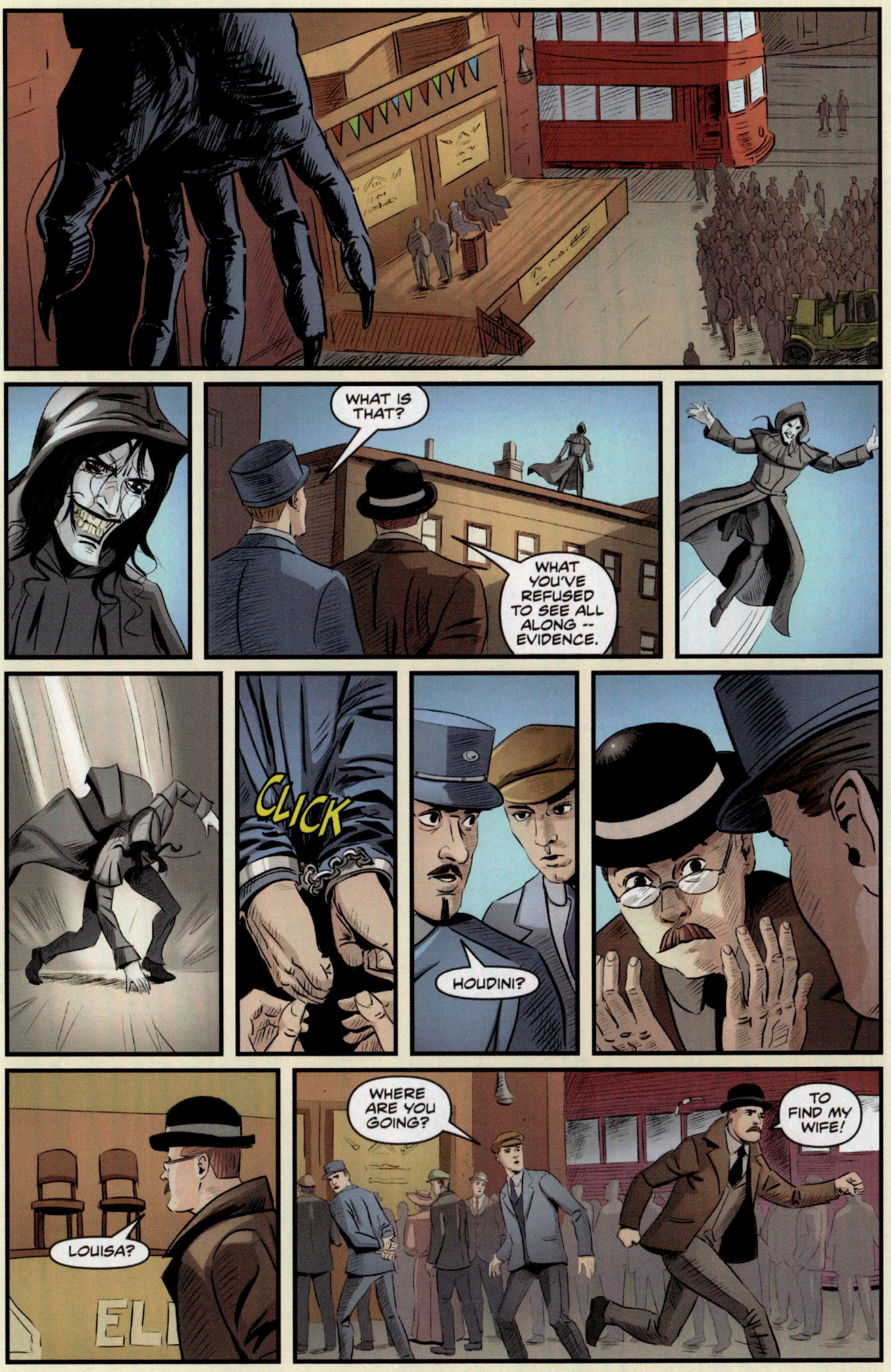
WHAT IS THAT?
WHAT YOU'VE REFUSED TO SEE ALL ALONG -- EVIDENCE.
CLICK
HOUDINI?
LOUISA?
WHERE ARE YOU GOING?
TO FIND MY WIFE!

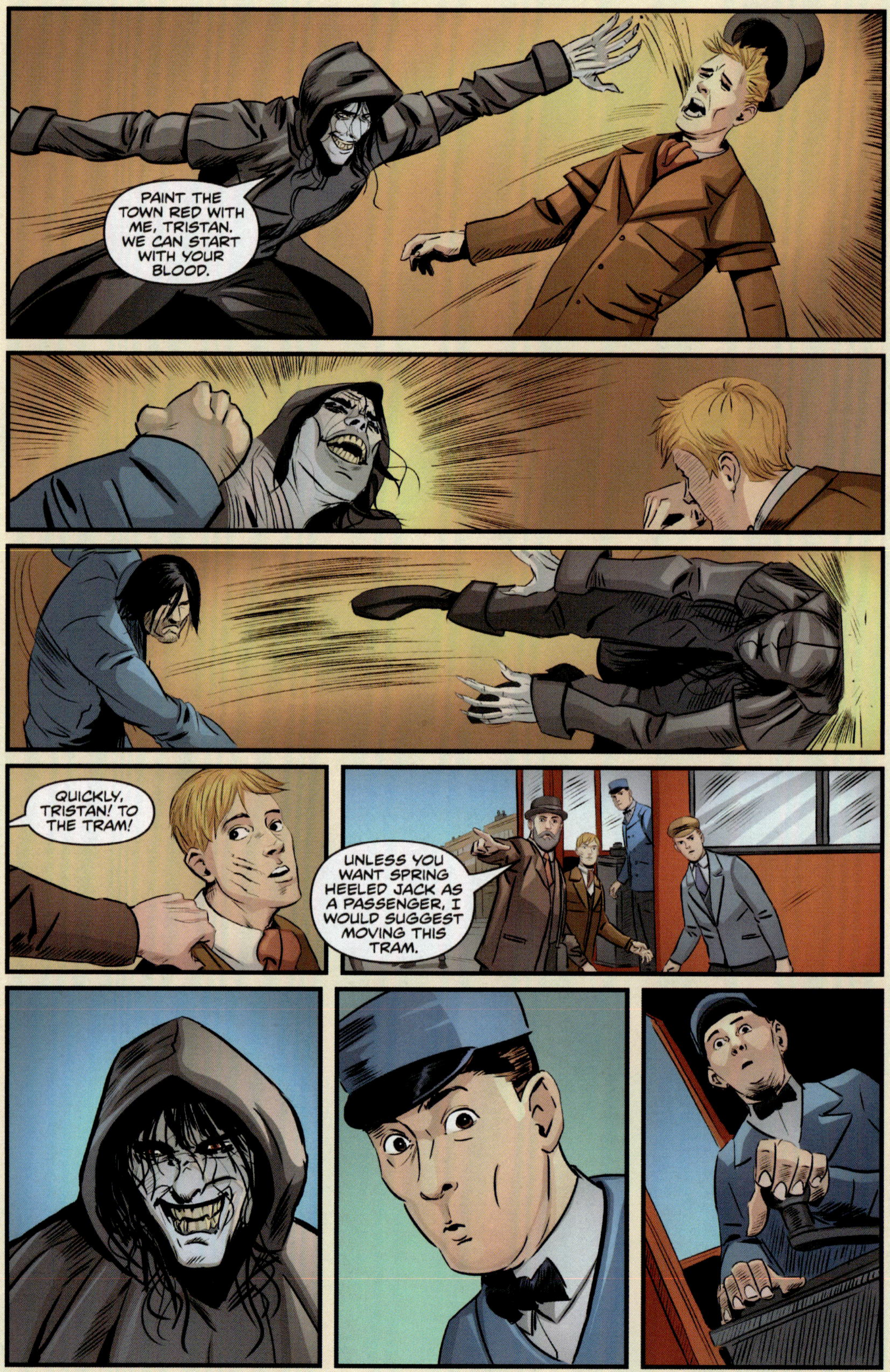
PAINT THE TOWN RED WITH ME, TRISTAN. WE CAN START WITH YOUR BLOOD.
QUICKLY, TRISTAN! TO THE TRAM!
UNLESS YOU WANT SPRING HEELED JACK AS A PASSENGER, I WOULD SUGGEST MOVING THIS TRAM.

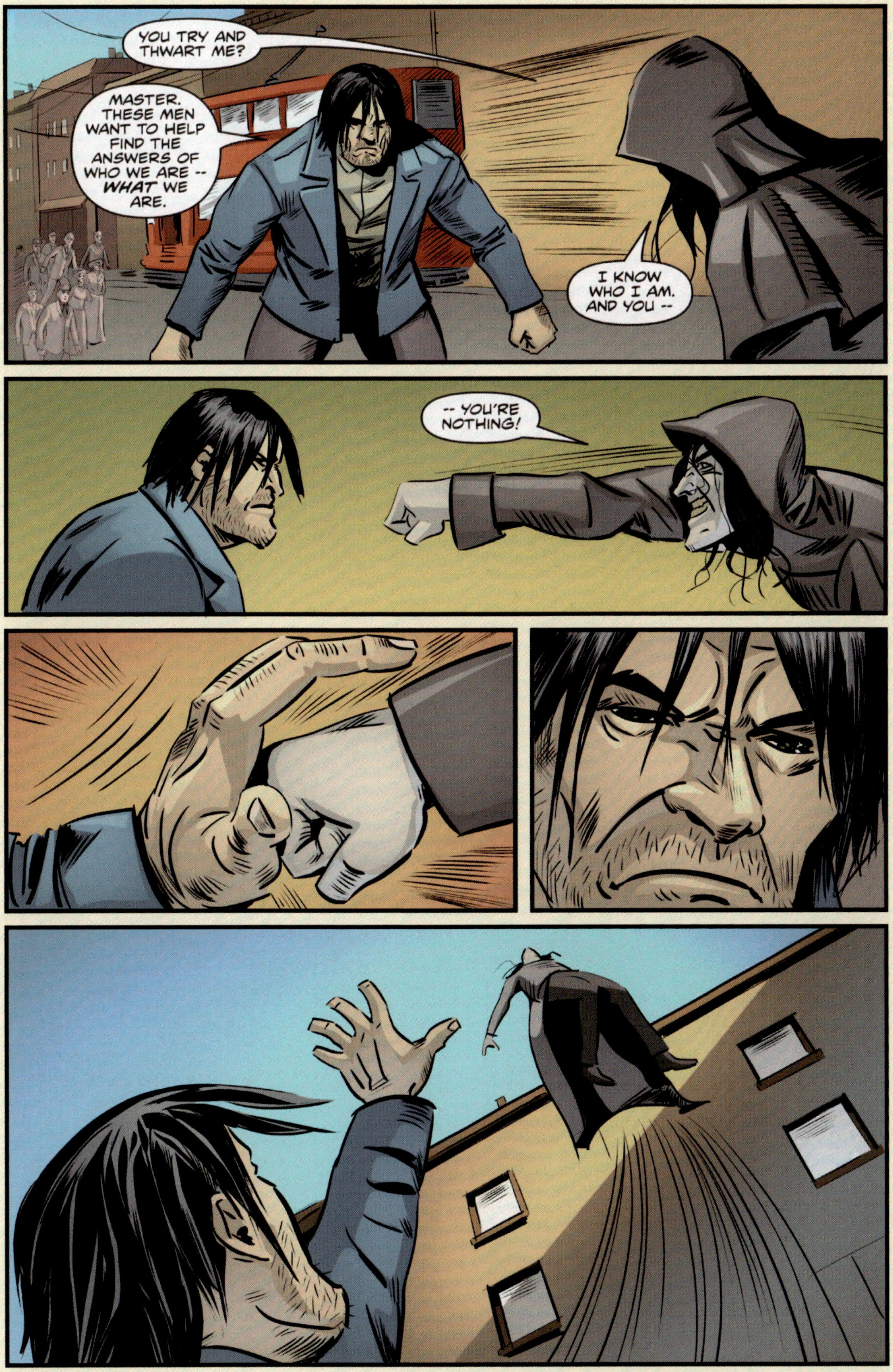
YOU TRY AND THWART ME?
MASTER. THESE MEN WANT TO HELP FIND THE ANSWERS OF WHO WE ARE -- *WHAT* WE ARE.
I KNOW WHO I AM. AND YOU --
-- YOU'RE NOTHING!

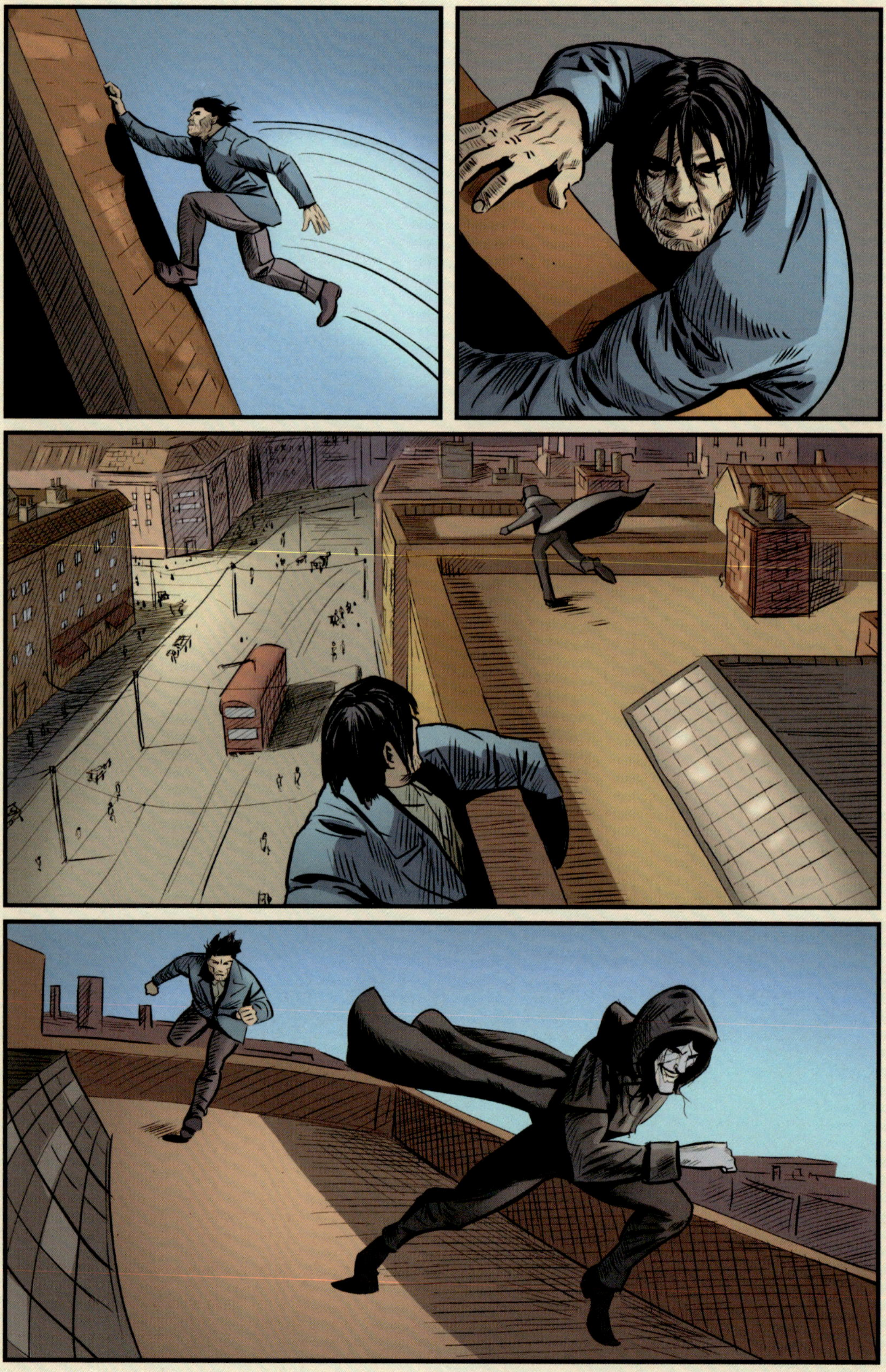

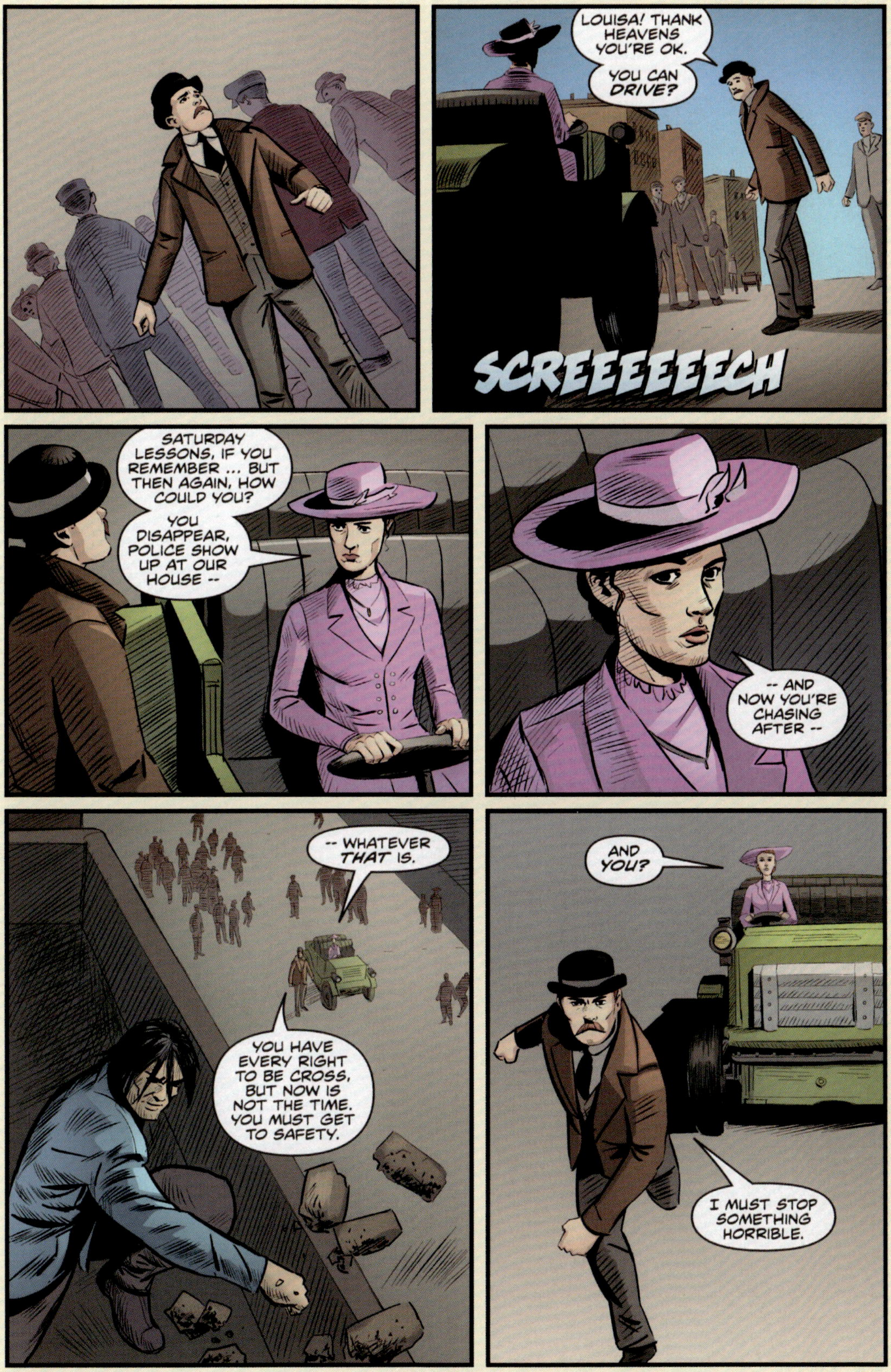
LOUISA! THANK HEAVENS YOU'RE OK.
YOU CAN *DRIVE?*
SCREEEEEECH
SATURDAY LESSONS, IF YOU REMEMBER ... BUT THEN AGAIN, HOW COULD YOU?
YOU DISAPPEAR, POLICE SHOW UP AT OUR HOUSE --
-- AND NOW YOU'RE CHASING AFTER --
-- WHATEVER *THAT* IS.
YOU HAVE EVERY RIGHT TO BE CROSS, BUT NOW IS NOT THE TIME. YOU MUST GET TO SAFETY.
AND *YOU?*
I MUST STOP SOMETHING HORRIBLE.

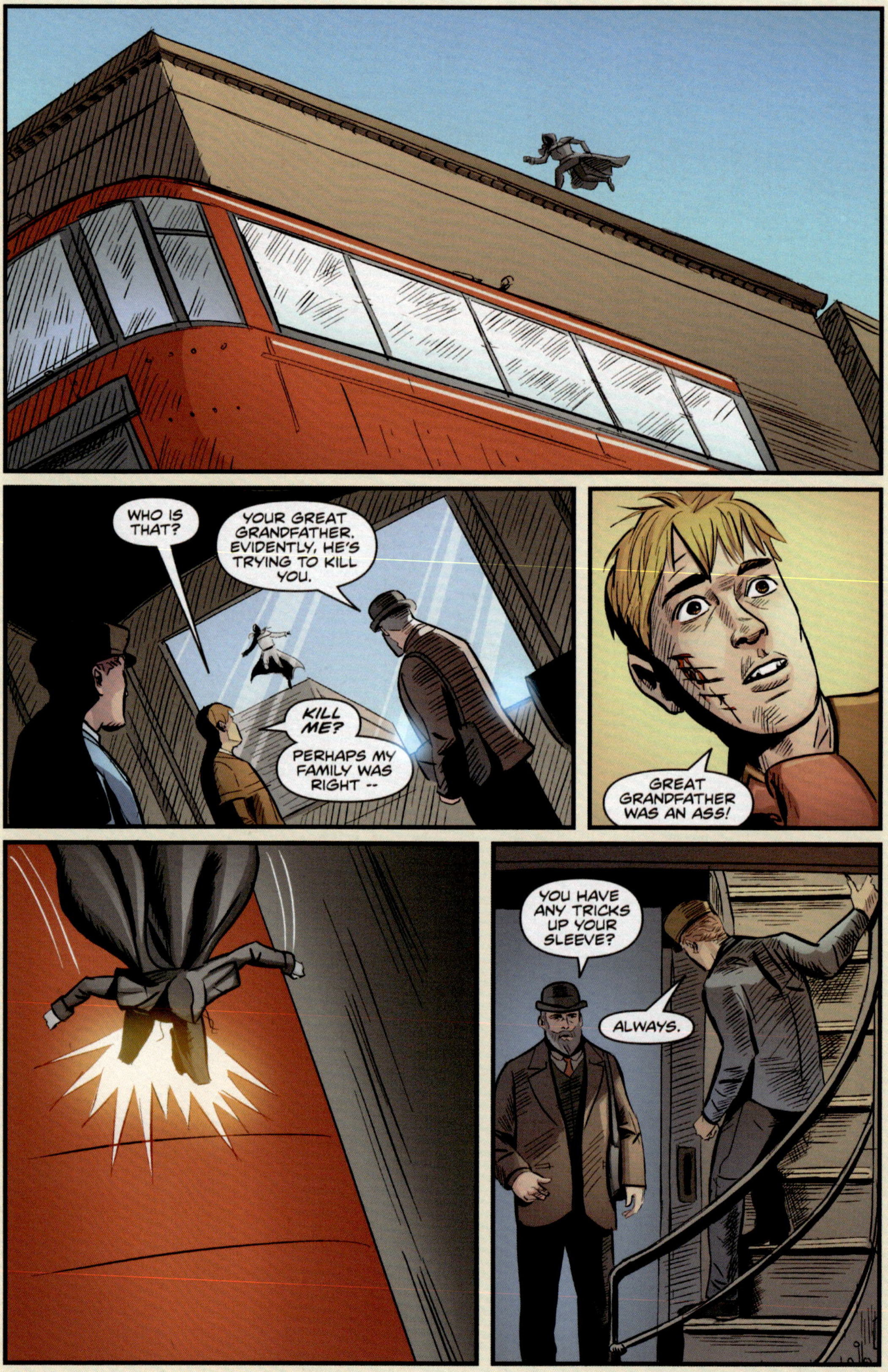
WHO IS THAT?
YOUR GREAT GRANDFATHER. EVIDENTLY, HE'S TRYING TO KILL YOU.
KILL ME?
PERHAPS MY FAMILY WAS RIGHT --
GREAT GRANDFATHER WAS AN ASS!
YOU HAVE ANY TRICKS UP YOUR SLEEVE?
ALWAYS.

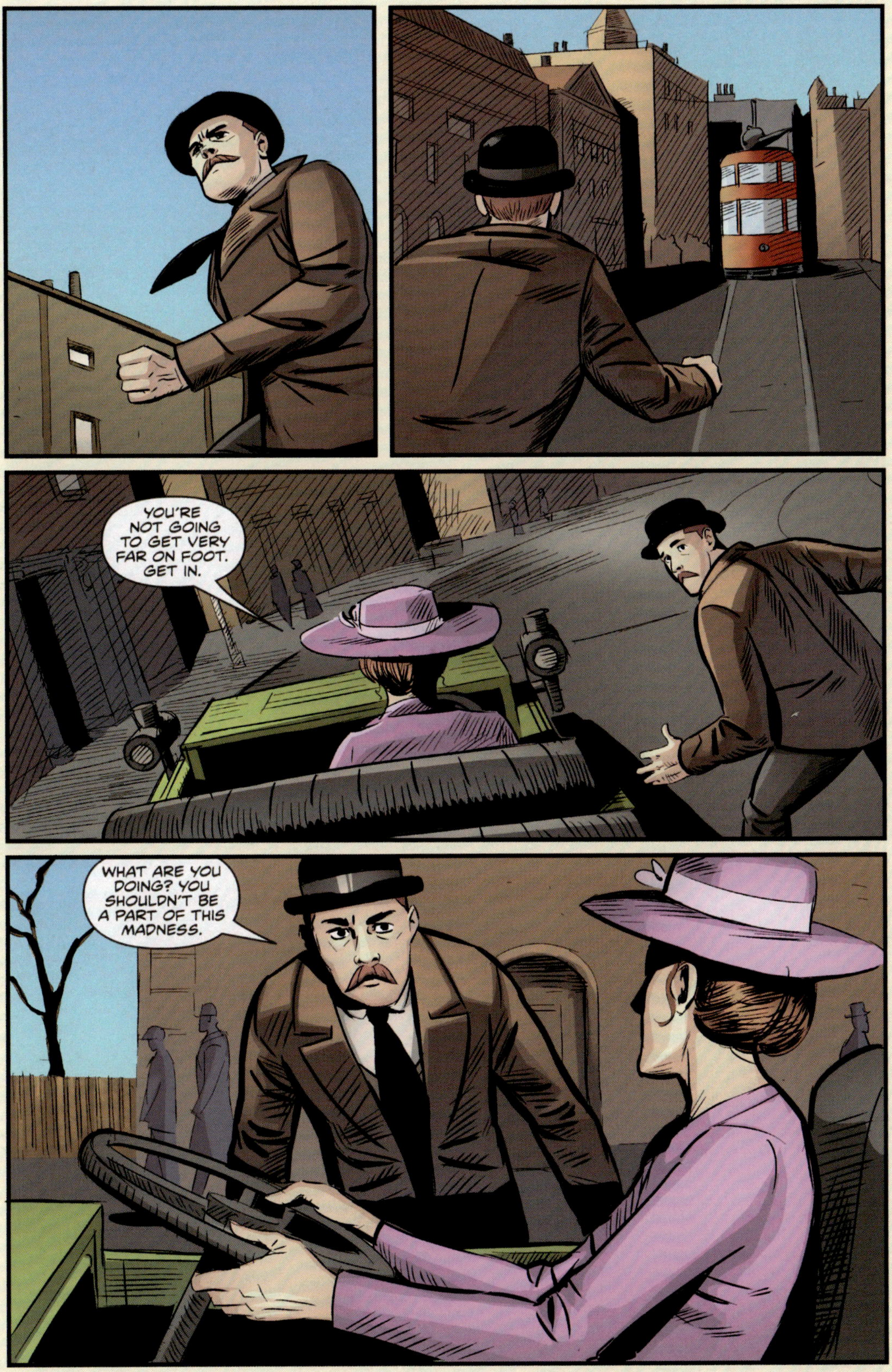

YOU'RE NOT GOING TO GET VERY FAR ON FOOT. GET IN.
WHAT ARE YOU DOING? YOU SHOULDN'T BE A PART OF THIS MADNESS.

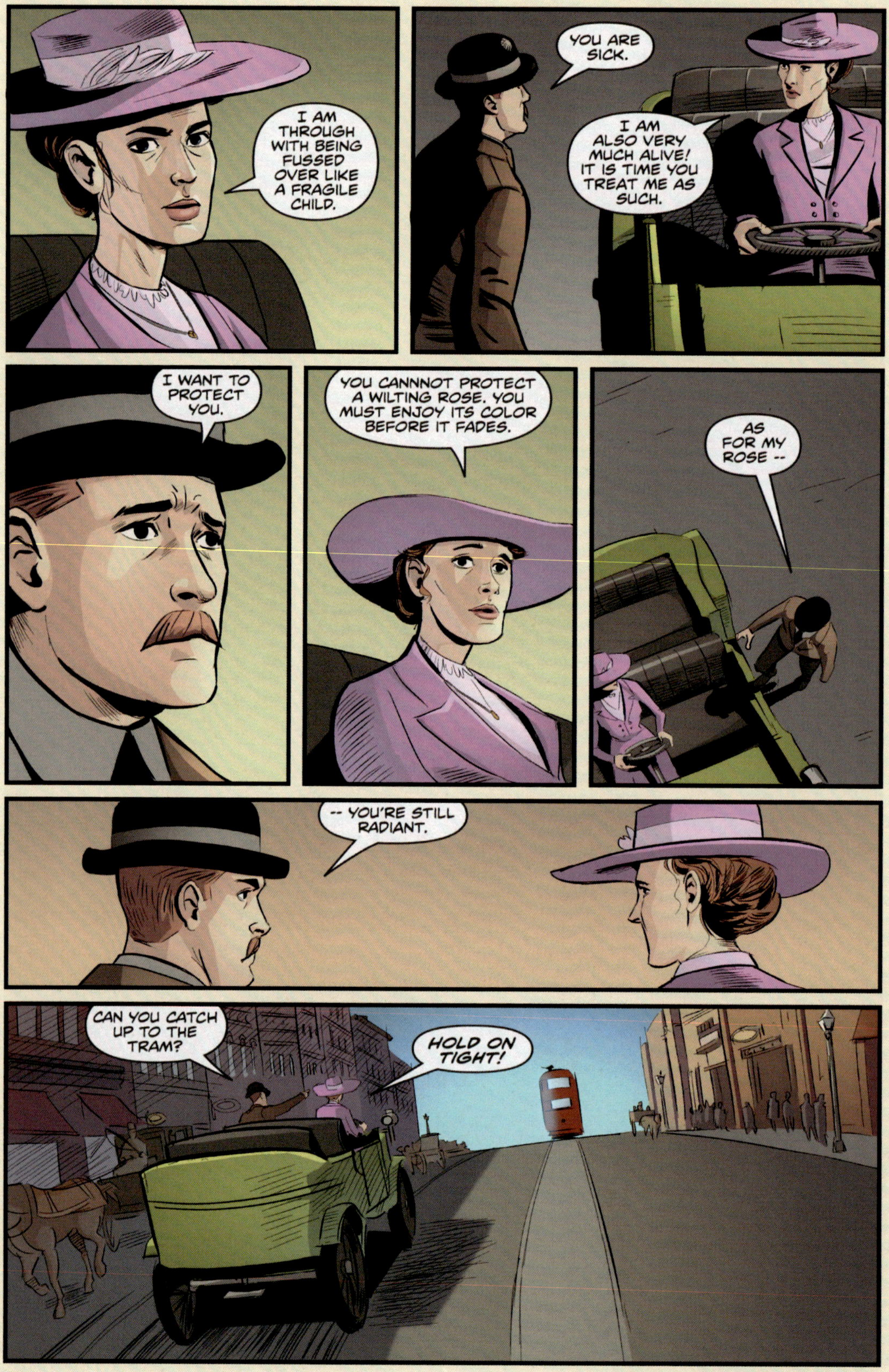
I AM THROUGH WITH BEING FUSSED OVER LIKE A FRAGILE CHILD.
YOU ARE SICK.
I AM ALSO VERY MUCH ALIVE! IT IS TIME YOU TREAT ME AS SUCH.
I WANT TO PROTECT YOU.
YOU CANNOT PROTECT A WILTING ROSE. YOU MUST ENJOY ITS COLOR BEFORE IT FADES.
AS FOR MY ROSE --
-- YOU'RE STILL RADIANT.
CAN YOU CATCH UP TO THE TRAM?
HOLD ON TIGHT!

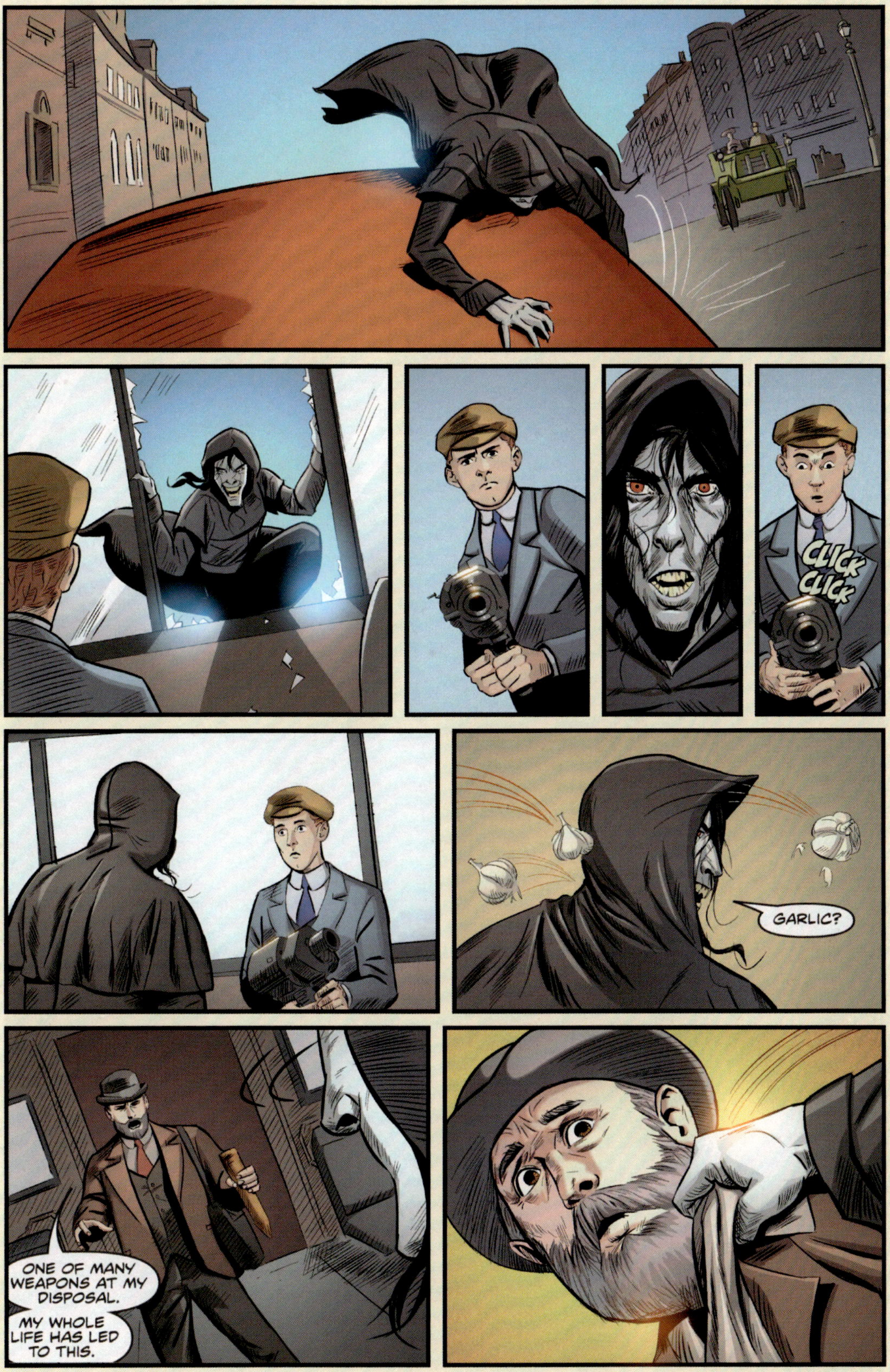
CLICK
CLICK
GARLIC?
ONE OF MANY WEAPONS AT MY DISPOSAL.
MY WHOLE LIFE HAS LED TO THIS.

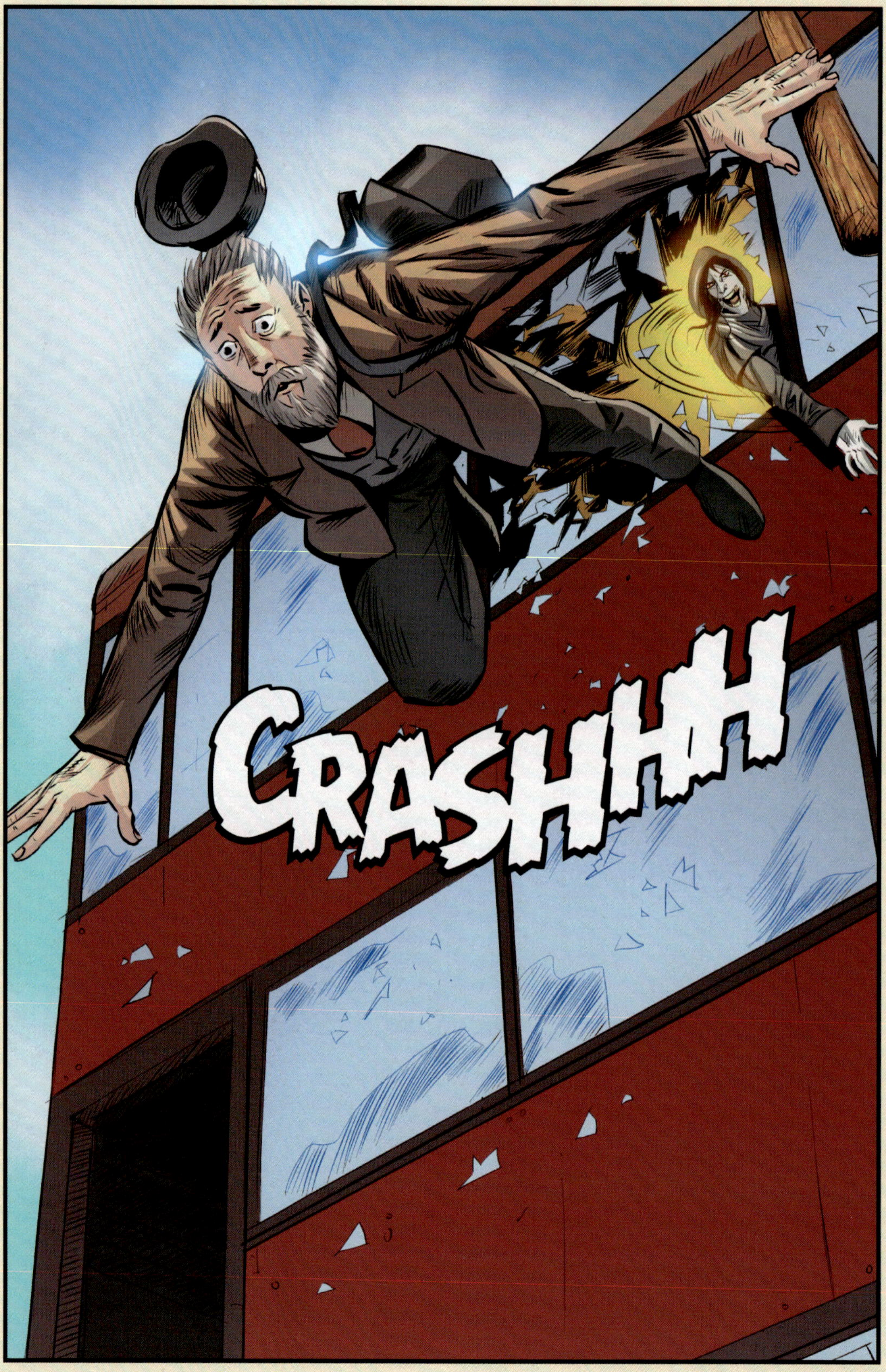
CRASHHH

chapter six

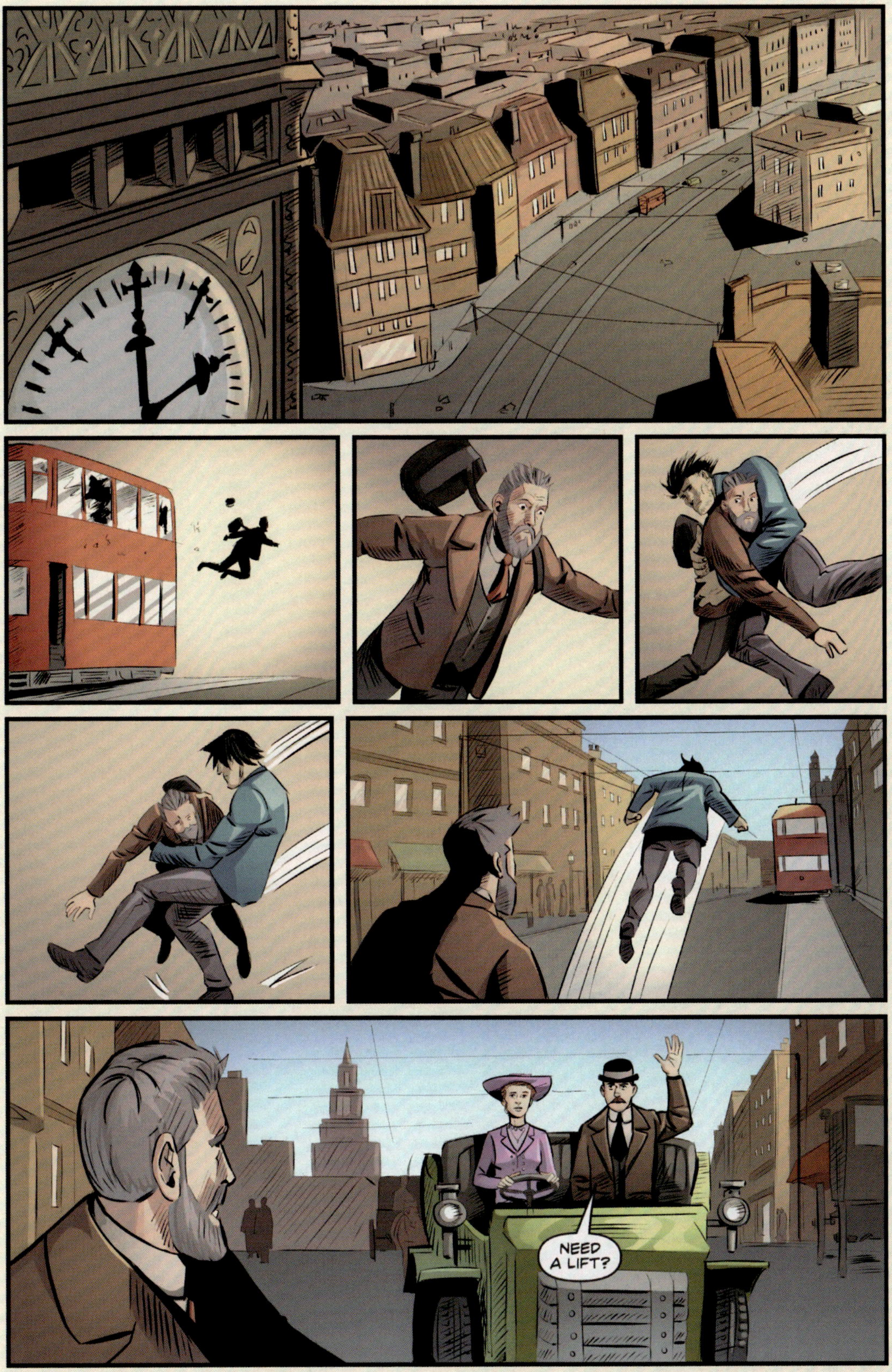
NEED A LIFT?

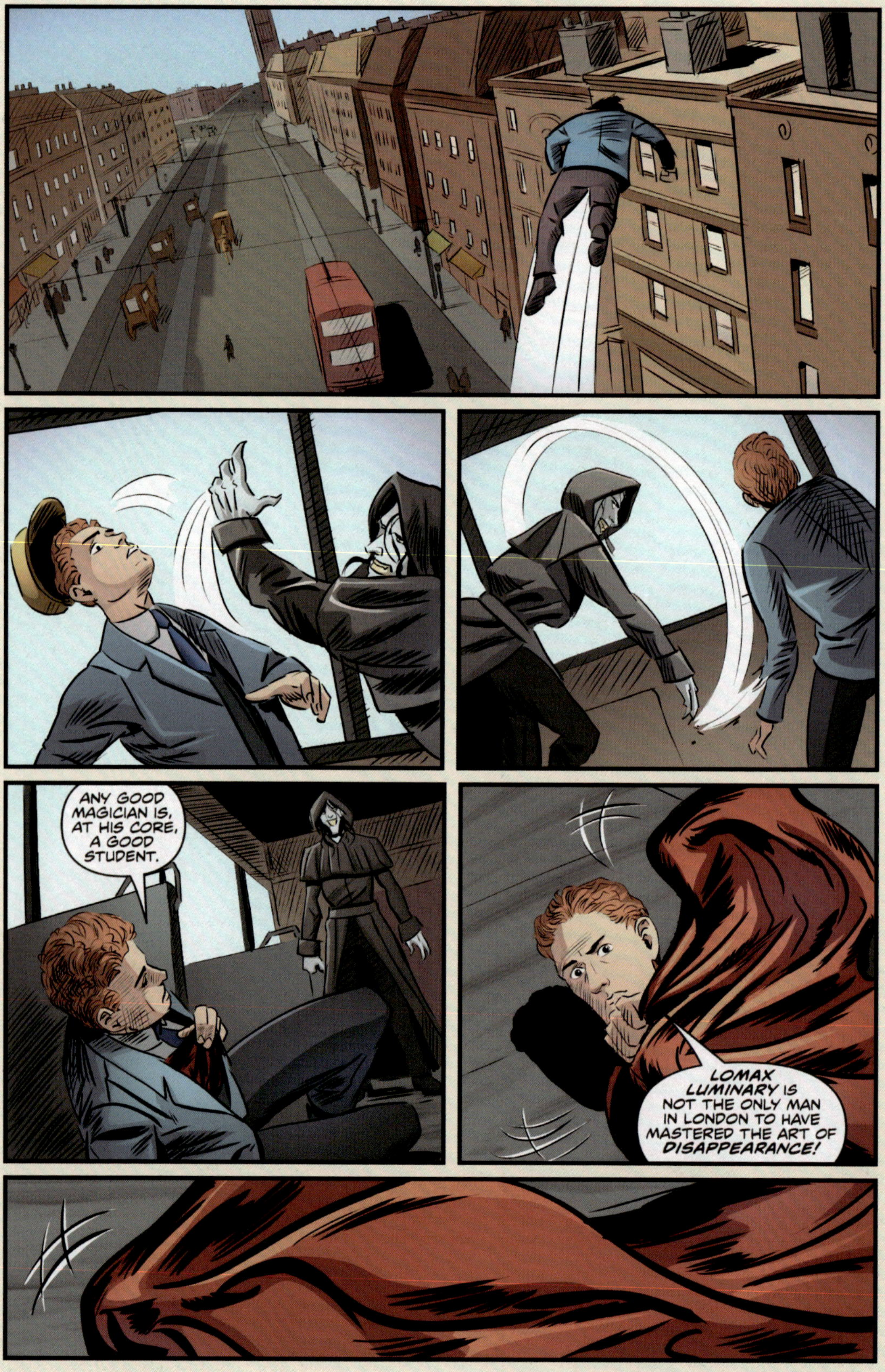
ANY GOOD MAGICIAN IS, AT HIS CORE, A GOOD STUDENT.
LOMAX LUMINARY IS NOT THE ONLY MAN IN LONDON TO HAVE MASTERED THE ART OF DISAPPEARANCE!

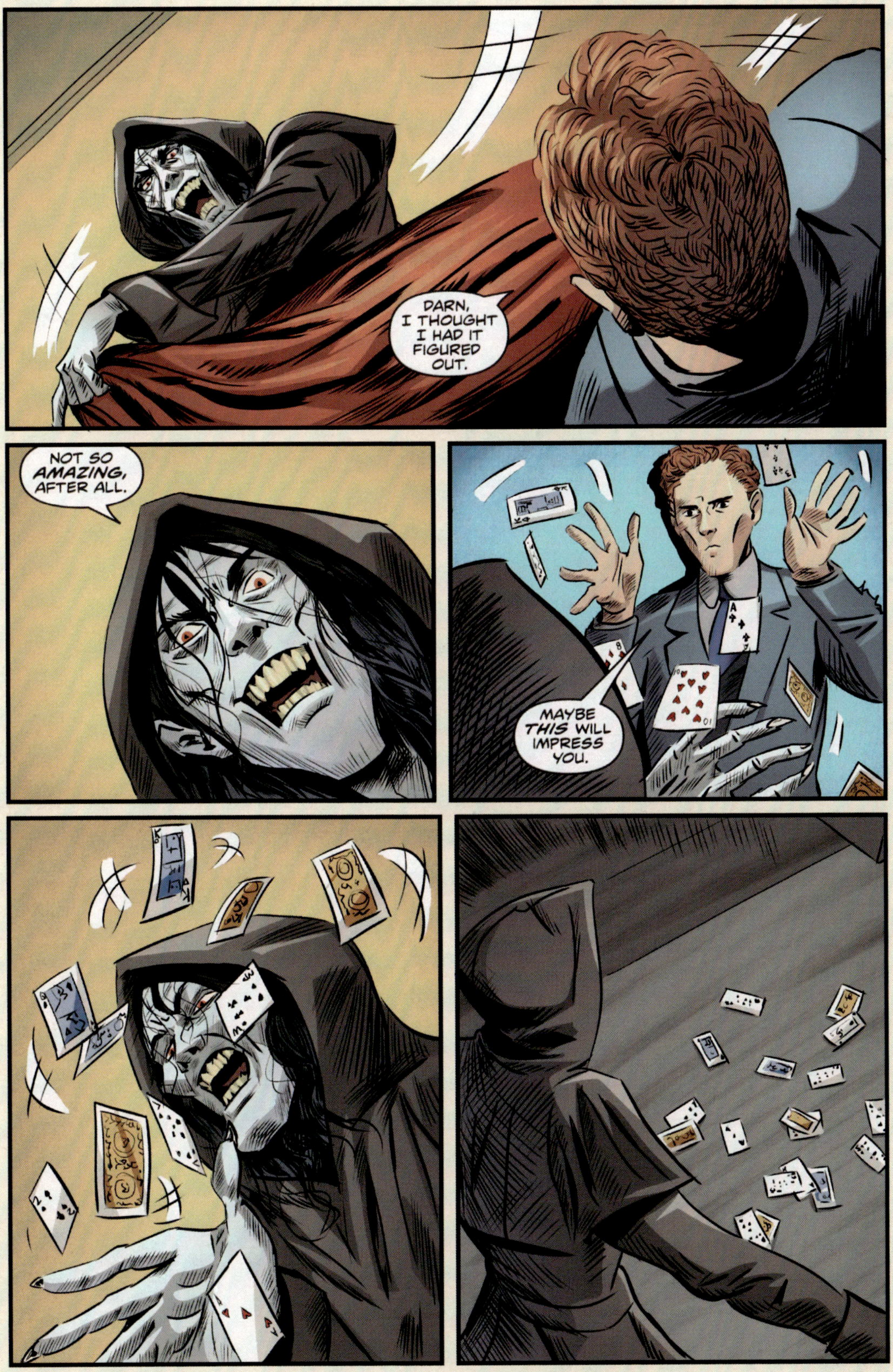
DARN, I THOUGHT I HAD IT FIGURED OUT.
NOT SO AMAZING, AFTER ALL.
MAYBE THIS WILL IMPRESS YOU.

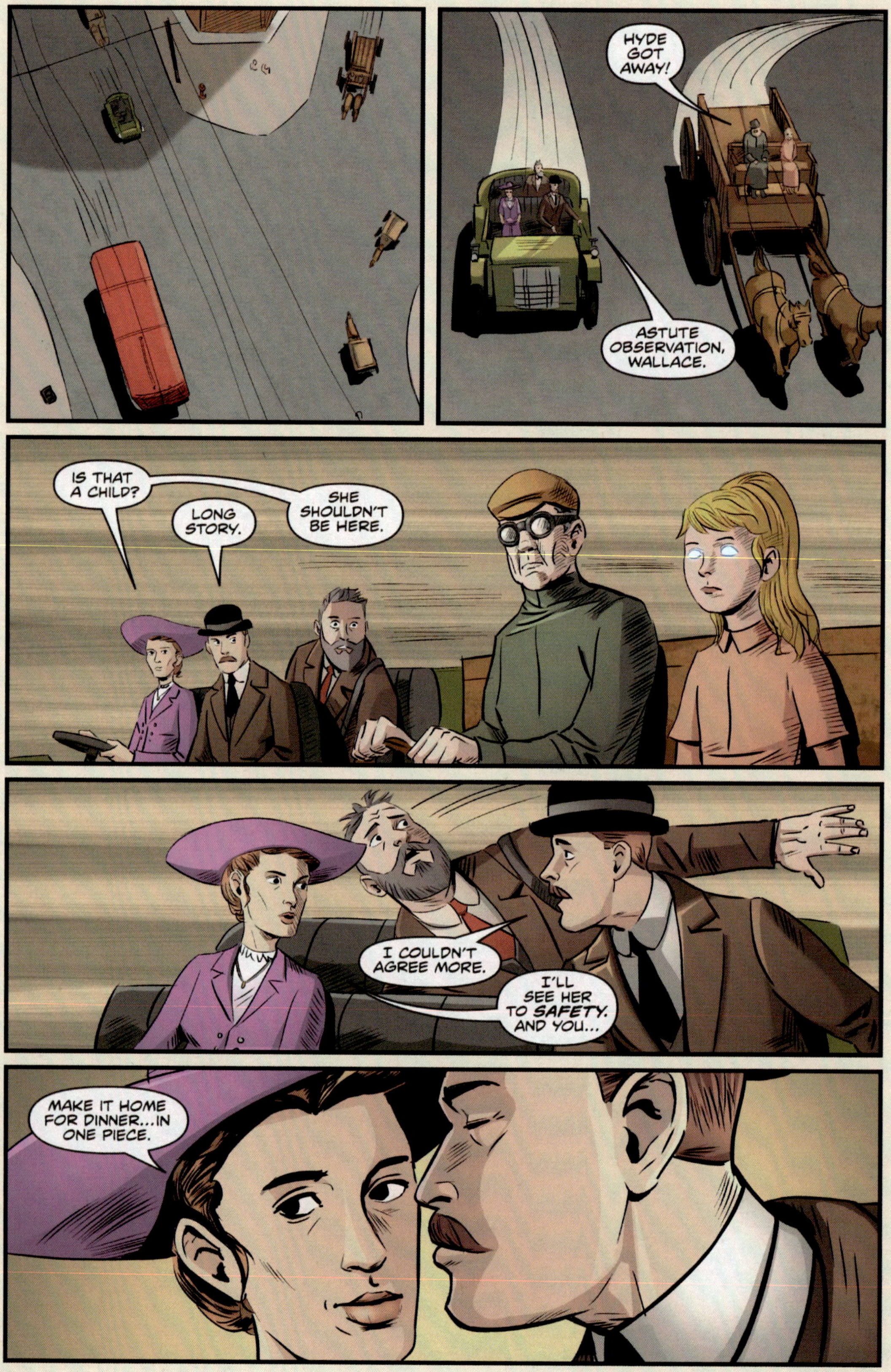
HYDE GOT AWAY!
ASTUTE OBSERVATION, WALLACE.
IS THAT A CHILD?
LONG STORY.
SHE SHOULDN'T BE HERE.
I COULDN'T AGREE MORE.
I'LL SEE HER TO SAFETY. AND YOU...
MAKE IT HOME FOR DINNER...IN ONE PIECE.

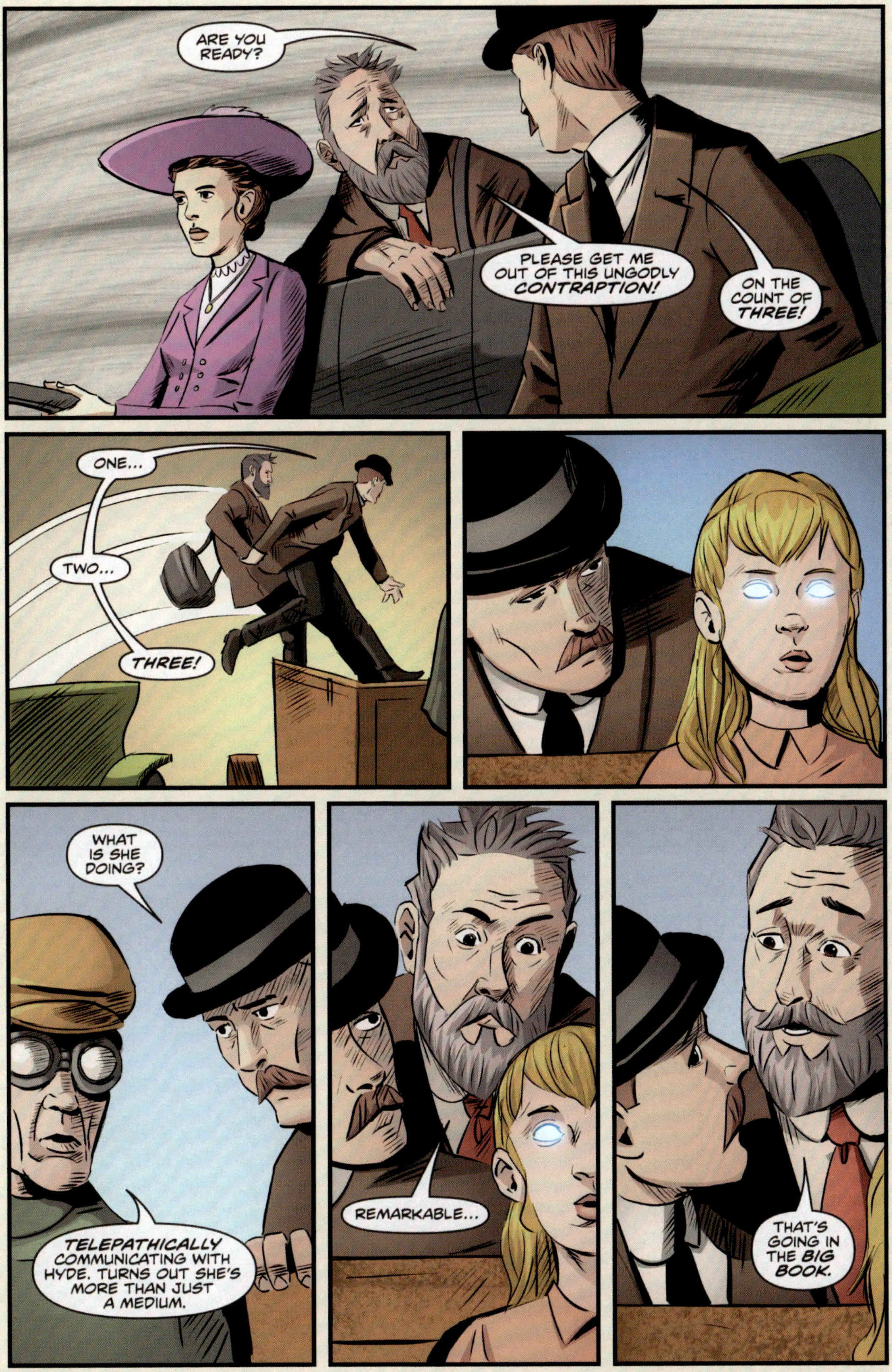
ARE YOU READY?
PLEASE GET ME OUT OF THIS UNGODLY *CONTRAPTION!*
ON THE COUNT OF *THREE!*
ONE...
TWO...
THREE!
WHAT IS SHE DOING?
TELEPATHICALLY COMMUNICATING WITH HYDE. TURNS OUT SHE'S MORE THAN JUST A MEDIUM.
REMARKABLE...
THAT'S GOING IN THE *BIG BOOK.*

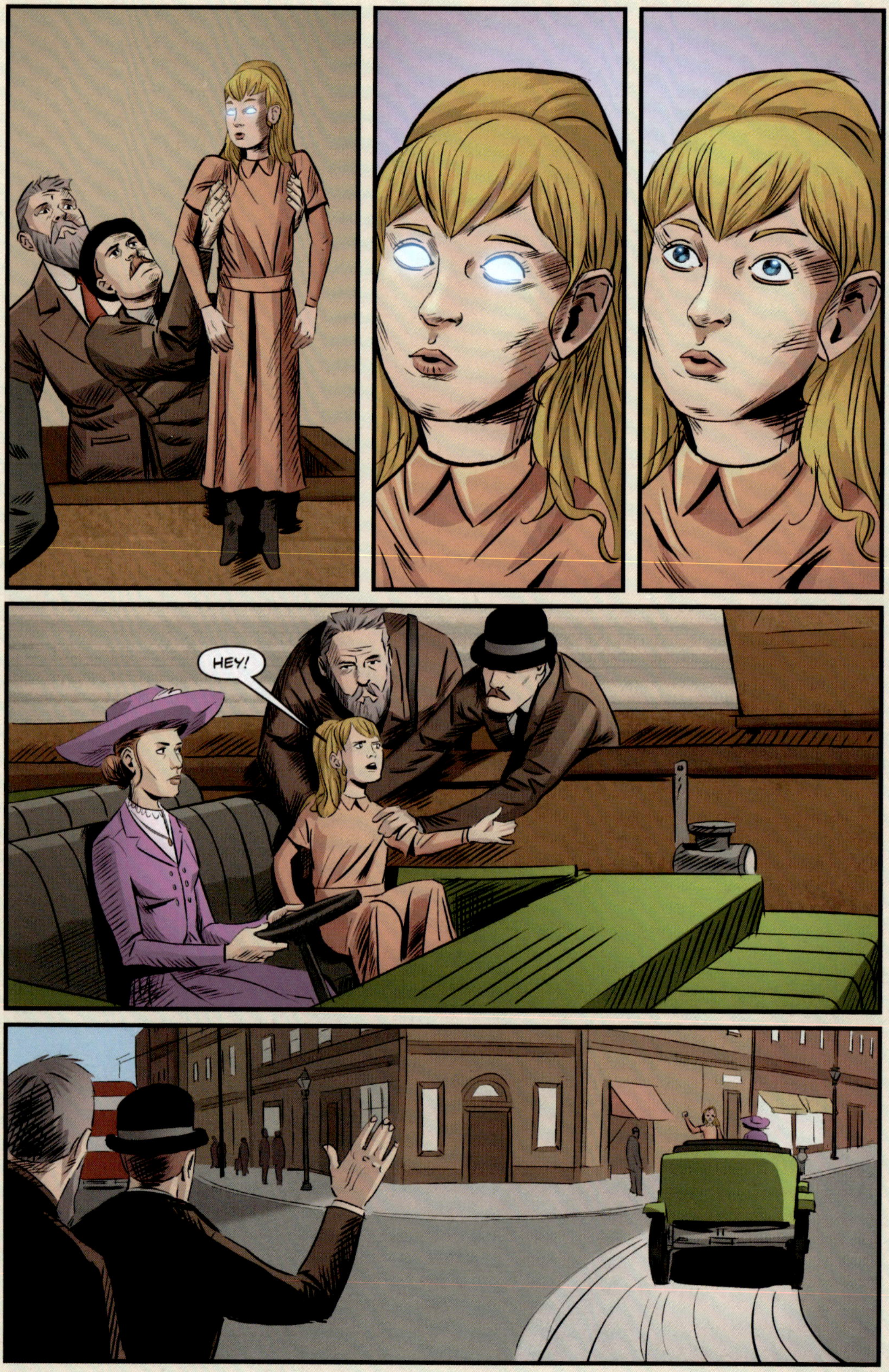
HEY!

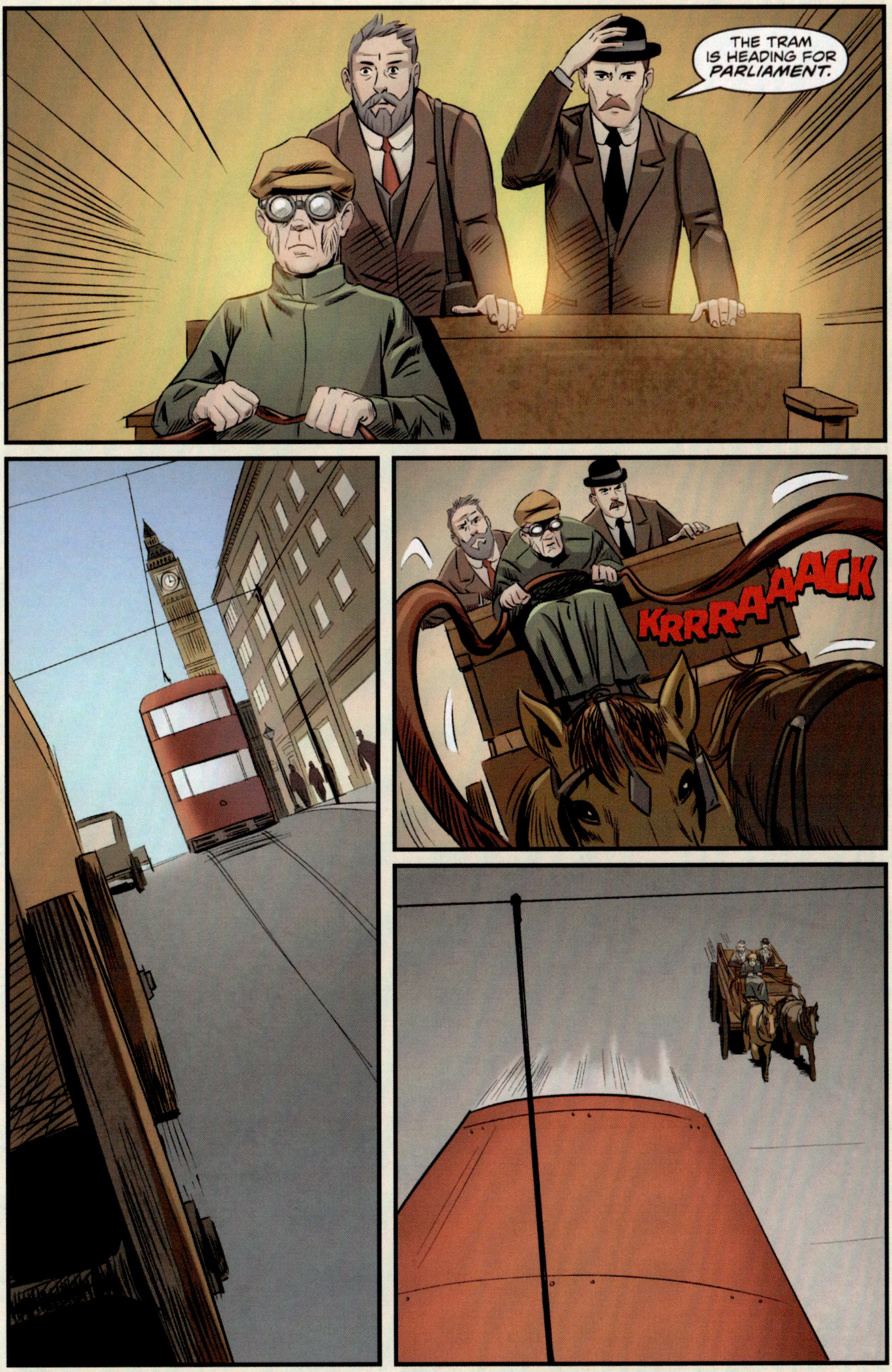
THE TRAM IS HEADING FOR *PARLIAMENT.*
KRRRAAACK

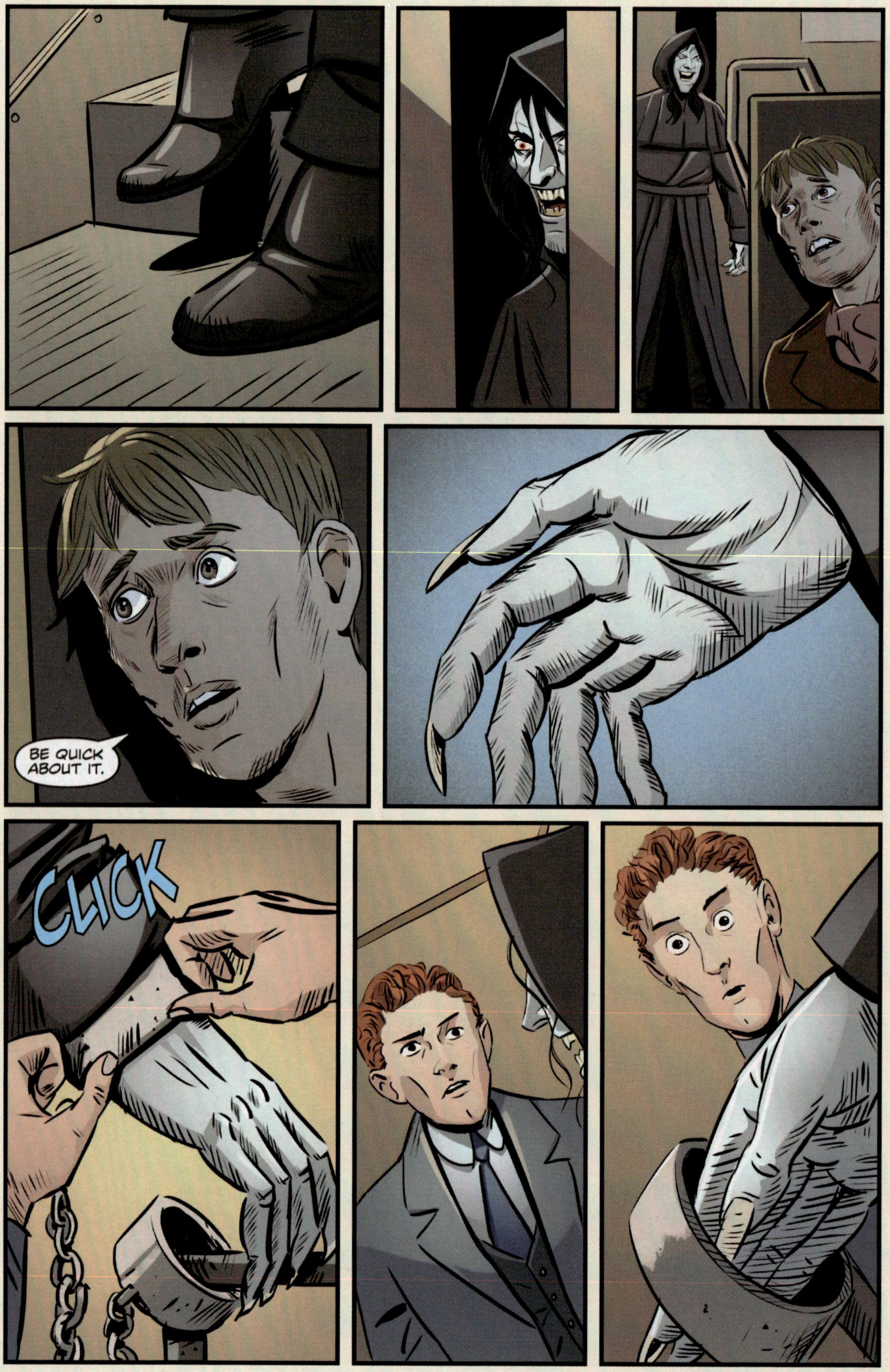
BE QUICK ABOUT IT.
CLICK

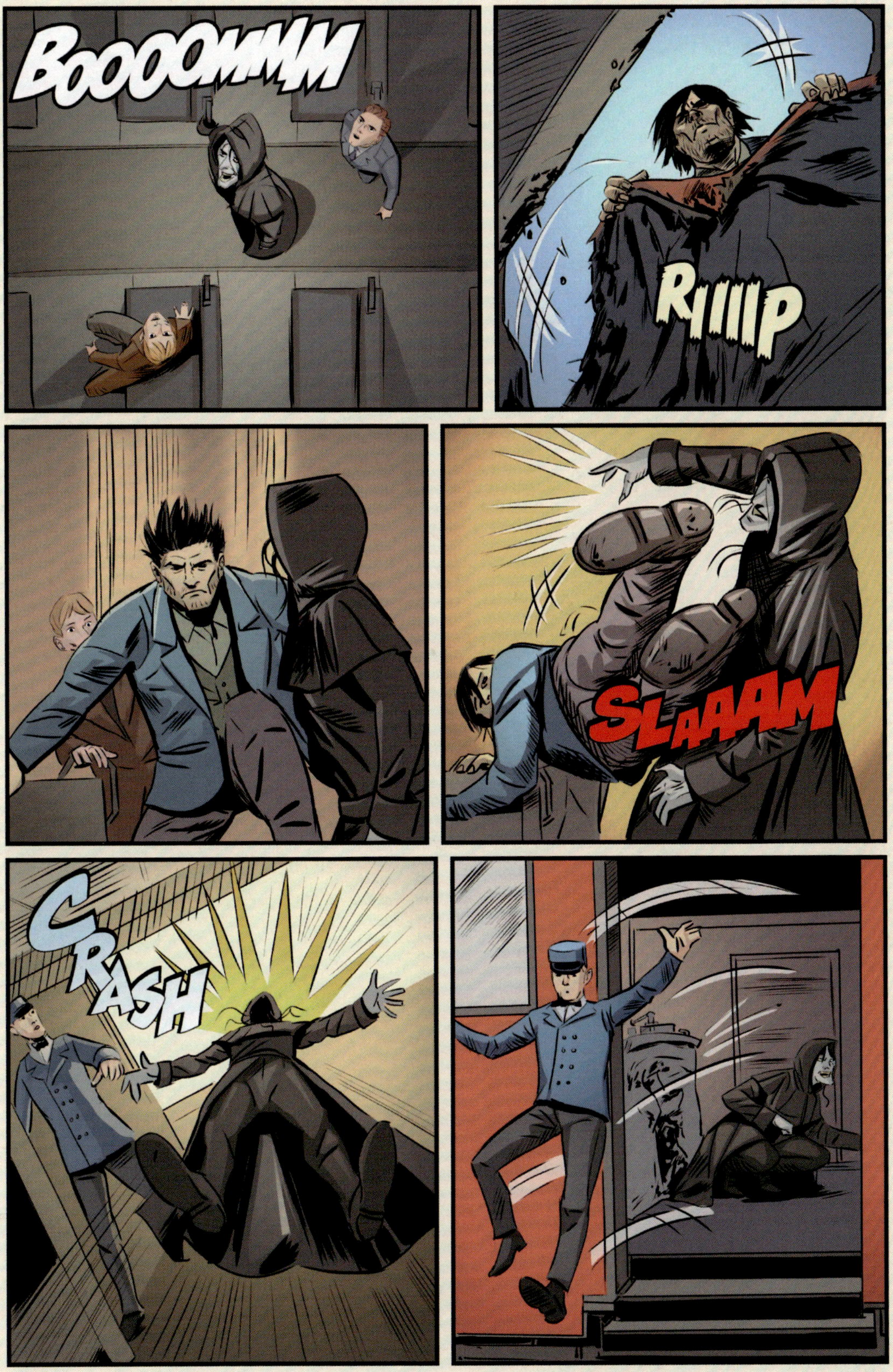
BOOOOMMM
RIIIP
SLAAAM
CRASH

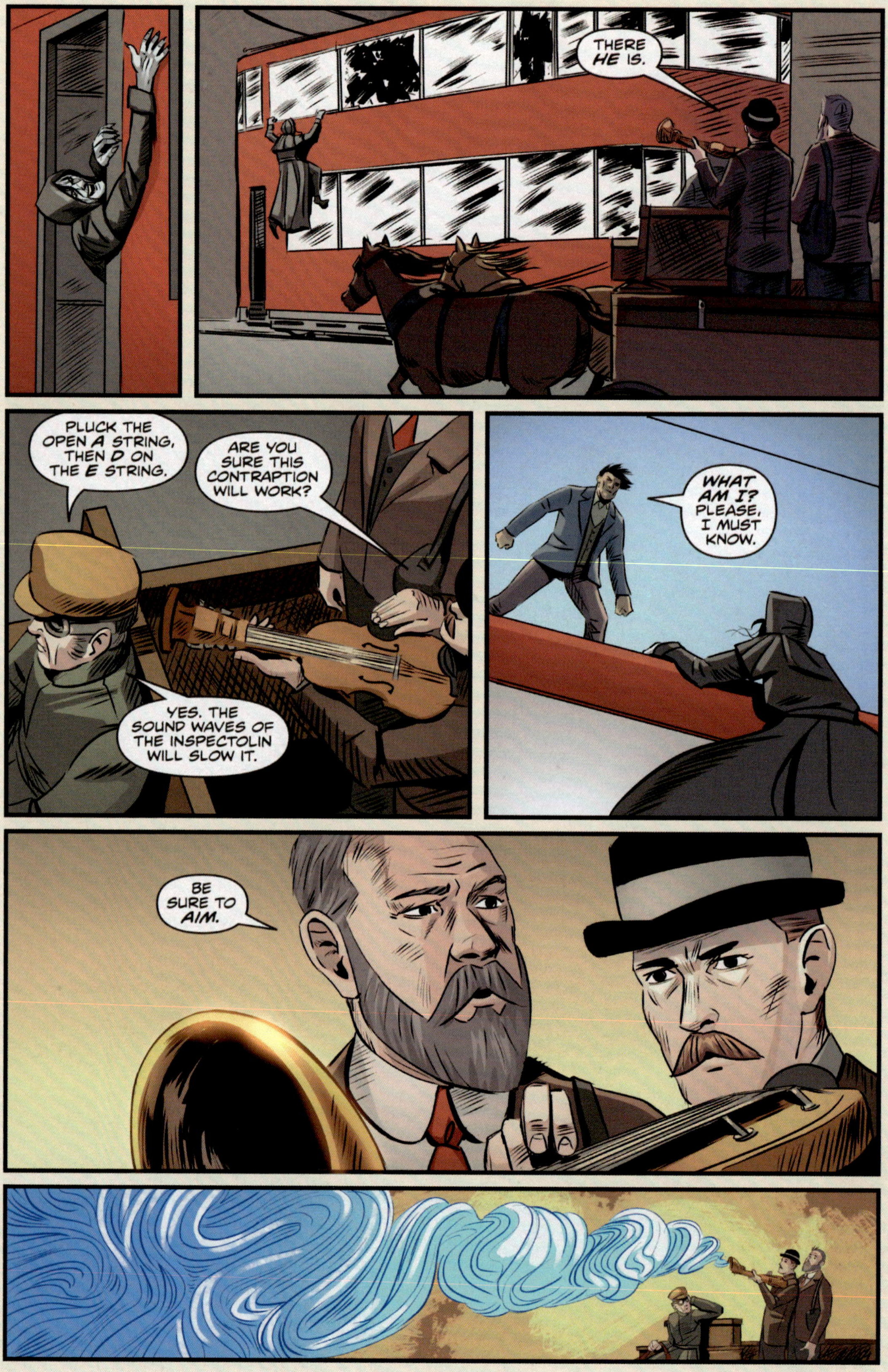
THERE HE IS.
PLUCK THE OPEN A STRING, THEN D ON THE E STRING.
ARE YOU SURE THIS CONTRAPTION WILL WORK?
YES. THE SOUND WAVES OF THE INSPECTOLIN WILL SLOW IT.
WHAT AM I? PLEASE, I MUST KNOW.
BE SURE TO AIM.

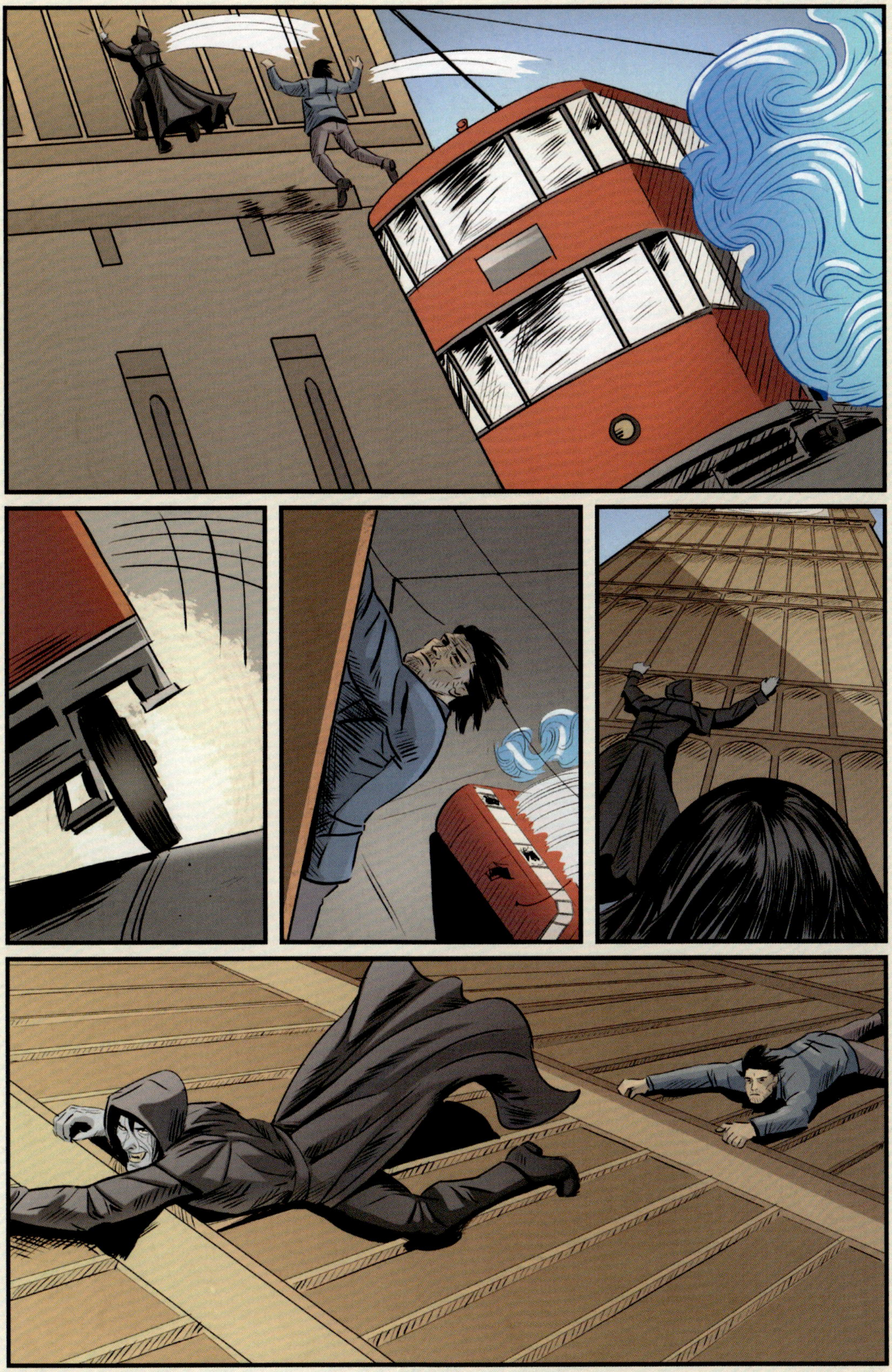

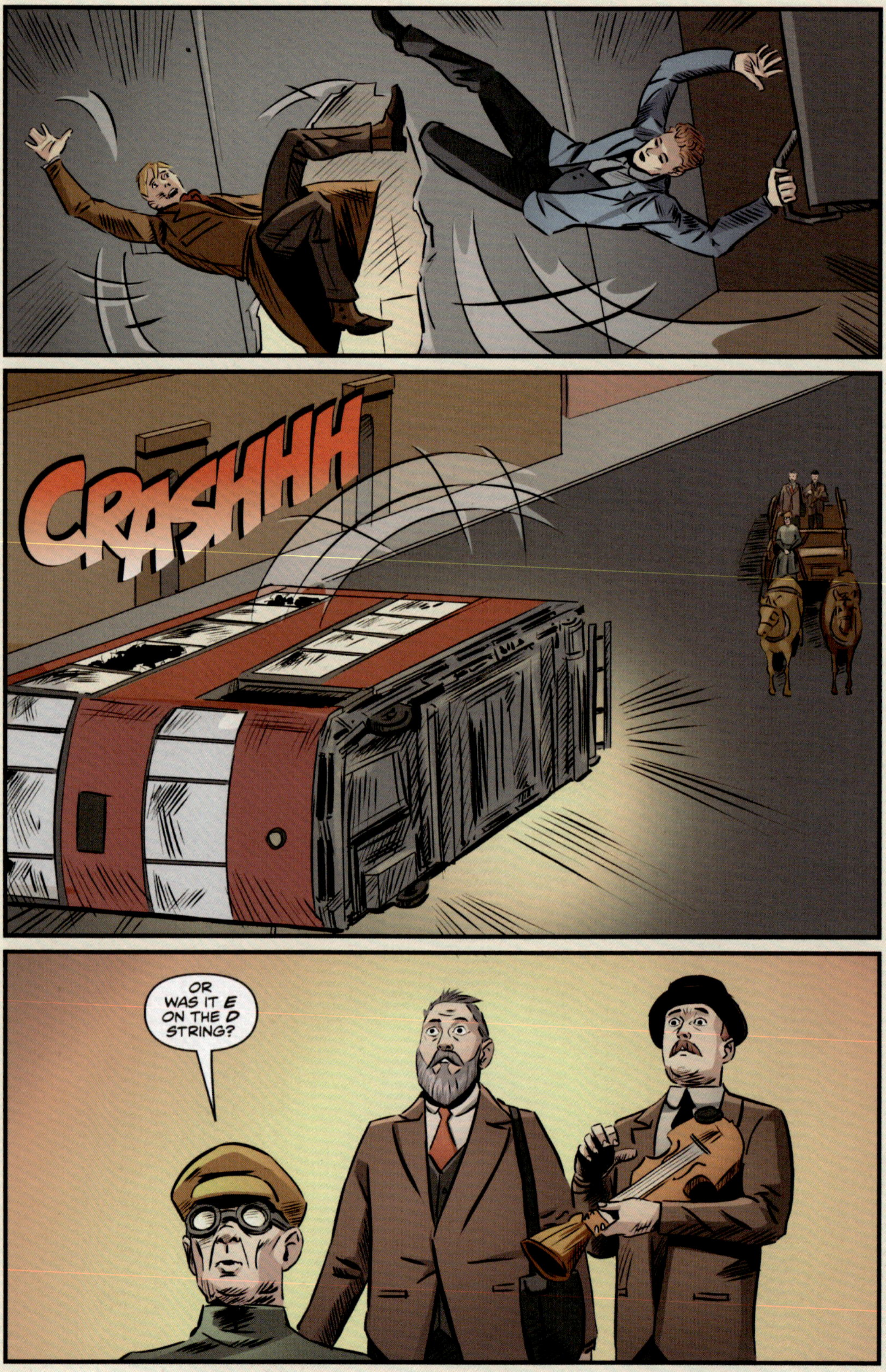
CRASHHH
OR WAS IT E ON THE D STRING?

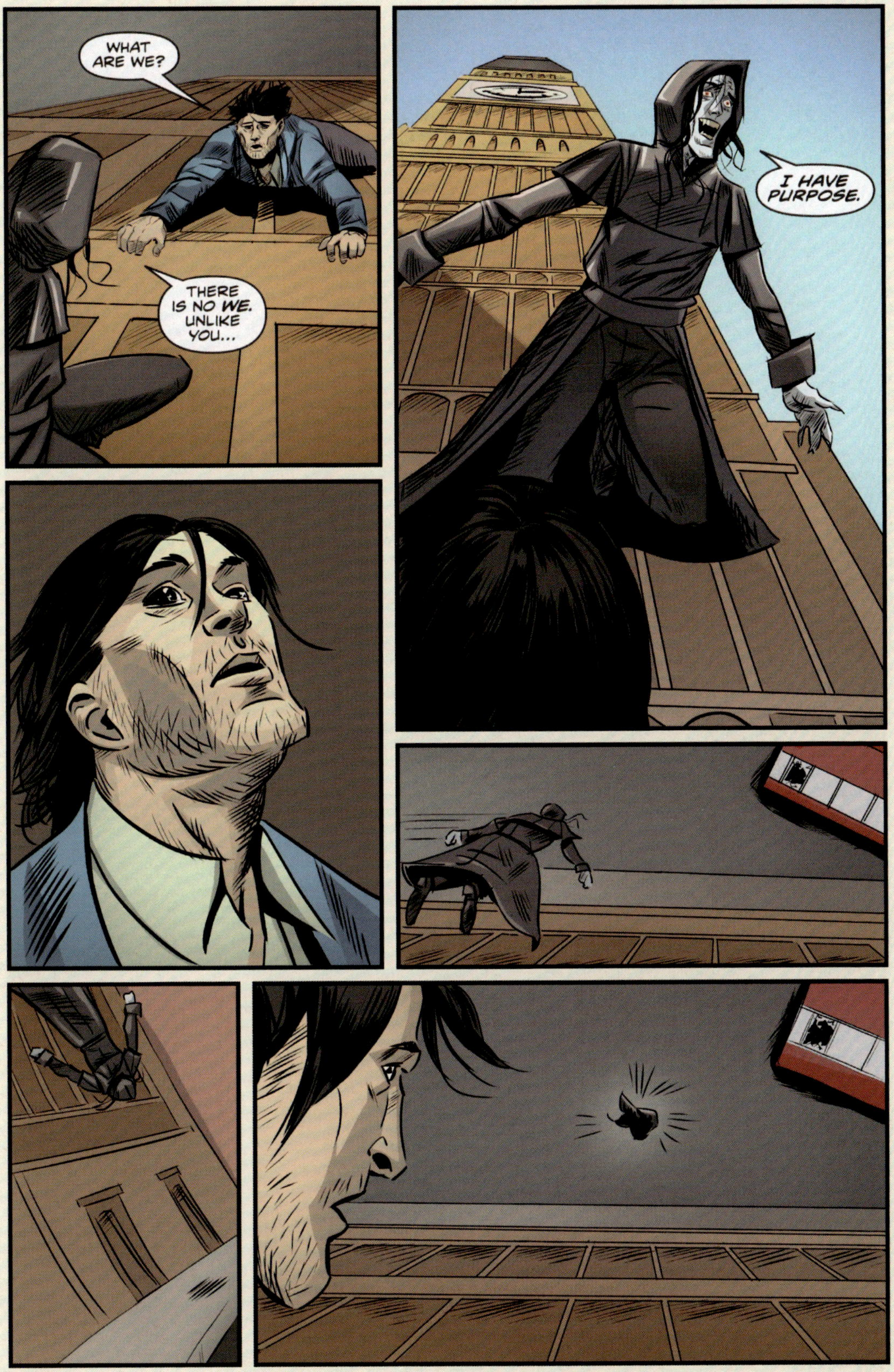
WHAT ARE WE?
THERE IS NO WE. UNLIKE YOU...
I HAVE PURPOSE.

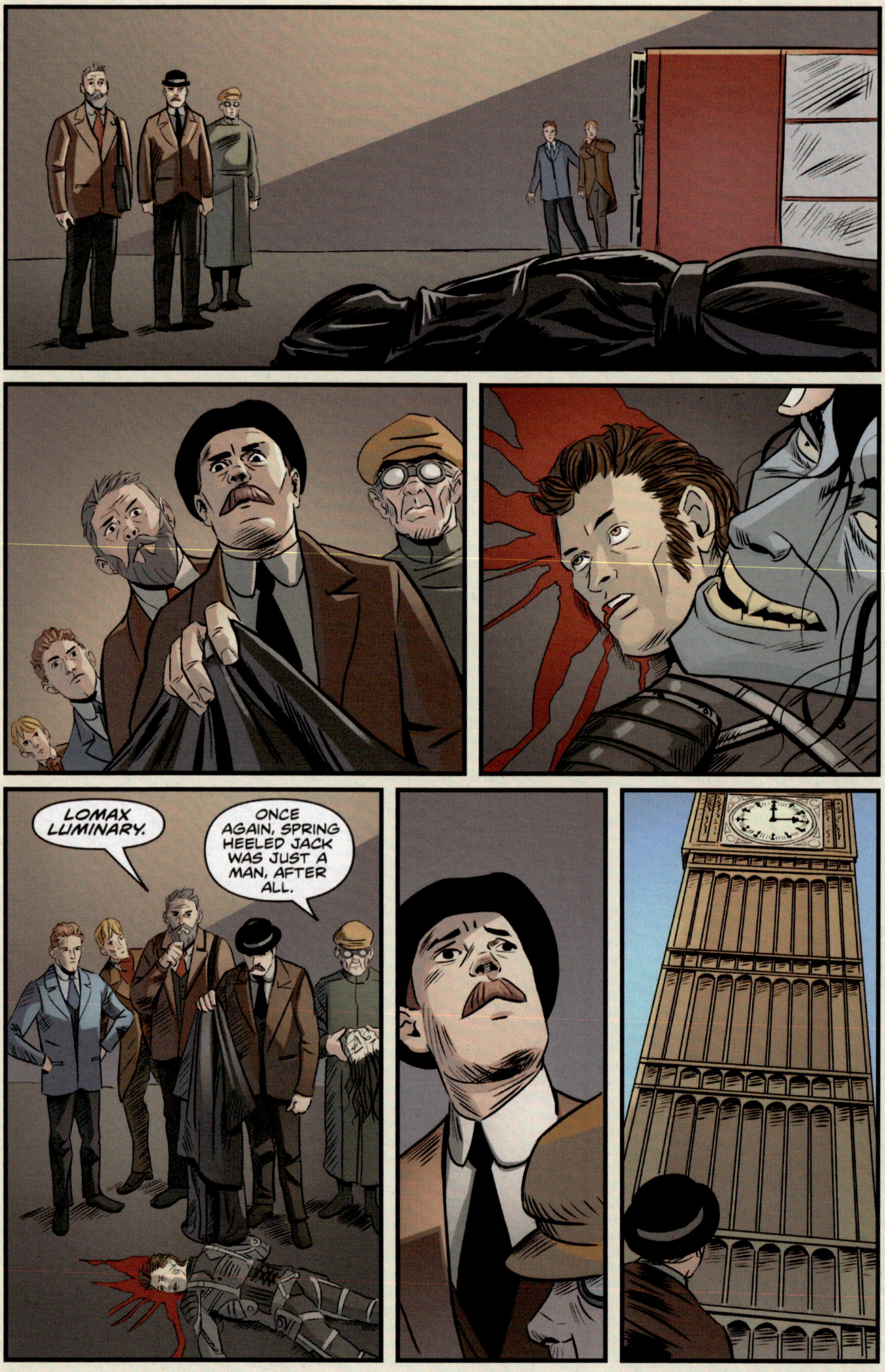
LOMAX LUMINARY.
ONCE AGAIN, SPRING HEELED JACK WAS JUST A MAN, AFTER ALL.

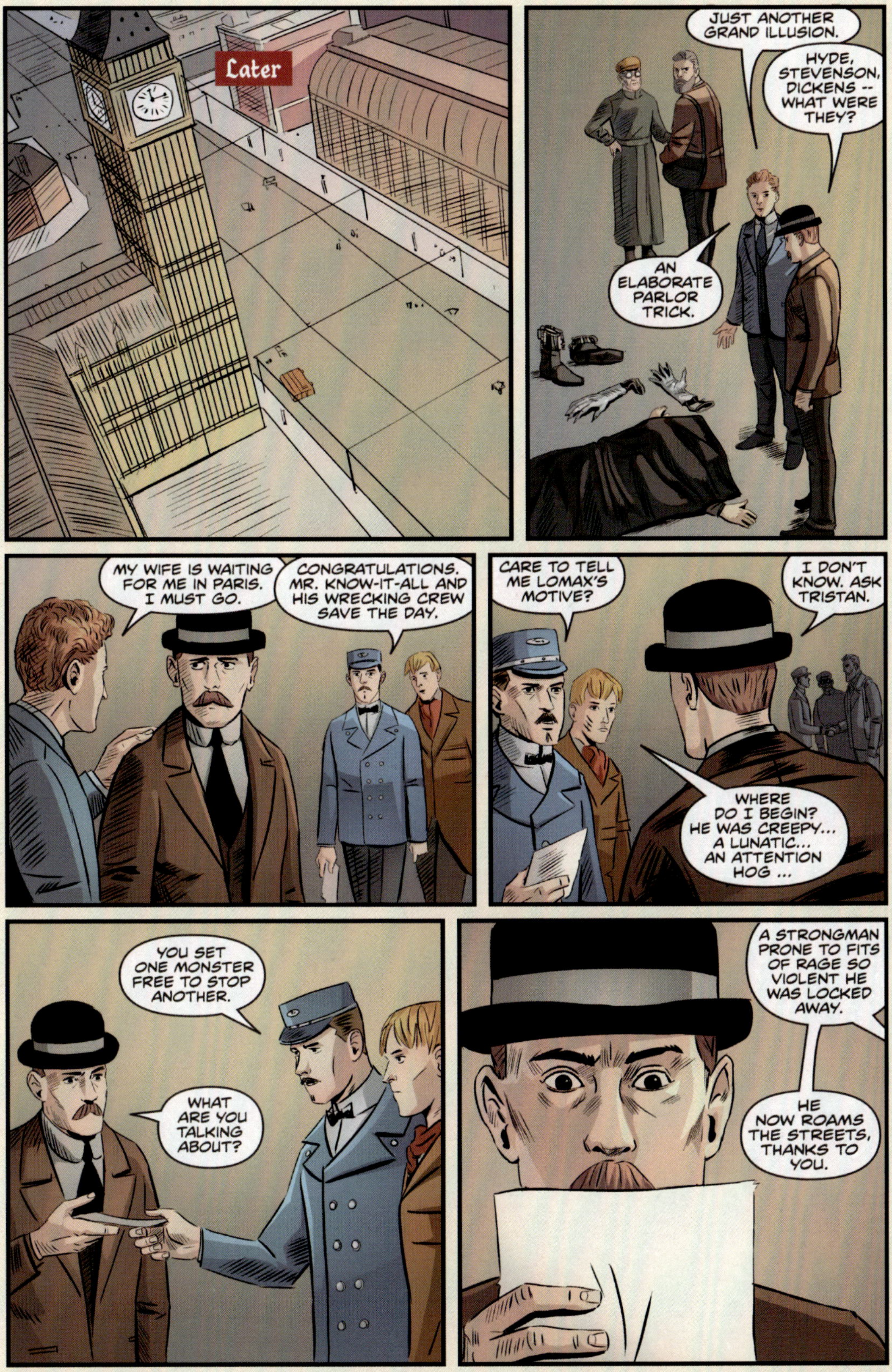
Later
JUST ANOTHER GRAND ILLUSION.
HYDE, STEVENSON, DICKENS -- WHAT WERE THEY?
AN ELABORATE PARLOR TRICK.
MY WIFE IS WAITING FOR ME IN PARIS. I MUST GO.
CONGRATULATIONS. MR. KNOW-IT-ALL AND HIS WRECKING CREW SAVE THE DAY.
CARE TO TELL ME LOMAX'S MOTIVE?
I DON'T KNOW. ASK TRISTAN.
WHERE DO I BEGIN? HE WAS CREEPY... A LUNATIC... AN ATTENTION HOG ...
YOU SET ONE MONSTER FREE TO STOP ANOTHER.
WHAT ARE YOU TALKING ABOUT?
A STRONGMAN PRONE TO FITS OF RAGE SO VIOLENT HE WAS LOCKED AWAY.
HE NOW ROAMS THE STREETS, THANKS TO YOU.

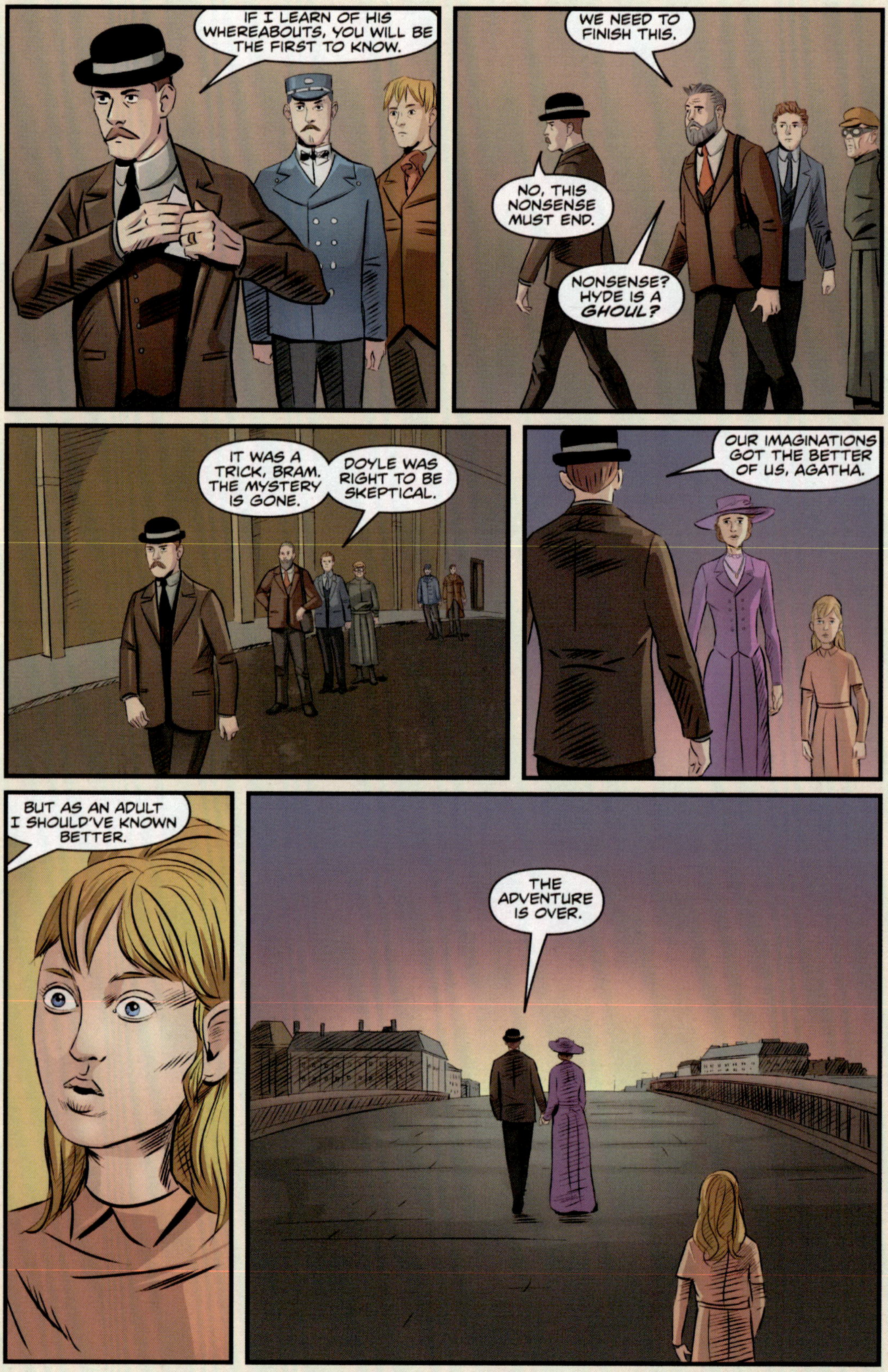
IF I LEARN OF HIS WHEREABOUTS, YOU WILL BE THE FIRST TO KNOW.
WE NEED TO FINISH THIS.
NO, THIS NONSENSE MUST END.
NONSENSE? HYDE IS A GHOUL?
IT WAS A TRICK, BRAM. THE MYSTERY IS GONE.
DOYLE WAS RIGHT TO BE SKEPTICAL.
OUR IMAGINATIONS GOT THE BETTER OF US, AGATHA.
BUT AS AN ADULT I SHOULD'VE KNOWN BETTER.
THE ADVENTURE IS OVER.

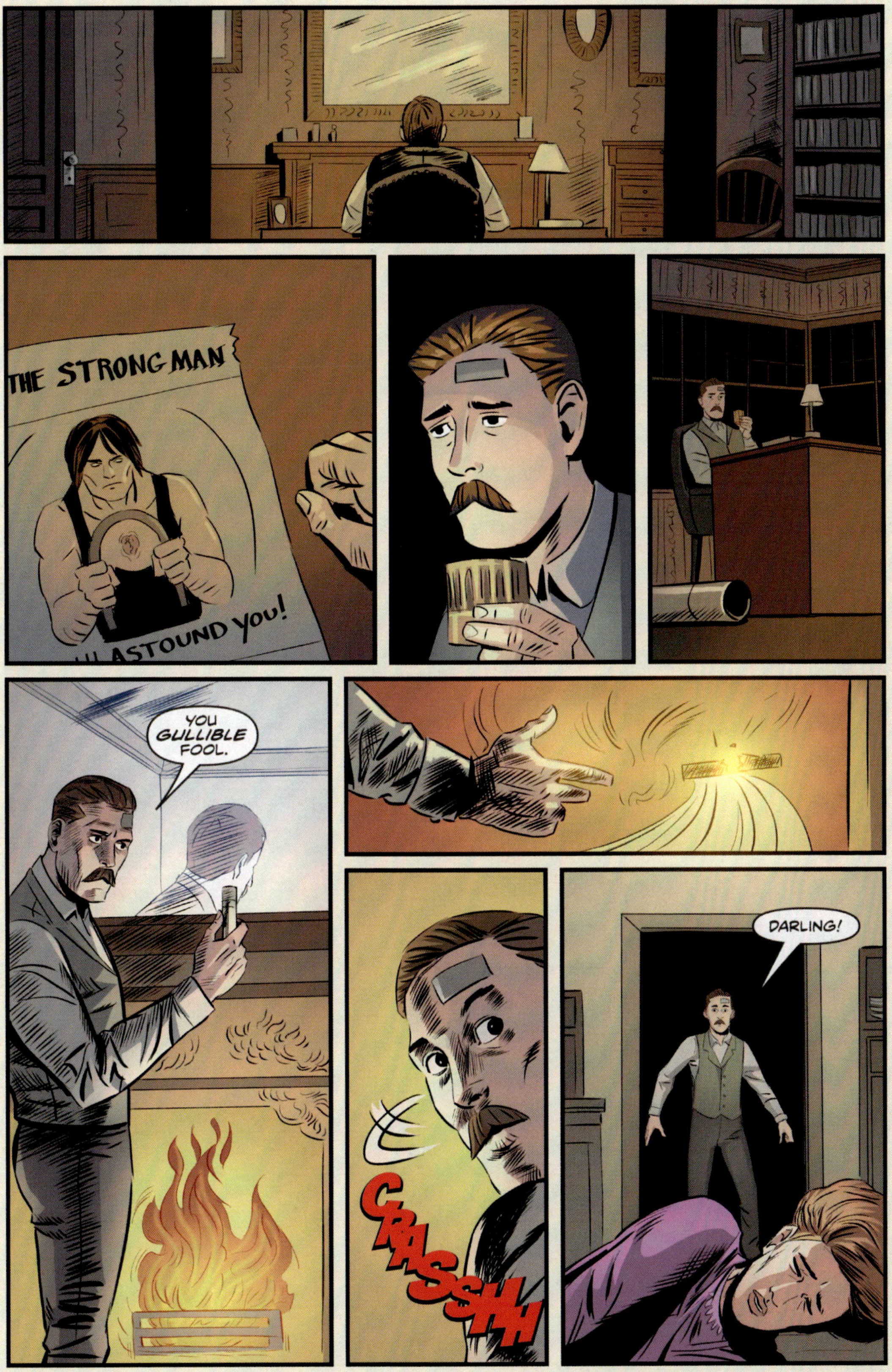
THE STRONG MAN
ASTOUND YOU!
YOU GULLIBLE FOOL.
CRASSHH
DARLING!

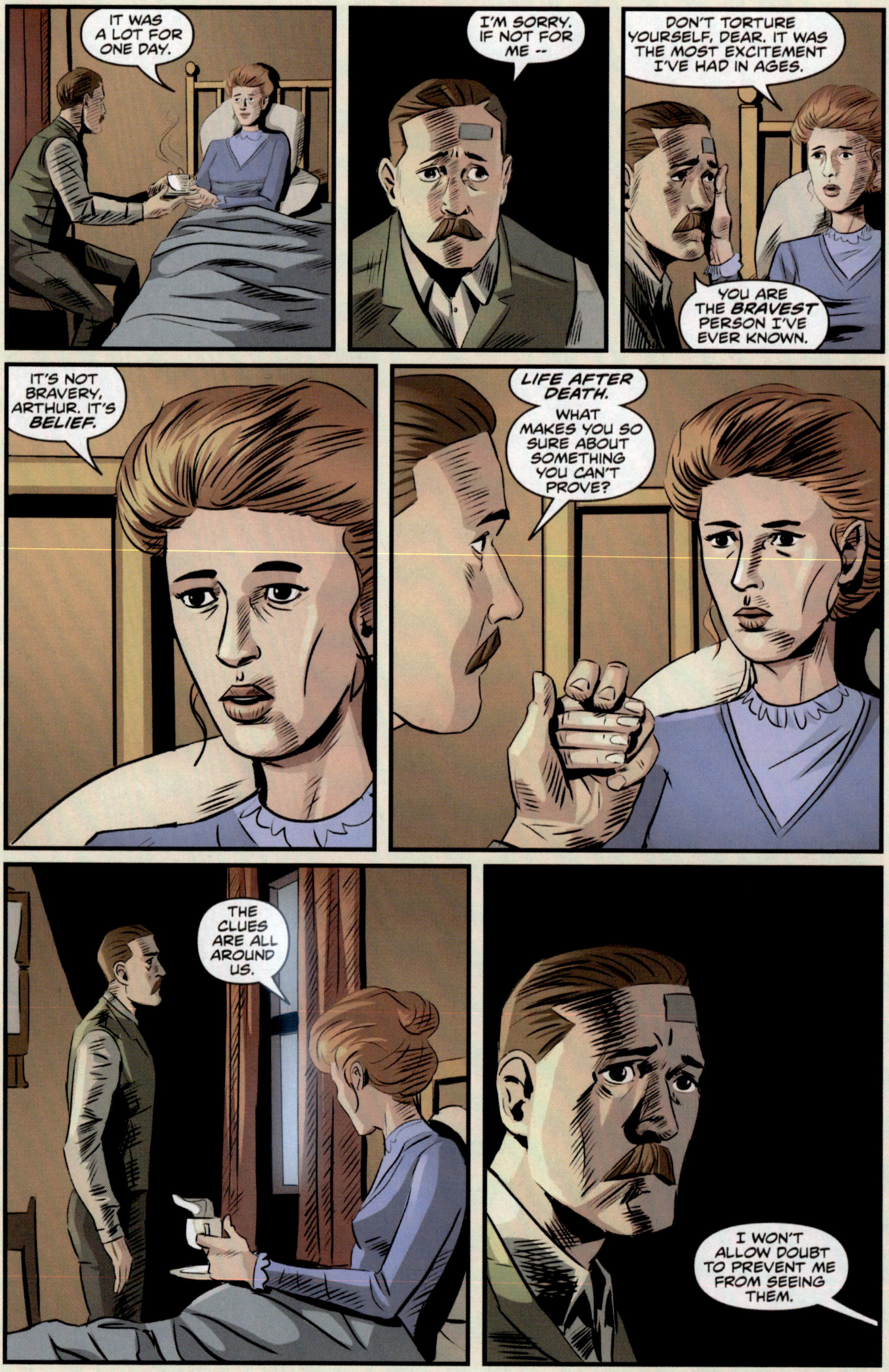
IT WAS A LOT FOR ONE DAY.
I'M SORRY. IF NOT FOR ME --
DON'T TORTURE YOURSELF, DEAR. IT WAS THE MOST EXCITEMENT I'VE HAD IN AGES.
YOU ARE THE **BRAVEST** PERSON I'VE EVER KNOWN.
IT'S NOT BRAVERY, ARTHUR. IT'S ***BELIEF.***
LIFE AFTER DEATH.
WHAT MAKES YOU SO SURE ABOUT SOMETHING YOU CAN'T PROVE?
THE CLUES ARE ALL AROUND US.
I WON'T ALLOW DOUBT TO PREVENT ME FROM SEEING THEM.

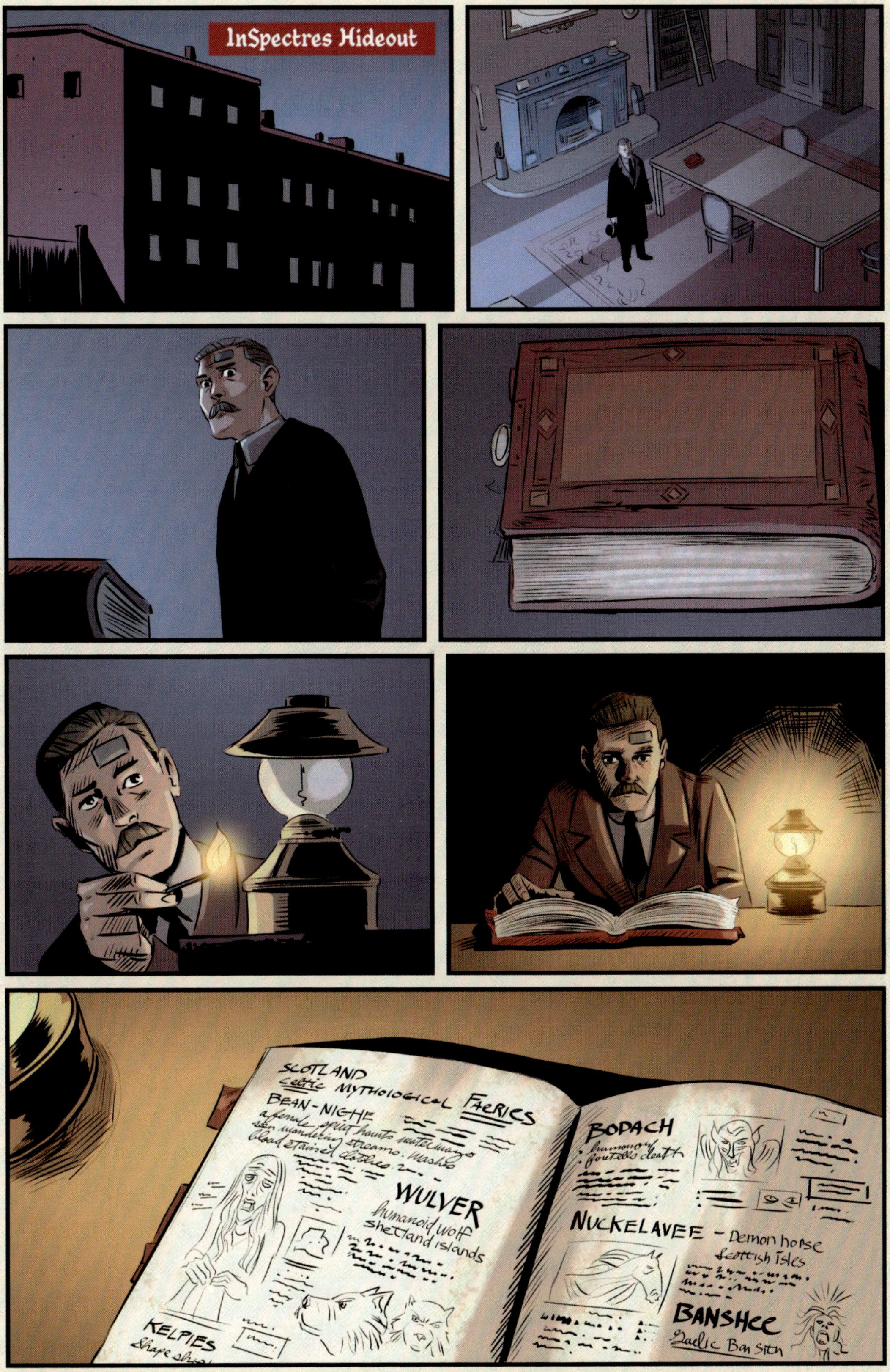
InSpectres Hideout
SCOTLAND
Celtic MYTHOLOGICAL FAERICS
BEAN-NIGHE
a female spirit haunts watermays
seen wandering streams. washes
blood stained clothes.
WULVER
humanoid wolf
shetland islands
KELPIES
BODACH
humanoid
foretells death
NUCKELAVEE - Demon horse
scottish Isles
BANSHEE
Gaelic Ban Sith

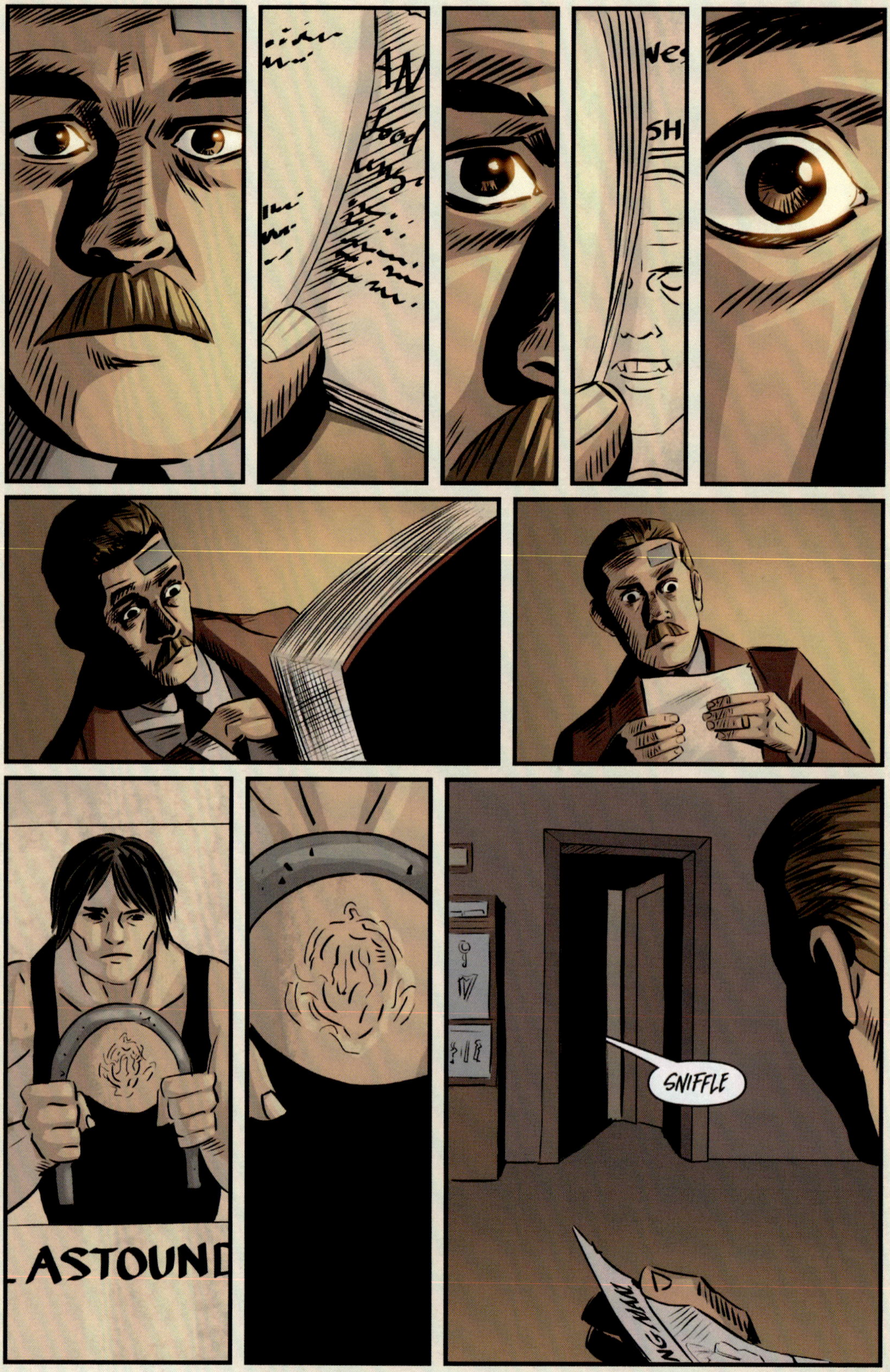
ASTOUND
SNIFFLE

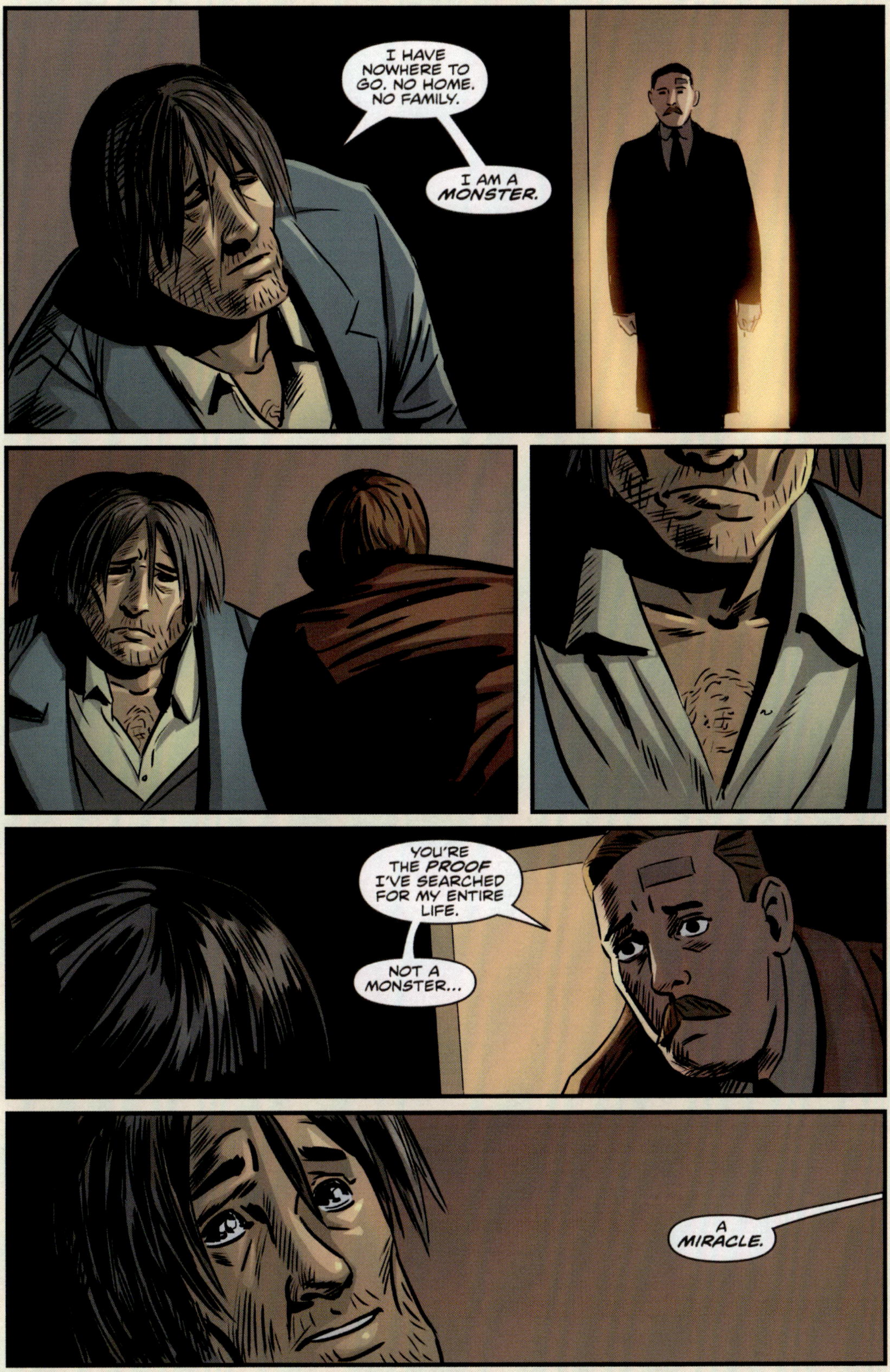
I HAVE NOWHERE TO GO. NO HOME. NO FAMILY.
I AM A *MONSTER.*
YOU'RE THE *PROOF* I'VE SEARCHED FOR MY ENTIRE LIFE.
NOT A MONSTER...
A *MIRACLE.*

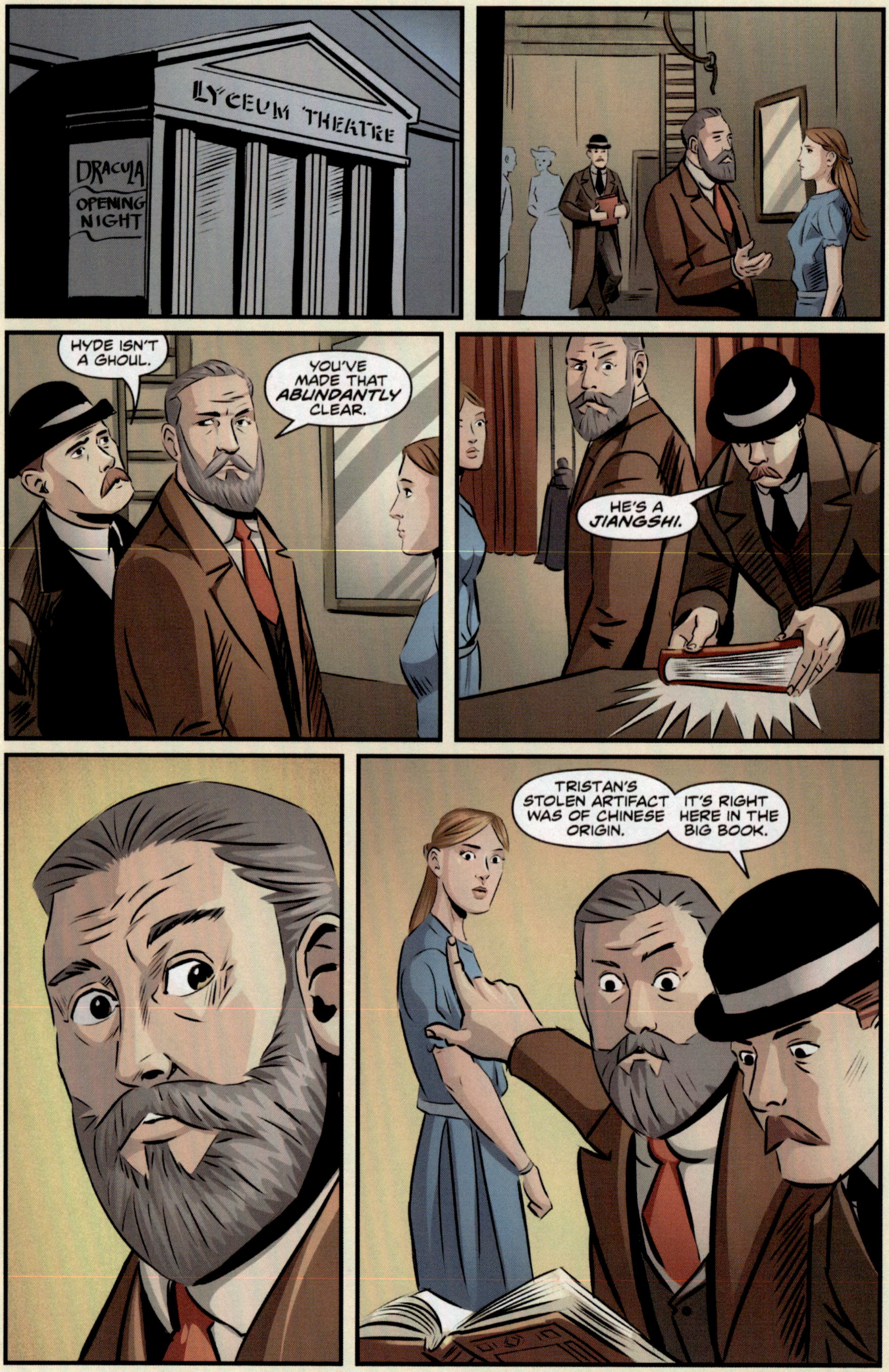
LYCEUM THEATRE
DRACULA OPENING NIGHT
HYDE ISN'T A GHOUL.
YOU'VE MADE THAT ABUNDANTLY CLEAR.
HE'S A JIANGSHI.
TRISTAN'S STOLEN ARTIFACT WAS OF CHINESE ORIGIN.
IT'S RIGHT HERE IN THE BIG BOOK.

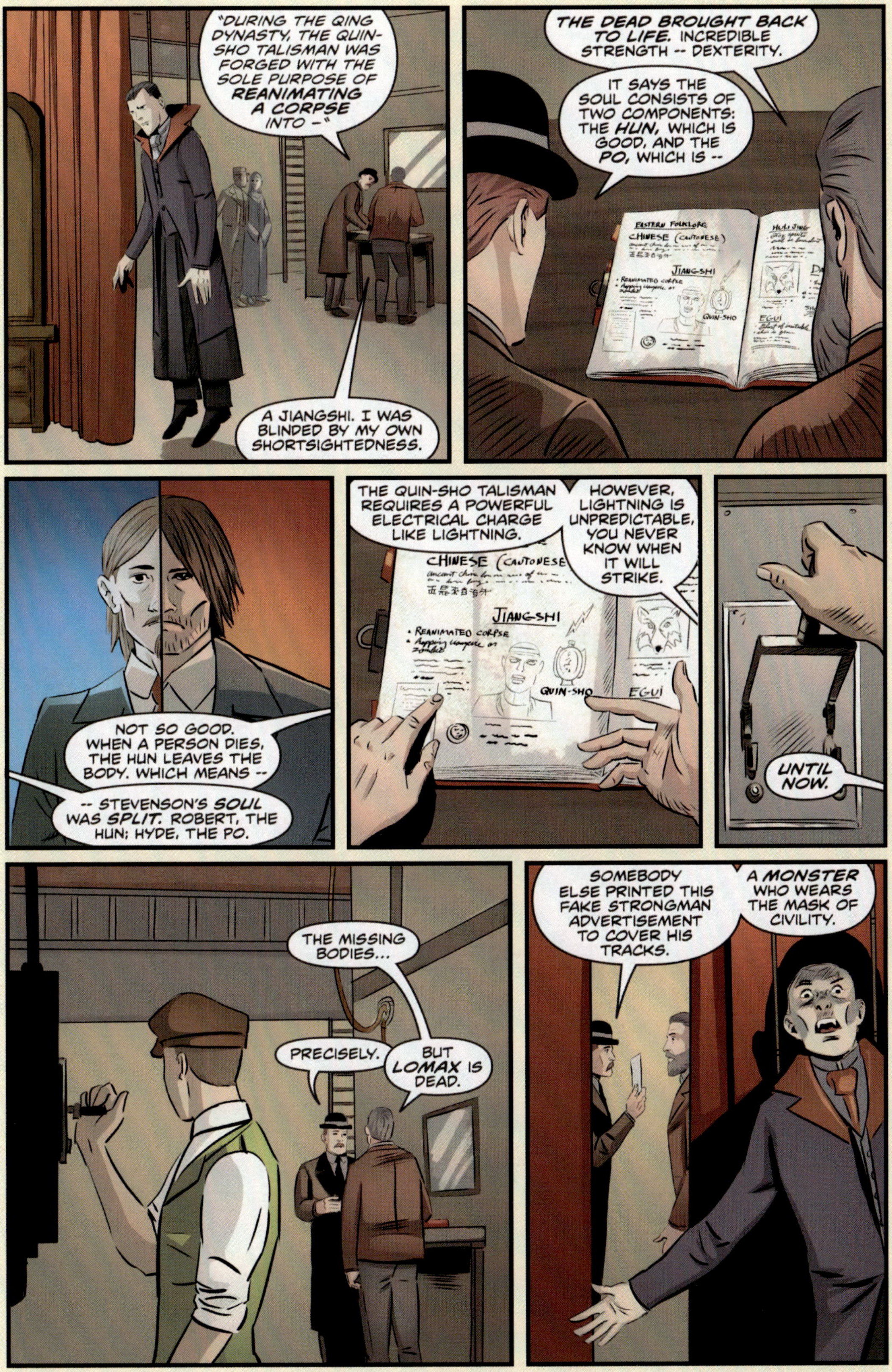

"DURING THE QING DYNASTY, THE QUIN-SHO TALISMAN WAS FORGED WITH THE SOLE PURPOSE OF ***REANIMATING A CORPSE*** INTO --"
A JIANGSHI. I WAS BLINDED BY MY OWN SHORTSIGHTEDNESS.
THE DEAD BROUGHT BACK TO LIFE. INCREDIBLE STRENGTH -- DEXTERITY.
IT SAYS THE SOUL CONSISTS OF TWO COMPONENTS: THE ***HUN,*** WHICH IS GOOD, AND THE ***PO,*** WHICH IS --
EASTERN FOLKLORE
CHINESE (CANTONESE)
JIANGSHI
QUIN-SHO
EGUI
NOT SO GOOD. WHEN A PERSON DIES, THE HUN LEAVES THE BODY. WHICH MEANS --
-- STEVENSON'S ***SOUL*** WAS ***SPLIT.*** ROBERT, THE HUN; HYDE, THE PO.
THE QUIN-SHO TALISMAN REQUIRES A POWERFUL ELECTRICAL CHARGE LIKE LIGHTNING.
HOWEVER, LIGHTNING IS UNPREDICTABLE, YOU NEVER KNOW WHEN IT WILL STRIKE.
CHINESE (CANTONESE
JIANGSHI
• REANIMATED CORPSE
QUIN-SHO
EGUI
UNTIL NOW.
THE MISSING BODIES...
PRECISELY.
BUT ***LOMAX*** IS DEAD.
SOMEBODY ELSE PRINTED THIS FAKE STRONGMAN ADVERTISEMENT TO COVER HIS TRACKS.
A ***MONSTER*** WHO WEARS THE MASK OF CIVILITY.

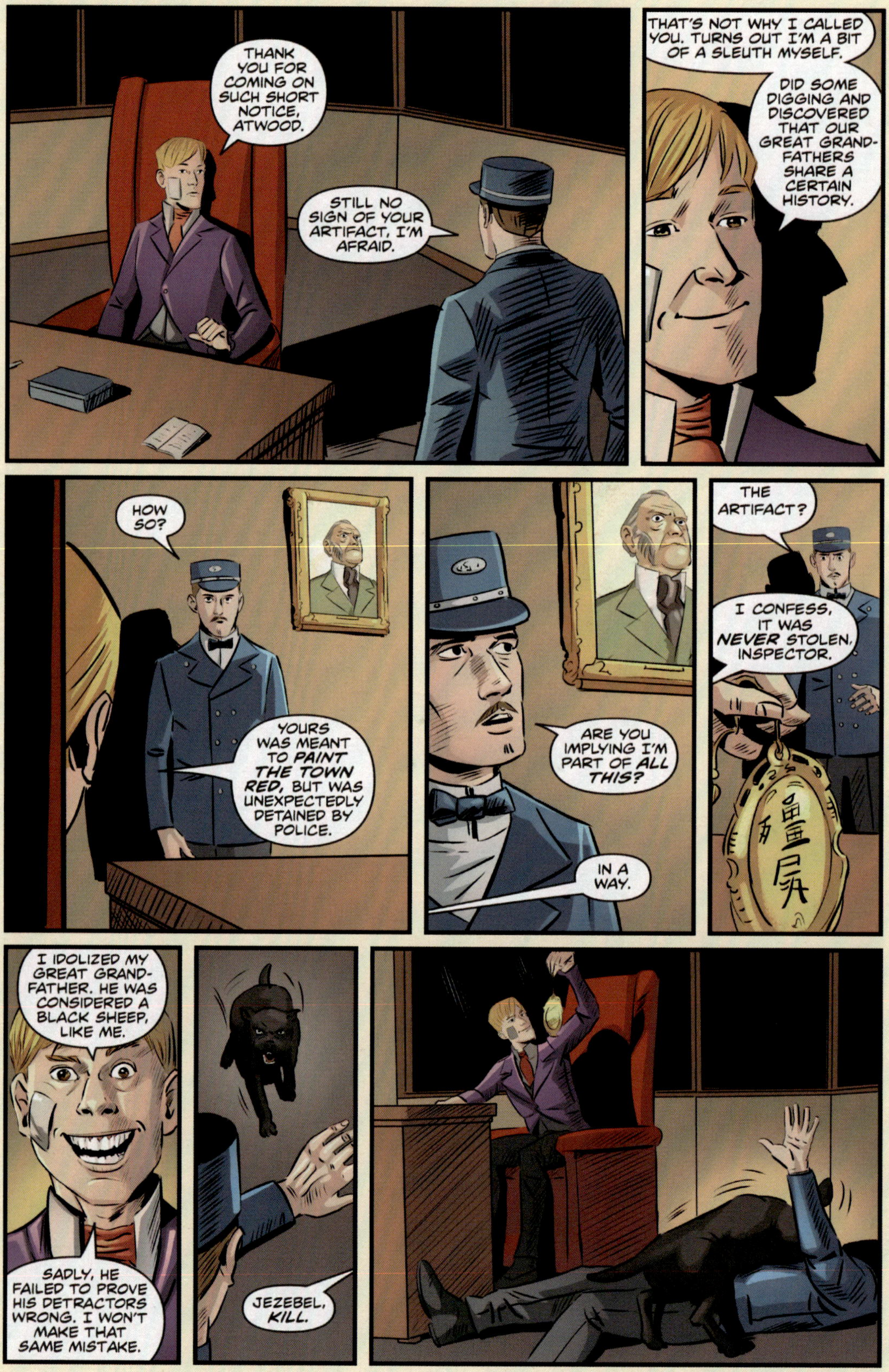
THANK YOU FOR COMING ON SUCH SHORT NOTICE, ATWOOD.
STILL NO SIGN OF YOUR ARTIFACT, I'M AFRAID.
THAT'S NOT WHY I CALLED YOU. TURNS OUT I'M A BIT OF A SLEUTH MYSELF.
DID SOME DIGGING AND DISCOVERED THAT OUR GREAT GRAND-FATHERS SHARE A CERTAIN HISTORY.
HOW SO?
YOURS WAS MEANT TO PAINT THE TOWN RED, BUT WAS UNEXPECTEDLY DETAINED BY POLICE.
ARE YOU IMPLYING I'M PART OF ALL THIS?
IN A WAY.
THE ARTIFACT?
I CONFESS, IT WAS NEVER STOLEN, INSPECTOR.
I IDOLIZED MY GREAT GRAND-FATHER. HE WAS CONSIDERED A BLACK SHEEP, LIKE ME.
SADLY, HE FAILED TO PROVE HIS DETRACTORS WRONG. I WON'T MAKE THAT SAME MISTAKE.
JEZEBEL, KILL.

Chapter Seven

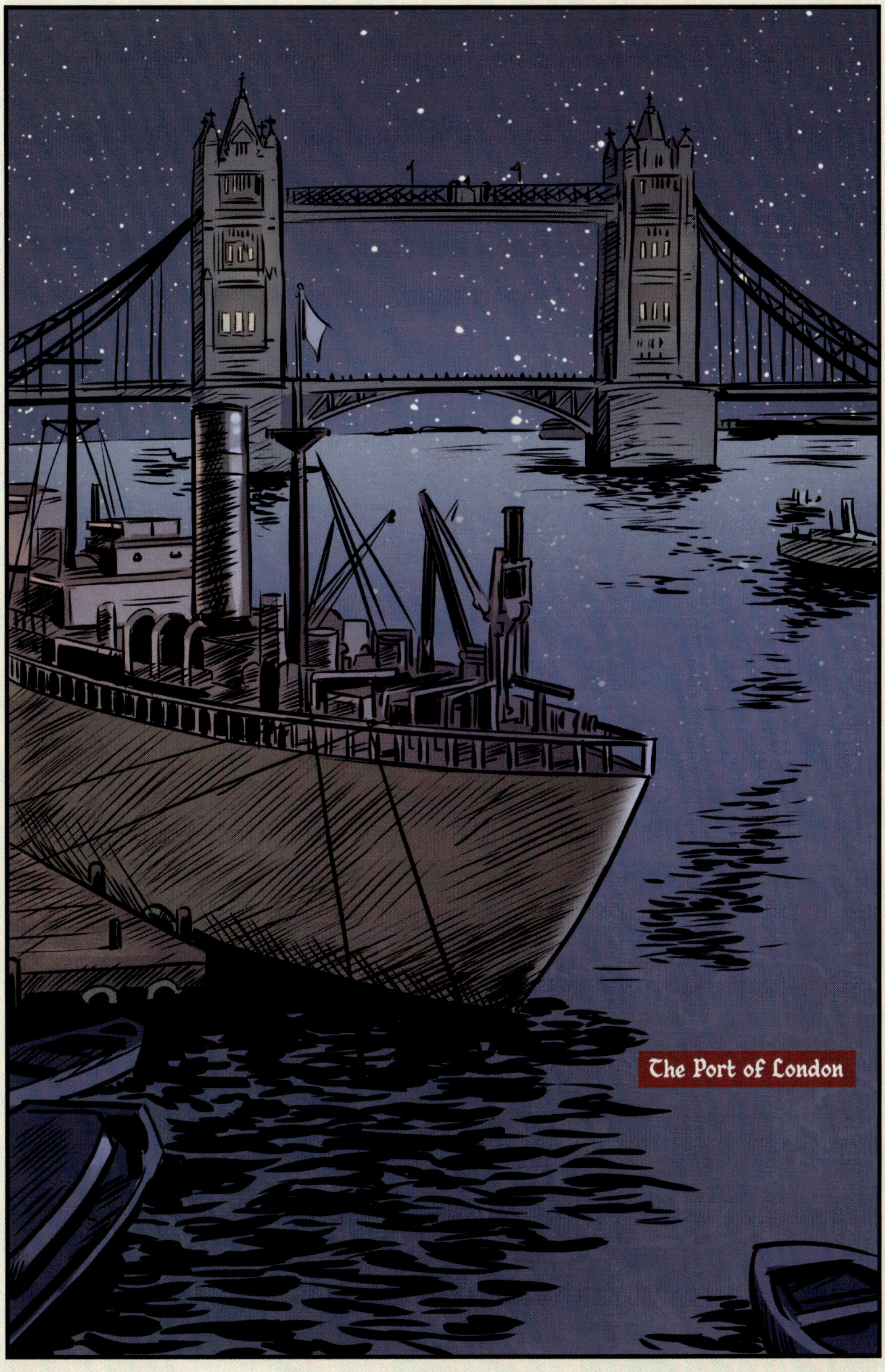
The Port of London

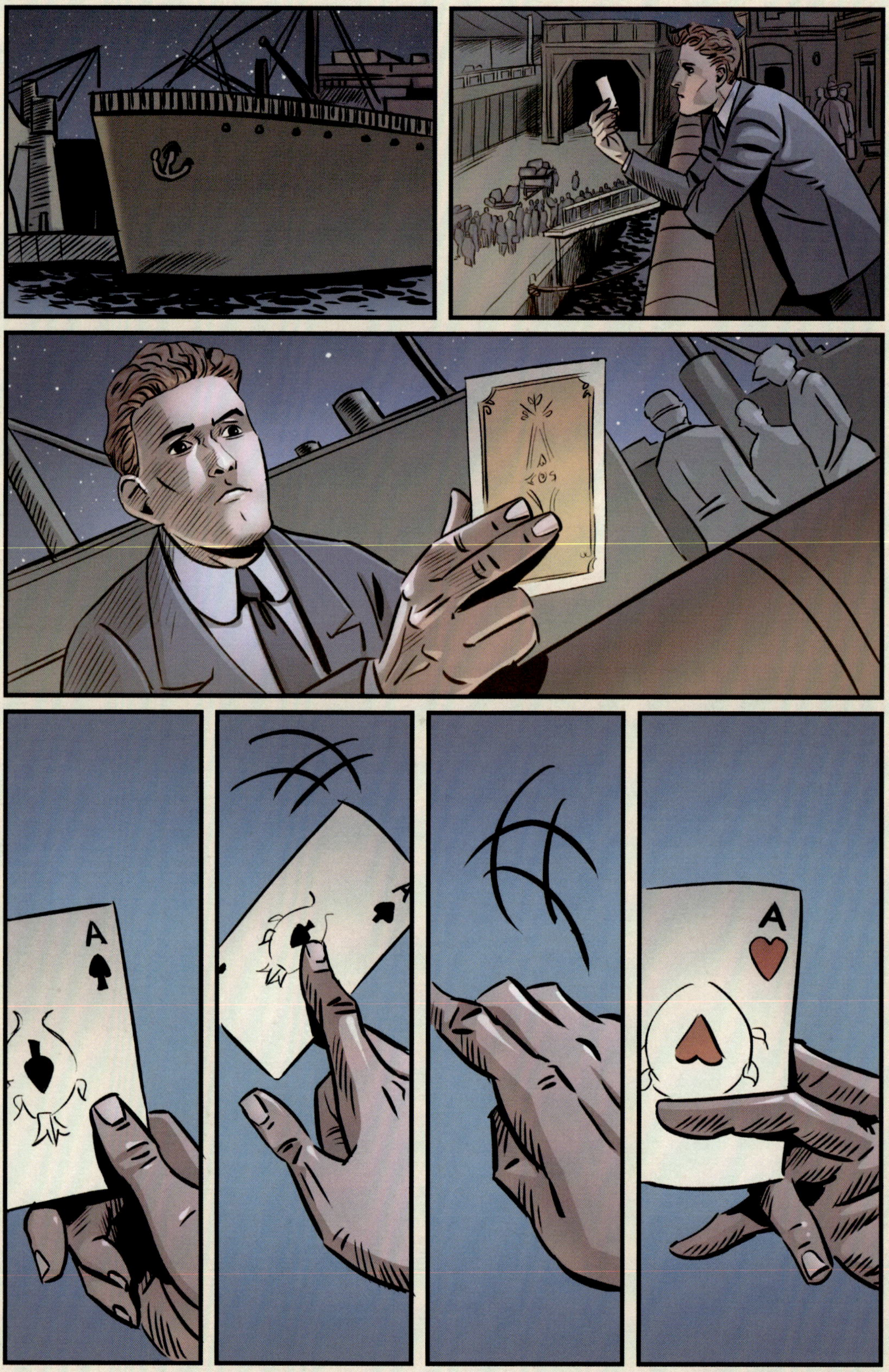

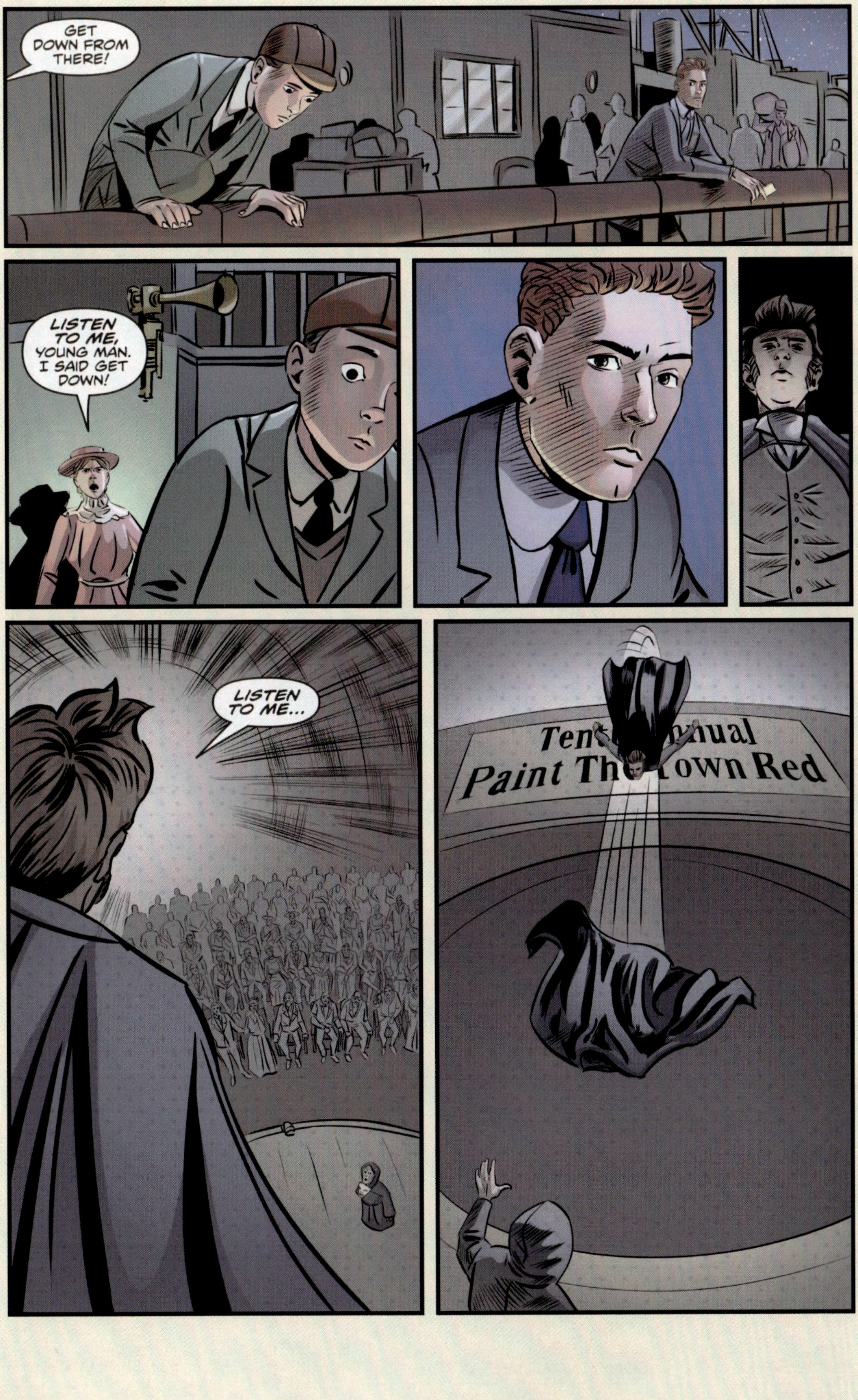
GET DOWN FROM THERE!
LISTEN TO ME, YOUNG MAN. I SAID GET DOWN!
LISTEN TO ME...
Paint Red

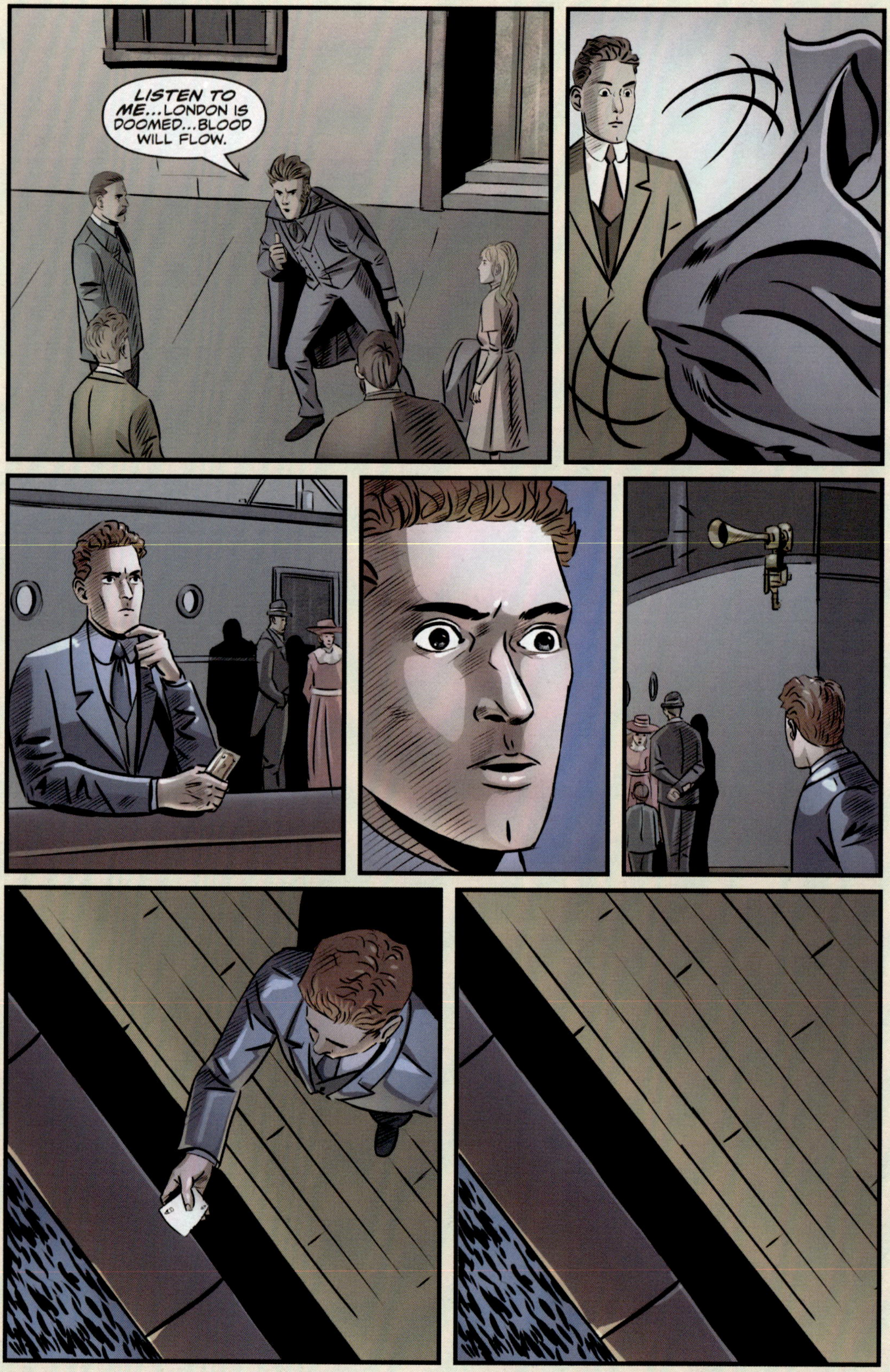
LISTEN TO ME...LONDON IS DOOMED...BLOOD WILL FLOW.

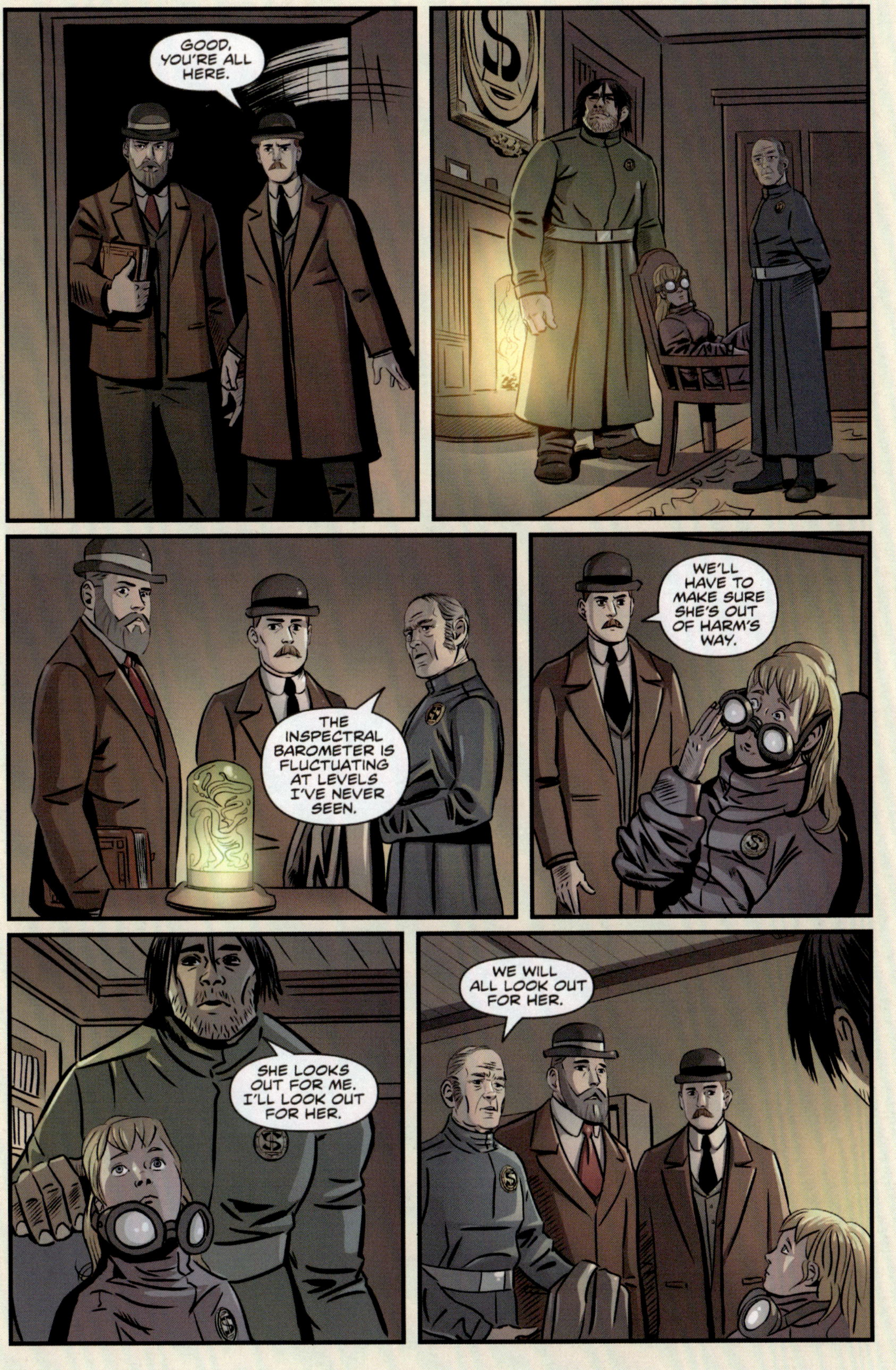
GOOD, YOU'RE ALL HERE.
THE INSPECTRAL BAROMETER IS FLUCTUATING AT LEVELS I'VE NEVER SEEN.
WE'LL HAVE TO MAKE SURE SHE'S OUT OF HARM'S WAY.
SHE LOOKS OUT FOR ME. I'LL LOOK OUT FOR HER.
WE WILL ALL LOOK OUT FOR HER.

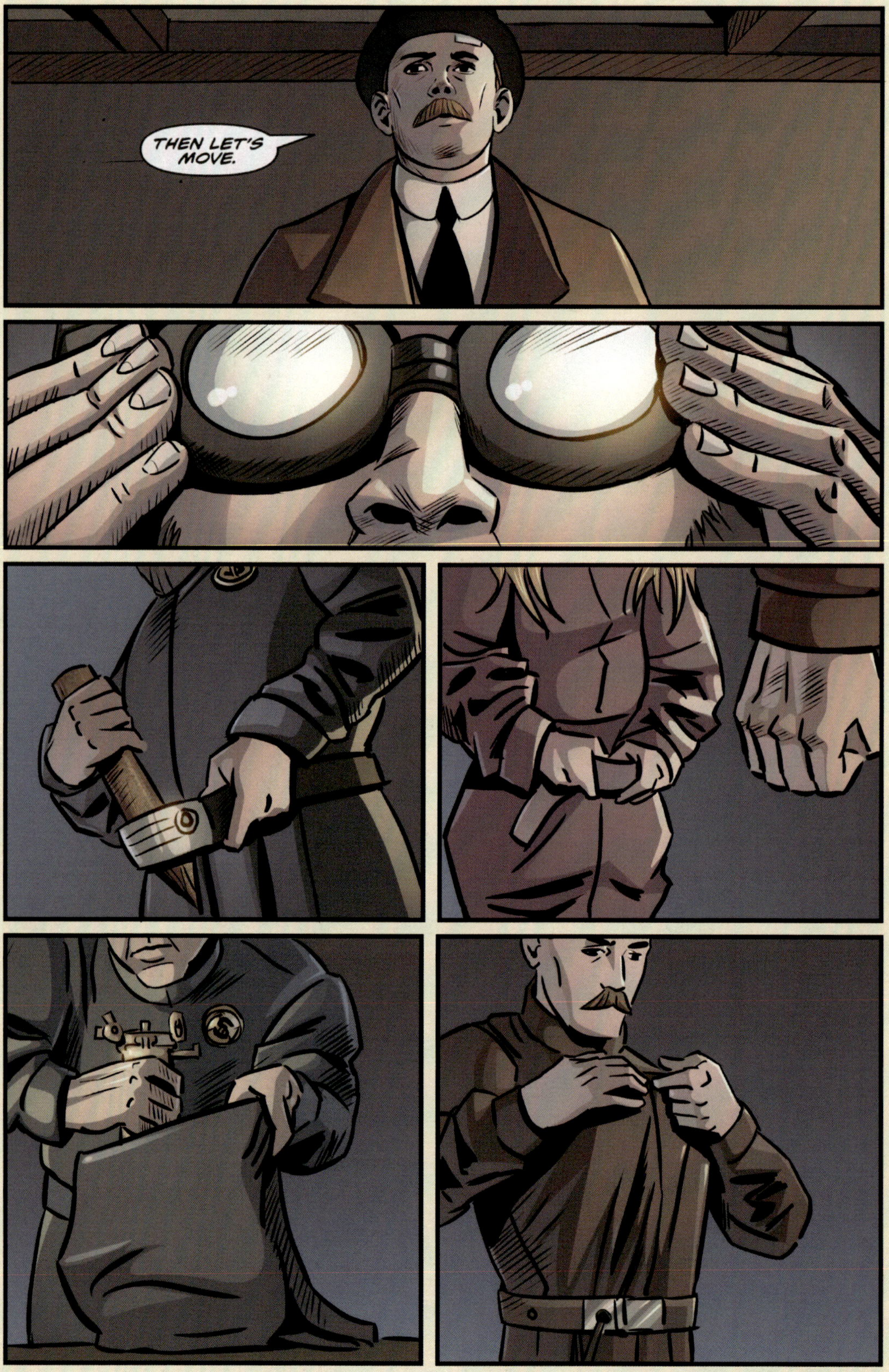
THEN LET'S MOVE.

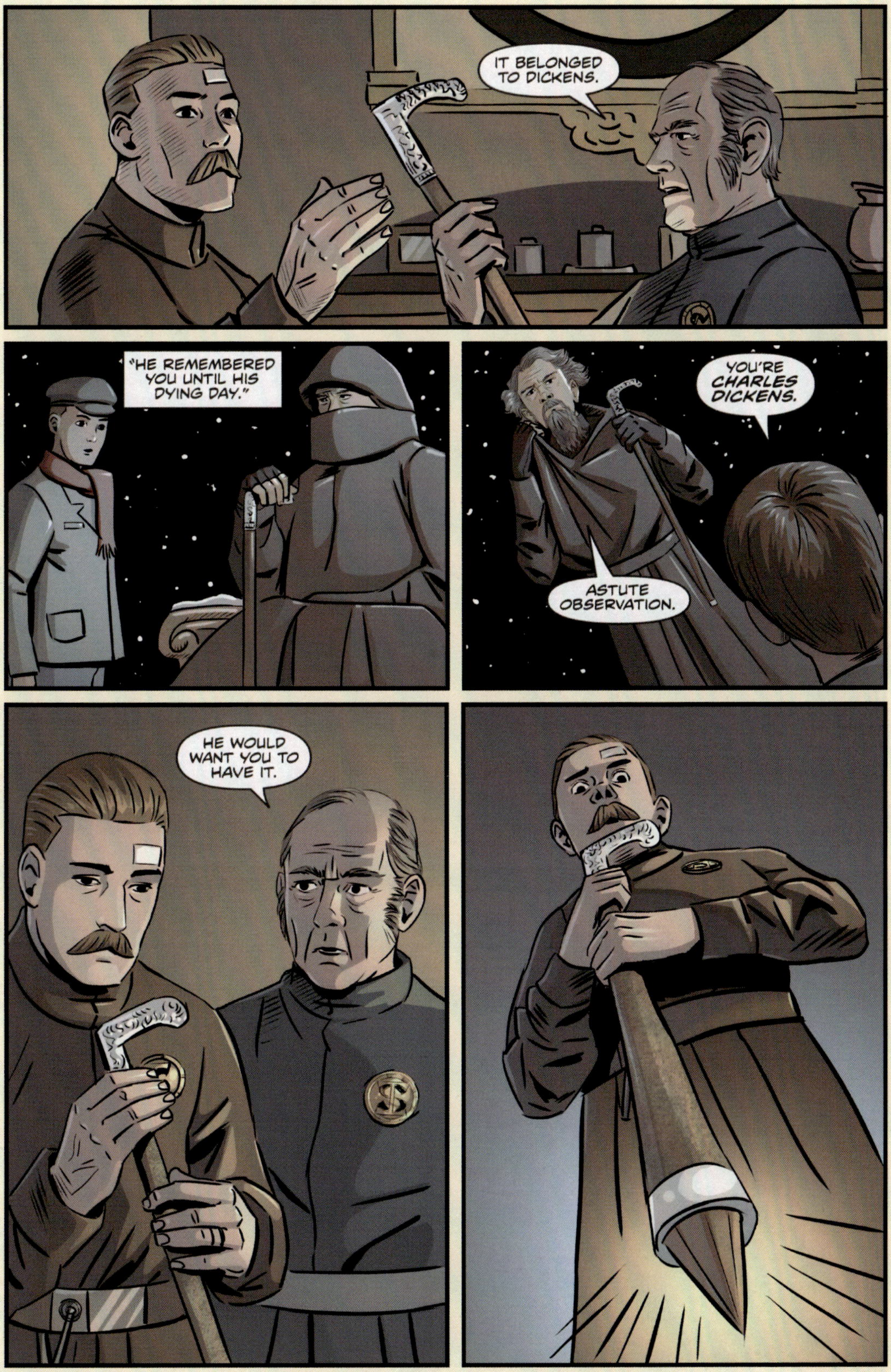
IT BELONGED TO DICKENS.
"HE REMEMBERED YOU UNTIL HIS DYING DAY."
YOU'RE CHARLES DICKENS.
ASTUTE OBSERVATION.
HE WOULD WANT YOU TO HAVE IT.

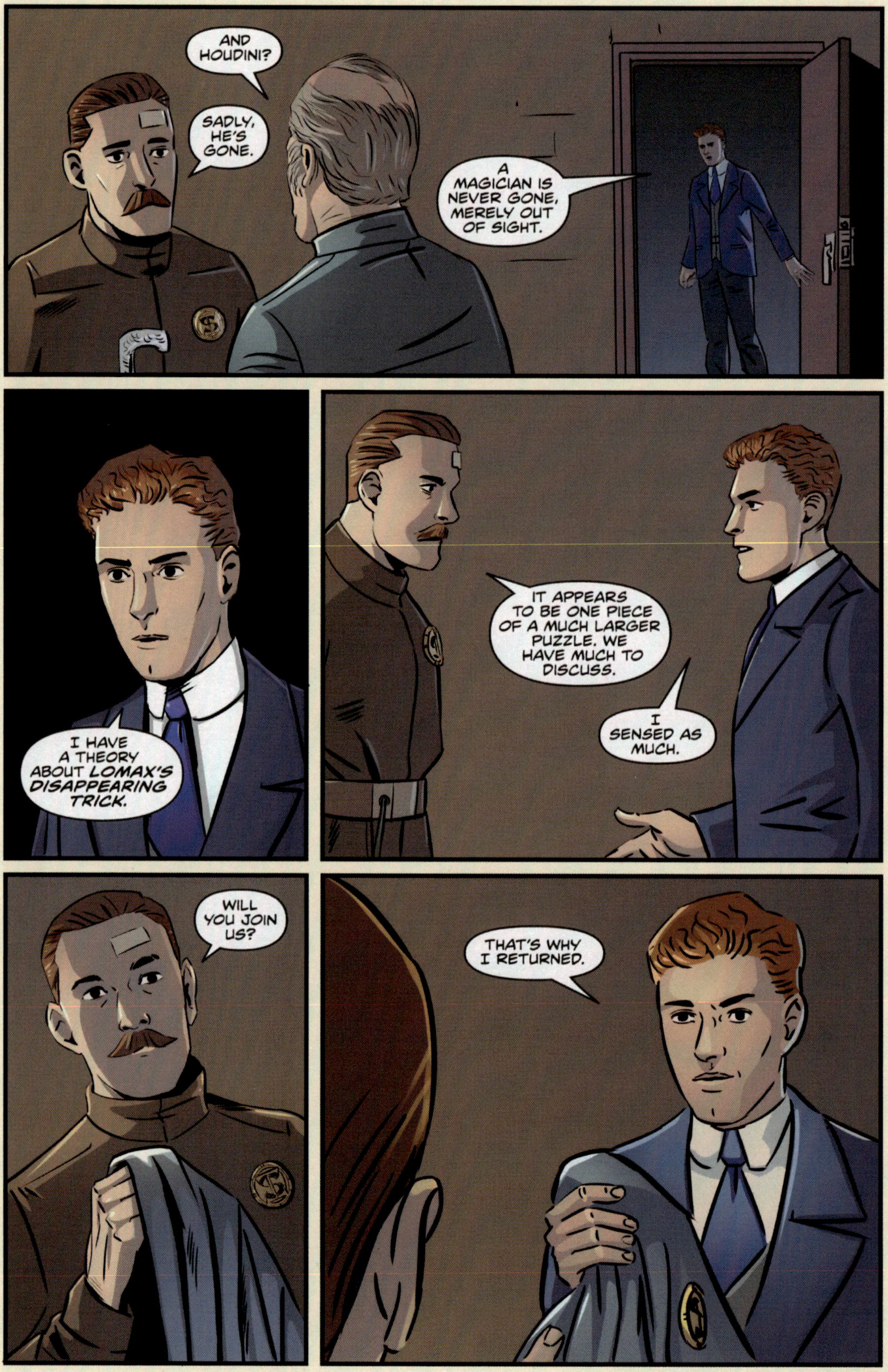
AND HOUDINI?
SADLY, HE'S GONE.
A MAGICIAN IS NEVER GONE, MERELY OUT OF SIGHT.
I HAVE A THEORY ABOUT *LOMAX'S DISAPPEARING TRICK.*
IT APPEARS TO BE ONE PIECE OF A MUCH LARGER PUZZLE. WE HAVE MUCH TO DISCUSS.
I SENSED AS MUCH.
WILL YOU JOIN US?
THAT'S WHY I RETURNED.

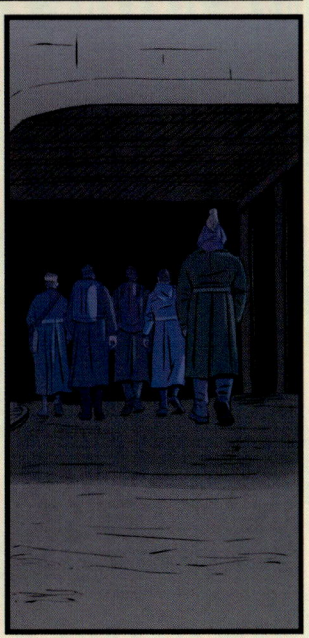

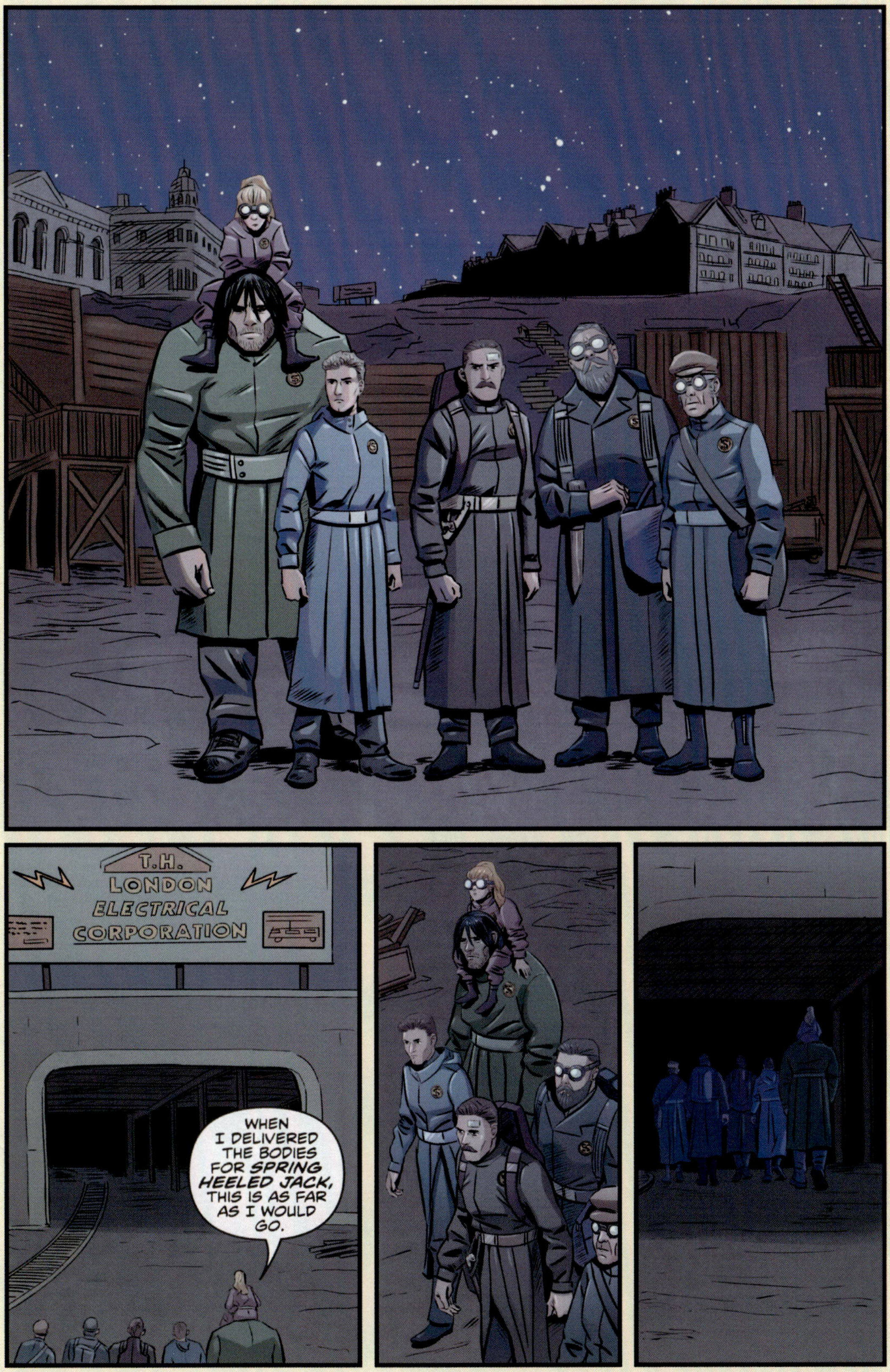
T.H.
LONDON
ELECTRICAL
CORPORATION
WHEN I DELIVERED THE BODIES FOR *SPRING HEELED JACK*, THIS IS AS FAR AS I WOULD GO.

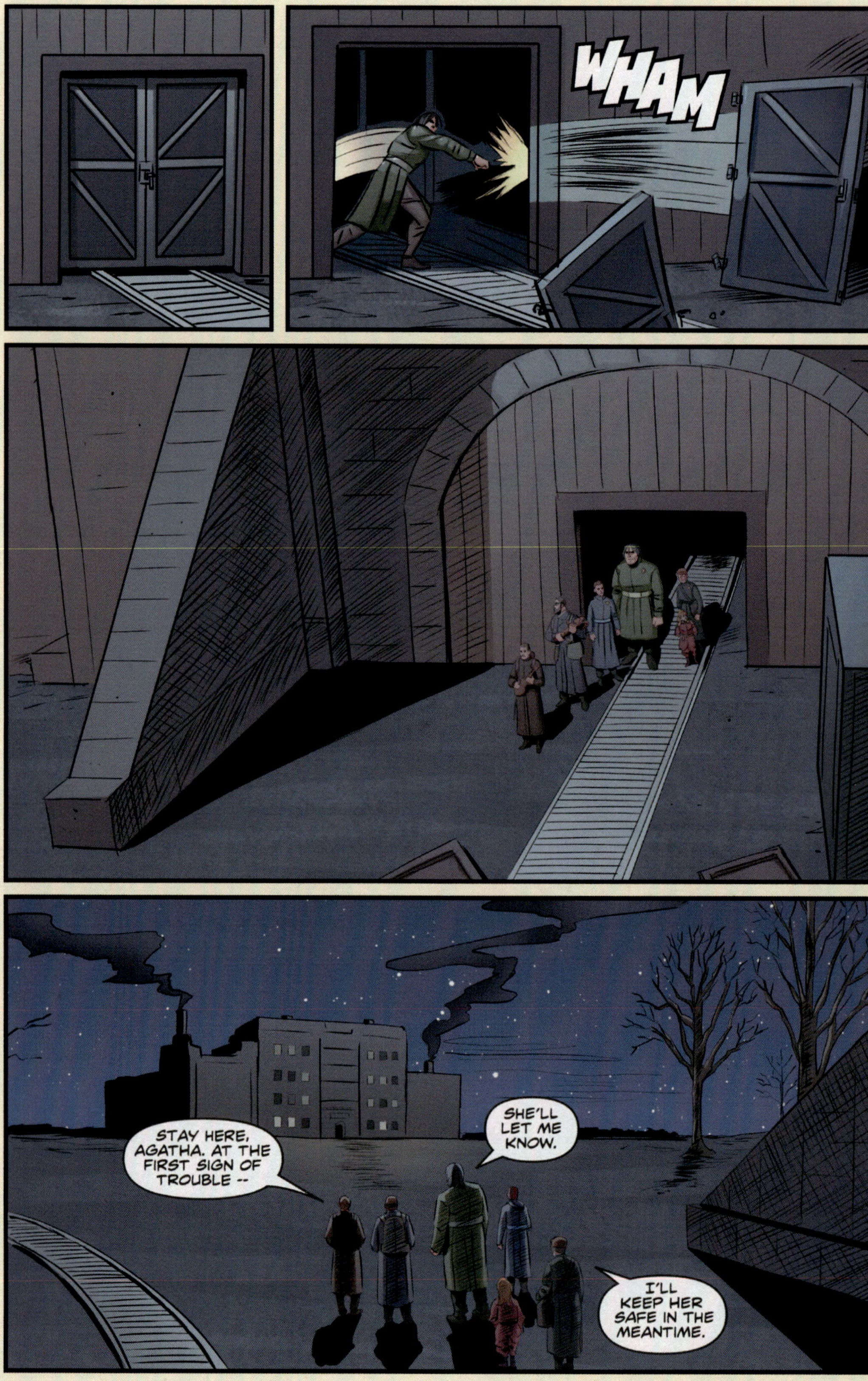
WHAM
STAY HERE, AGATHA. AT THE FIRST SIGN OF TROUBLE --
SHE'LL LET ME KNOW.
I'LL KEEP HER SAFE IN THE MEANTIME.

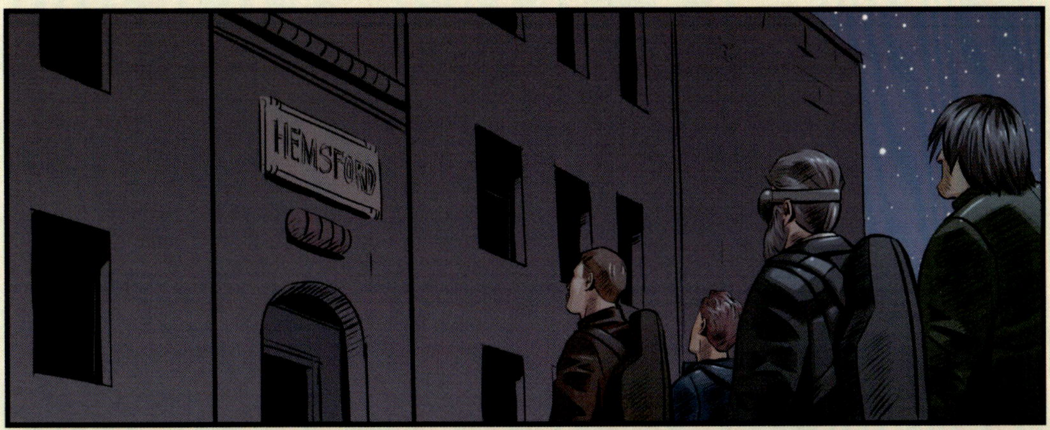
HEMSFORD

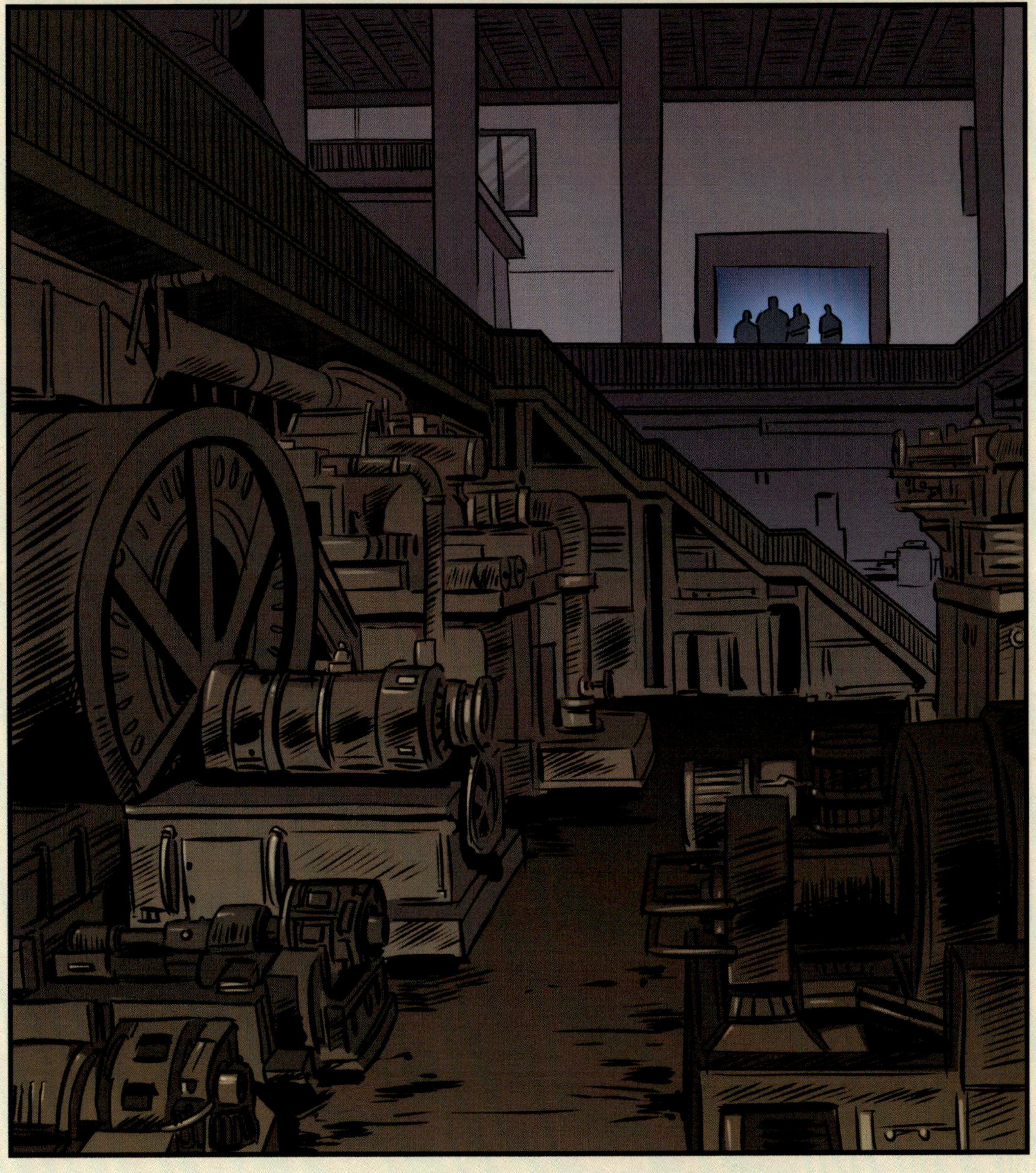

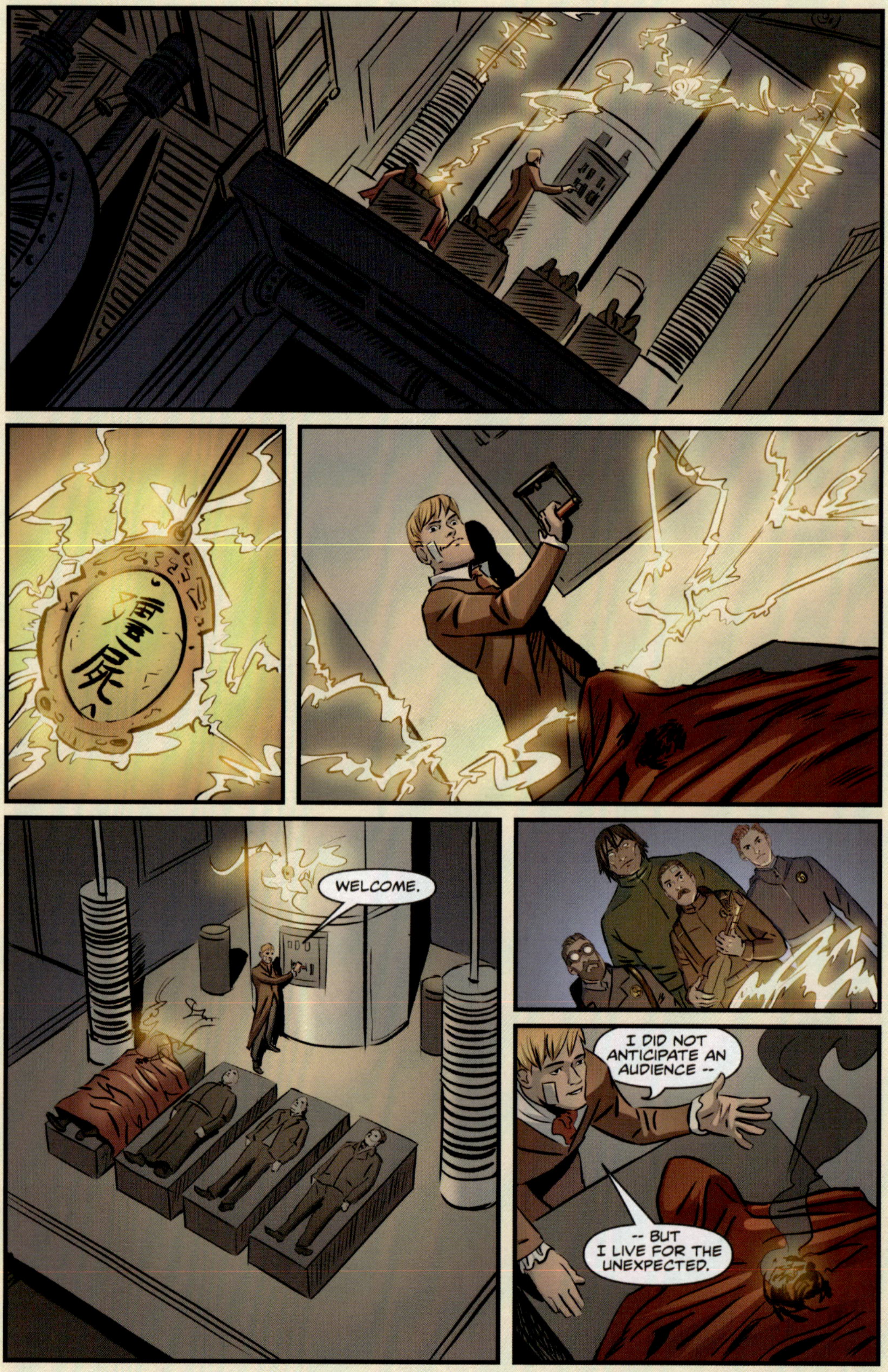
WELCOME.
I DID NOT ANTICIPATE AN AUDIENCE --
-- BUT I LIVE FOR THE UNEXPECTED.

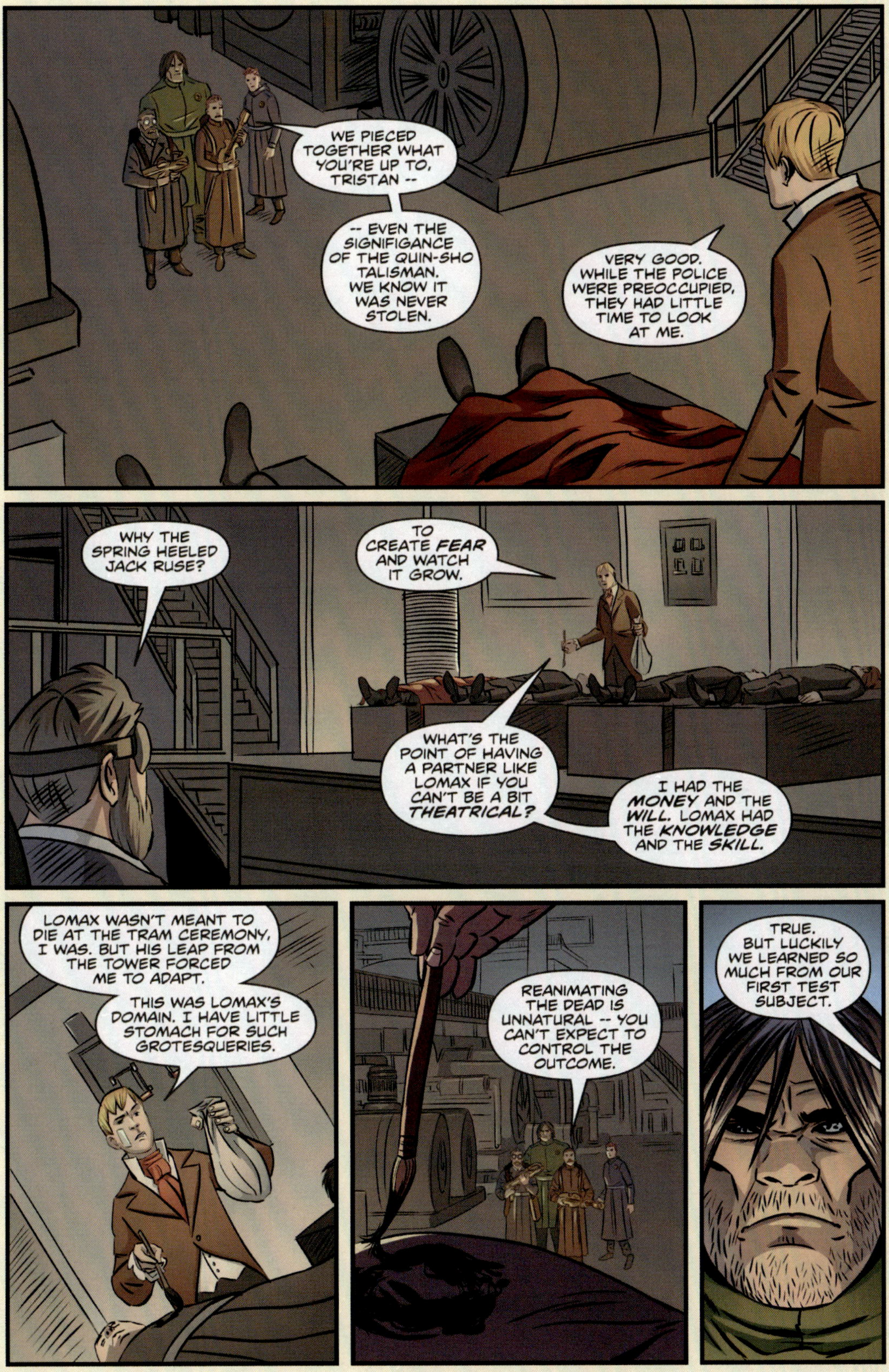
WE PIECED TOGETHER WHAT YOU'RE UP TO, TRISTAN --
-- EVEN THE SIGNIFIGANCE OF THE QUIN-SHO TALISMAN. WE KNOW IT WAS NEVER STOLEN.
VERY GOOD. WHILE THE POLICE WERE PREOCCUPIED, THEY HAD LITTLE TIME TO LOOK AT ME.
WHY THE SPRING HEELED JACK RUSE?
TO CREATE FEAR AND WATCH IT GROW.
WHAT'S THE POINT OF HAVING A PARTNER LIKE LOMAX IF YOU CAN'T BE A BIT THEATRICAL?
I HAD THE MONEY AND THE WILL. LOMAX HAD THE KNOWLEDGE AND THE SKILL.
LOMAX WASN'T MEANT TO DIE AT THE TRAM CEREMONY, I WAS. BUT HIS LEAP FROM THE TOWER FORCED ME TO ADAPT.
THIS WAS LOMAX'S DOMAIN. I HAVE LITTLE STOMACH FOR SUCH GROTESQUERIES.
REANIMATING THE DEAD IS UNNATURAL -- YOU CAN'T EXPECT TO CONTROL THE OUTCOME.
TRUE. BUT LUCKILY WE LEARNED SO MUCH FROM OUR FIRST TEST SUBJECT.

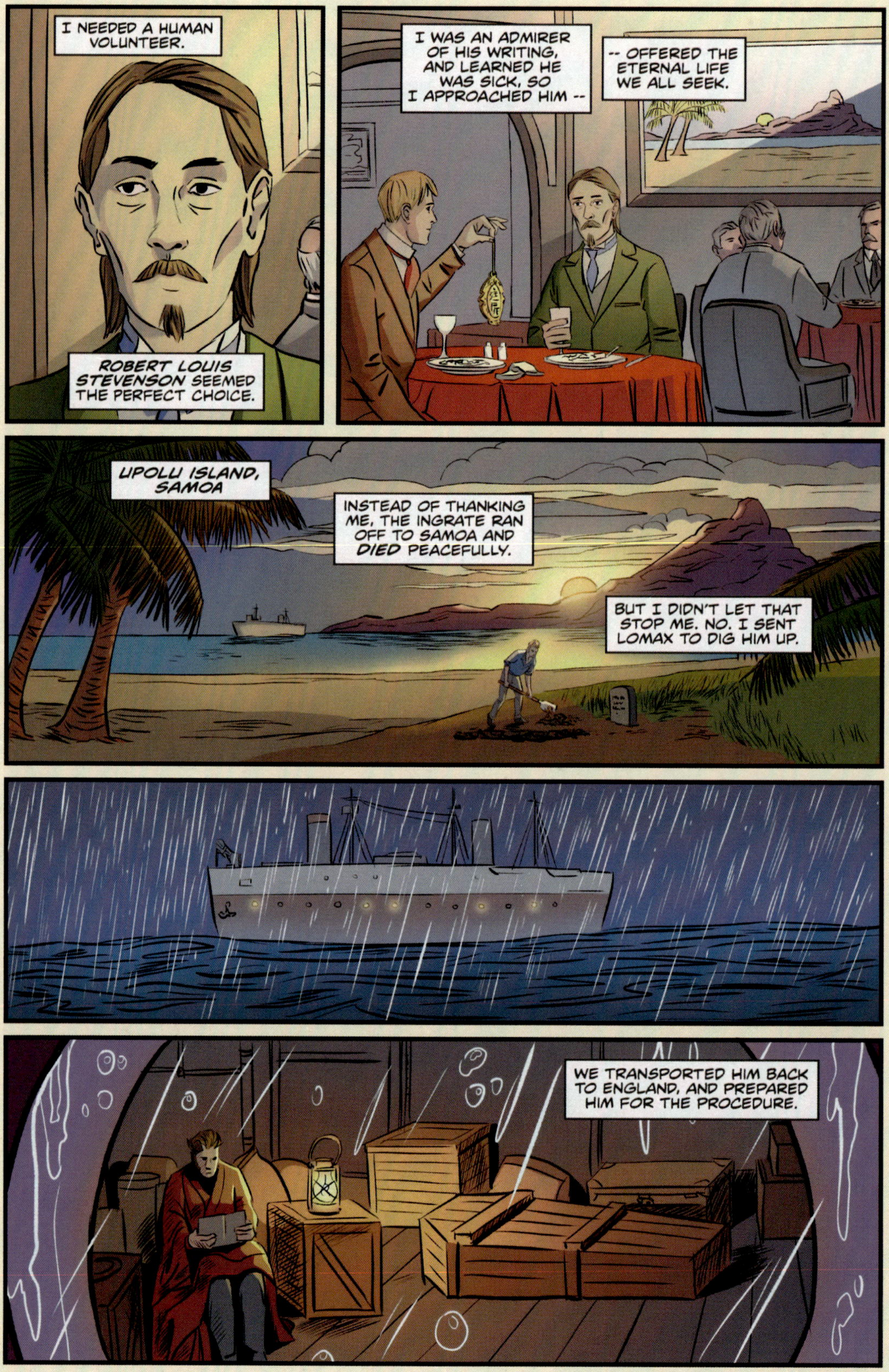
I NEEDED A HUMAN VOLUNTEER.
ROBERT LOUIS STEVENSON SEEMED THE PERFECT CHOICE.
I WAS AN ADMIRER OF HIS WRITING, AND LEARNED HE WAS SICK, SO I APPROACHED HIM --
-- OFFERED THE ETERNAL LIFE WE ALL SEEK.
UPOLU ISLAND, SAMOA
INSTEAD OF THANKING ME, THE INGRATE RAN OFF TO SAMOA AND DIED PEACEFULLY.
BUT I DIDN'T LET THAT STOP ME. NO. I SENT LOMAX TO DIG HIM UP.
WE TRANSPORTED HIM BACK TO ENGLAND, AND PREPARED HIM FOR THE PROCEDURE.

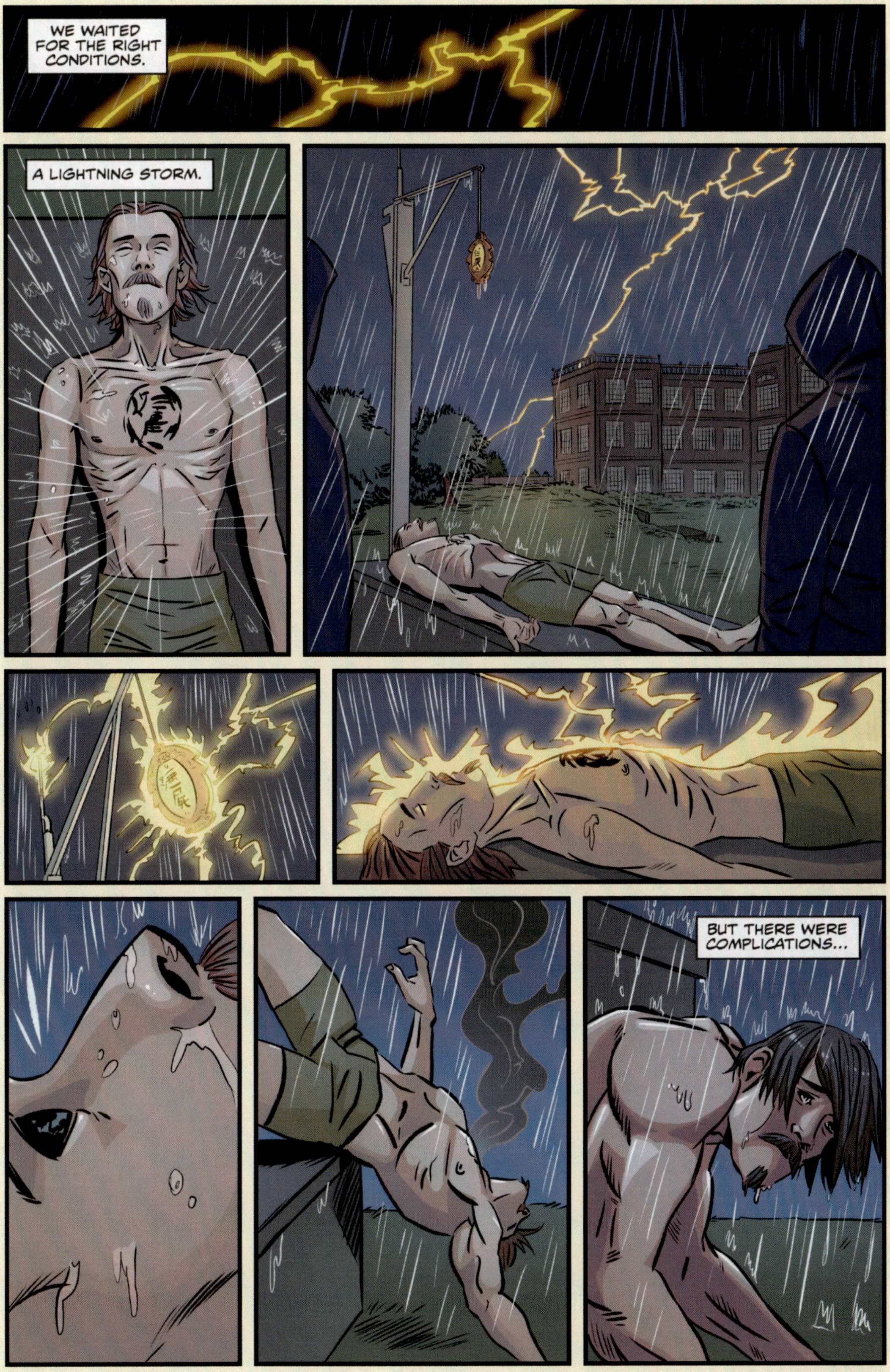
WE WAITED FOR THE RIGHT CONDITIONS.
A LIGHTNING STORM.
BUT THERE WERE COMPLICATIONS...

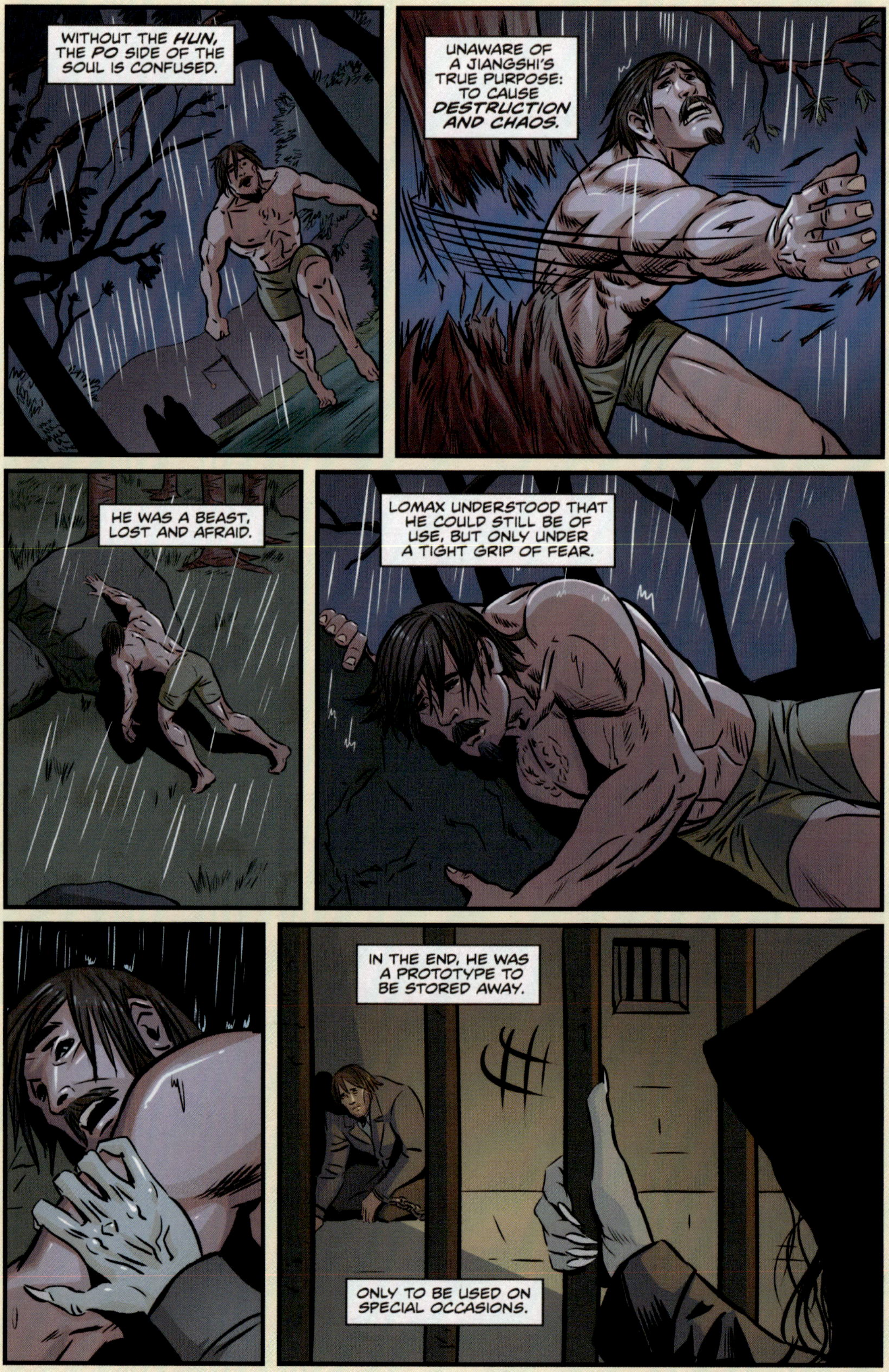
WITHOUT THE HUN, THE PO SIDE OF THE SOUL IS CONFUSED.
UNAWARE OF A JIANGSHI'S TRUE PURPOSE: TO CAUSE DESTRUCTION AND CHAOS.
HE WAS A BEAST, LOST AND AFRAID.
LOMAX UNDERSTOOD THAT HE COULD STILL BE OF USE, BUT ONLY UNDER A TIGHT GRIP OF FEAR.
IN THE END, HE WAS A PROTOTYPE TO BE STORED AWAY.
ONLY TO BE USED ON SPECIAL OCCASIONS.

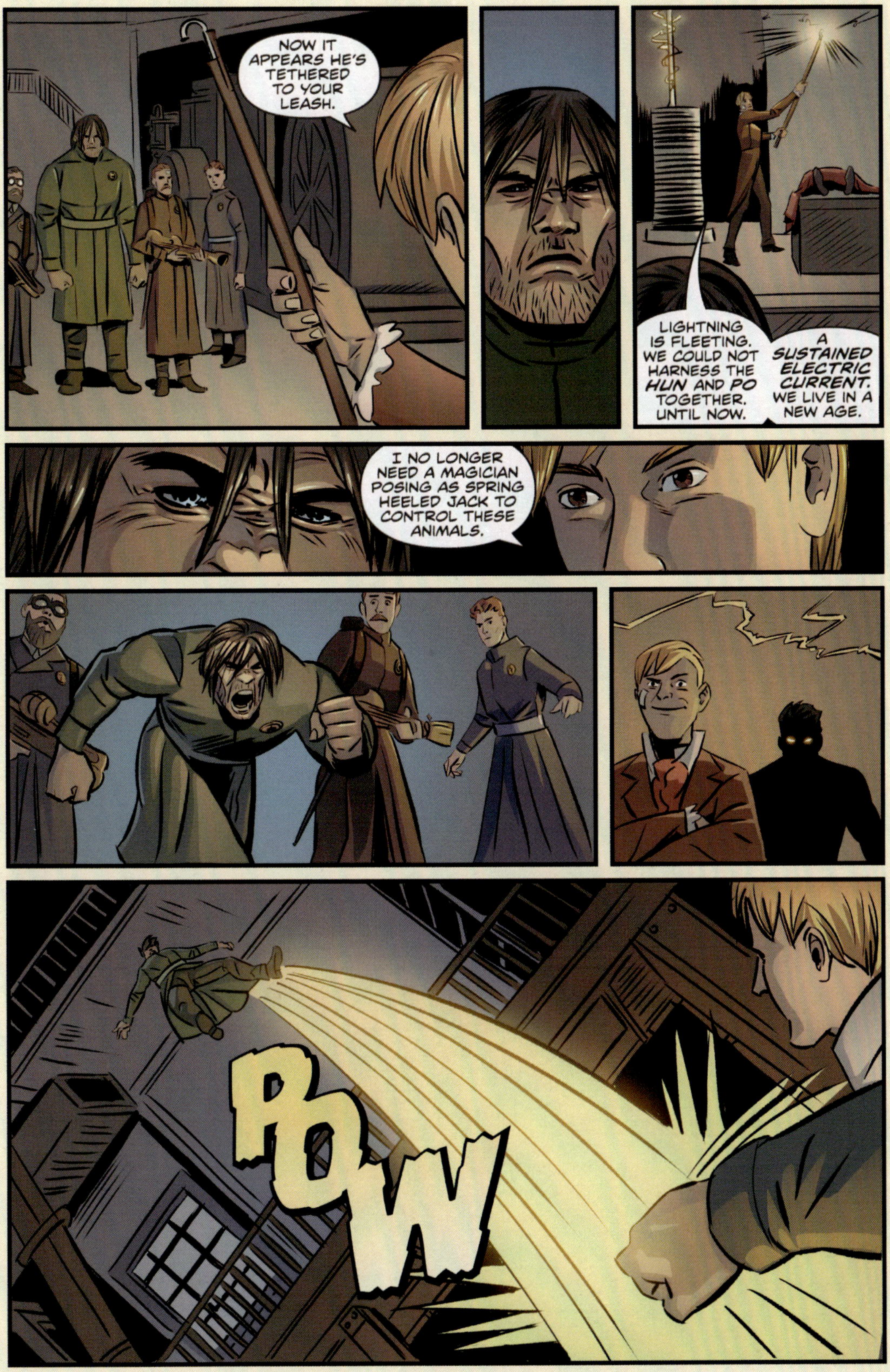
NOW IT APPEARS HE'S TETHERED TO YOUR LEASH.
LIGHTNING IS FLEETING. WE COULD NOT HARNESS THE *HUN* AND *PO* TOGETHER. UNTIL NOW.
A *SUSTAINED ELECTRIC CURRENT.* WE LIVE IN A NEW AGE.
I NO LONGER NEED A MAGICIAN POSING AS SPRING HEELED JACK TO CONTROL THESE ANIMALS.
POW

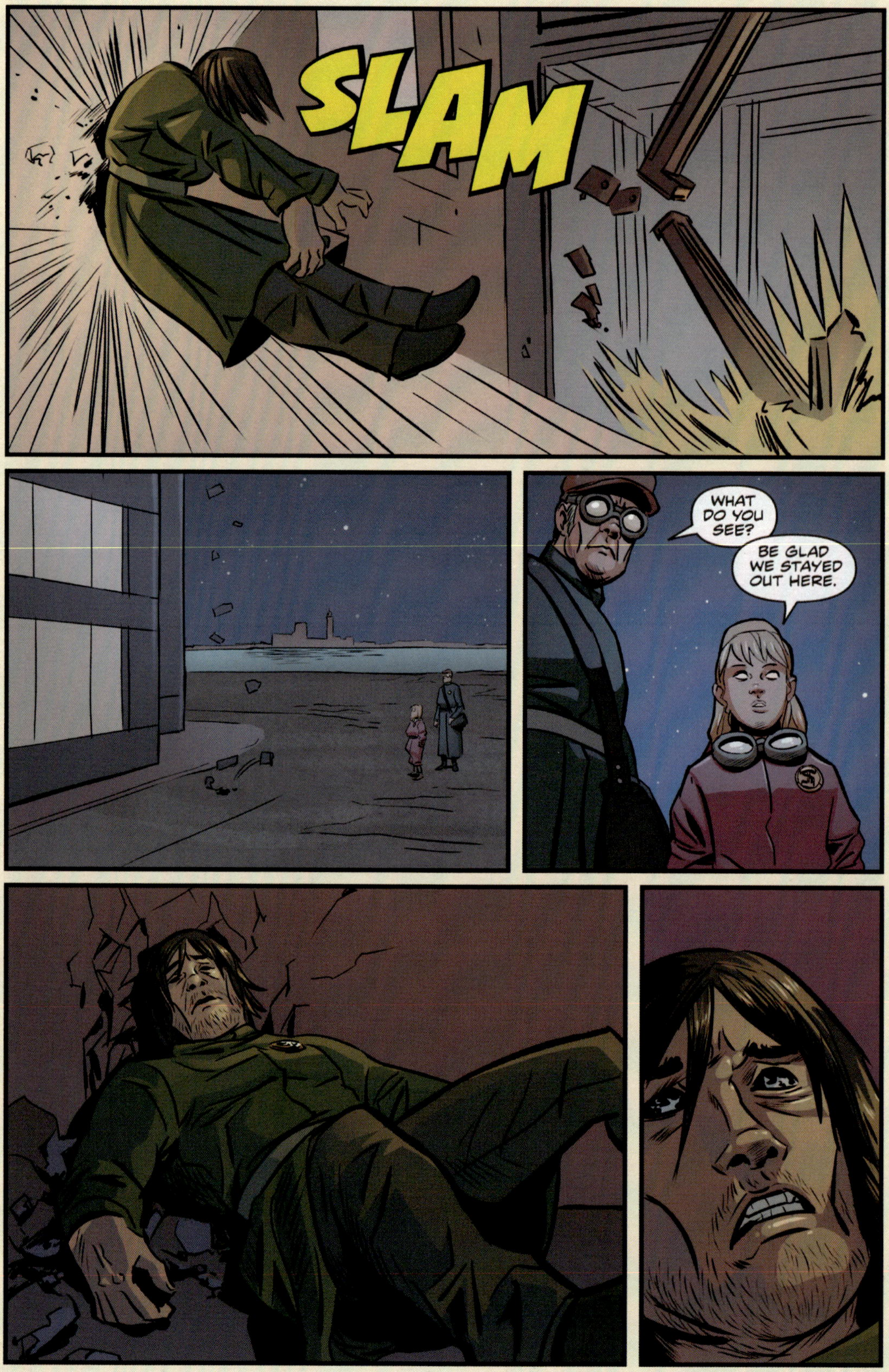
SLAM
WHAT DO YOU SEE?
BE GLAD WE STAYED OUT HERE.

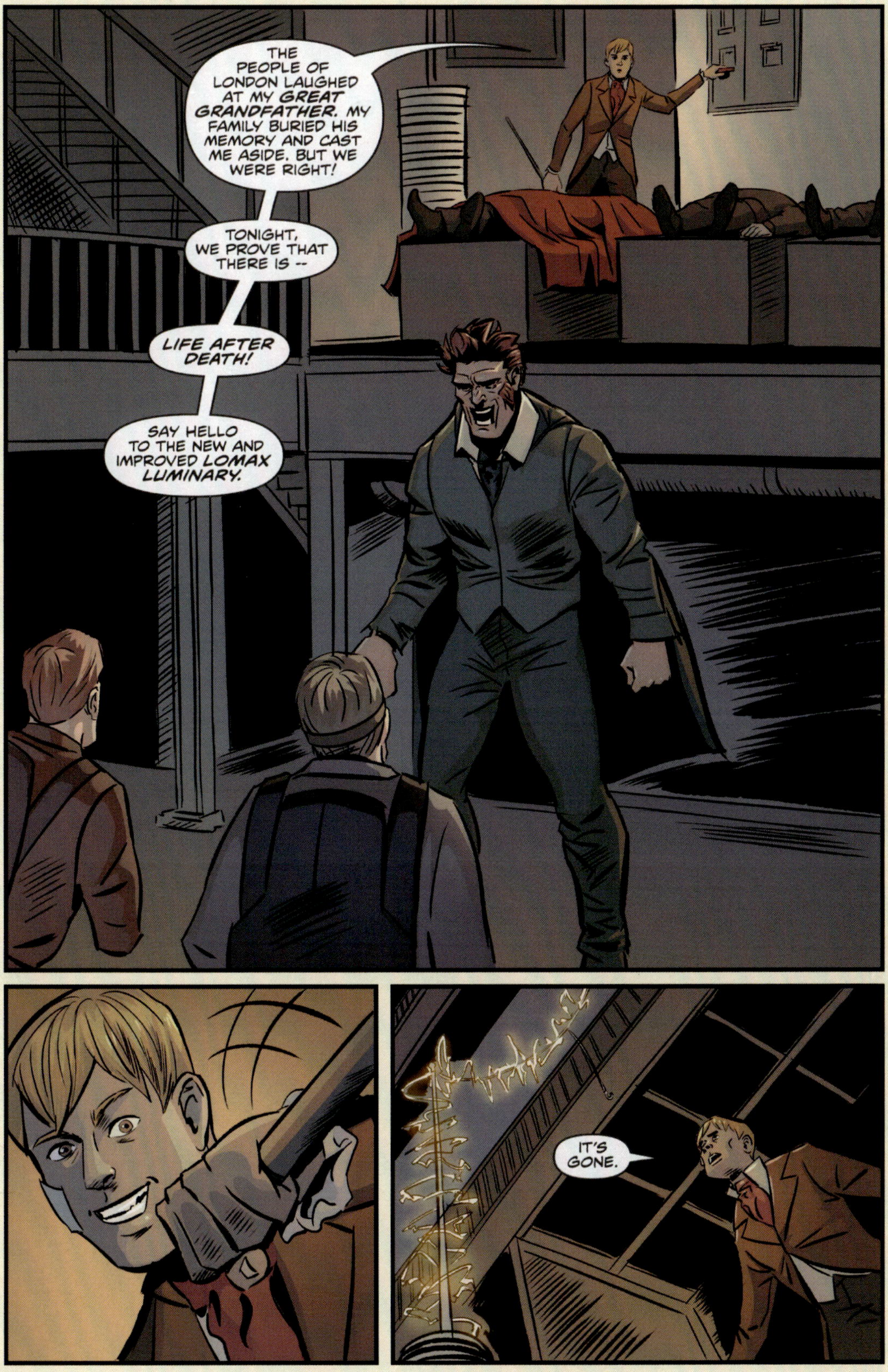
THE PEOPLE OF LONDON LAUGHED AT MY GREAT GRANDFATHER. MY FAMILY BURIED HIS MEMORY AND CAST ME ASIDE. BUT WE WERE RIGHT!
TONIGHT, WE PROVE THAT THERE IS --
LIFE AFTER DEATH!
SAY HELLO TO THE NEW AND IMPROVED LOMAX LUMINARY.
IT'S GONE.

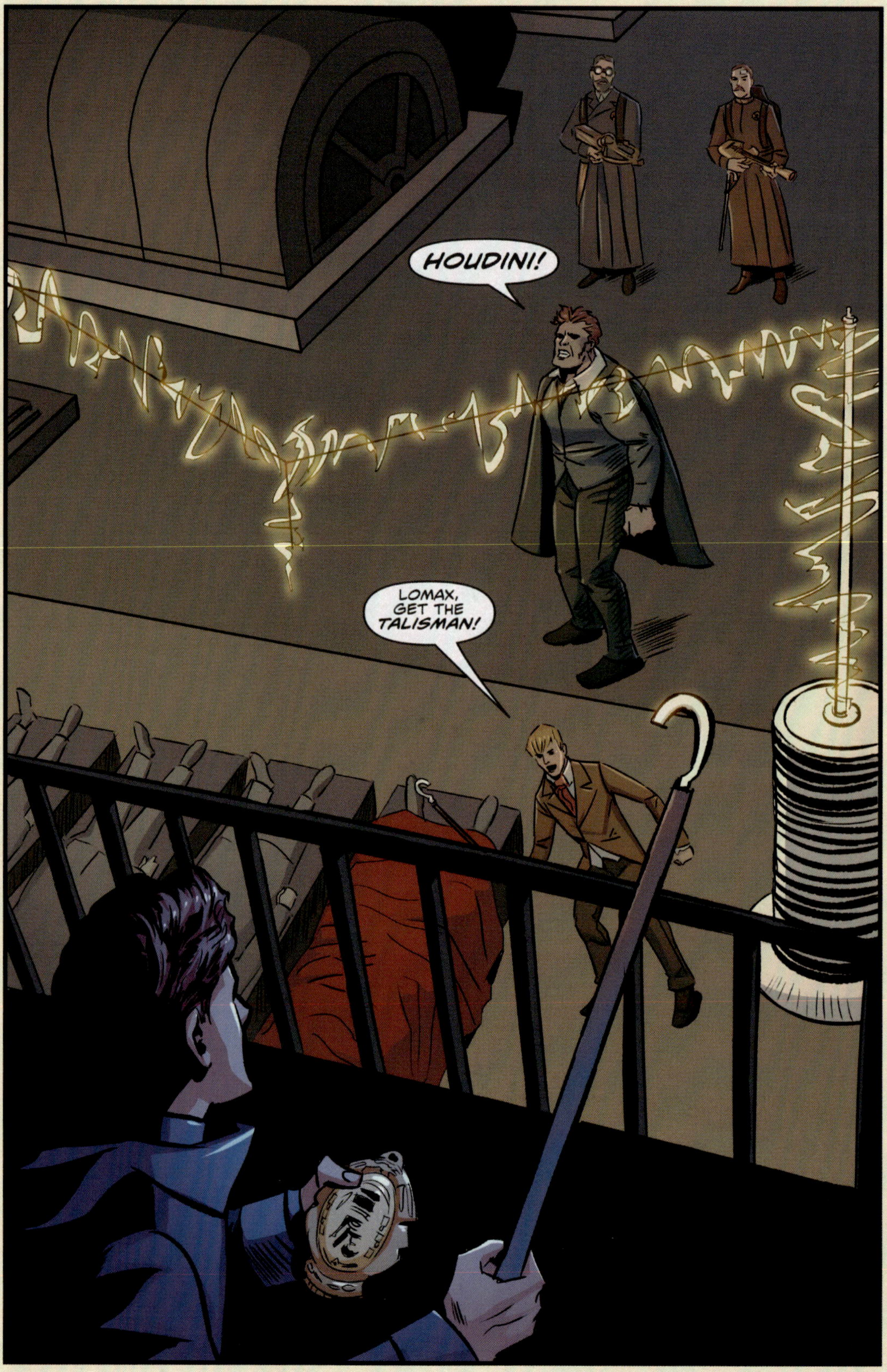
HOUDINI!
LOMAX, GET THE TALISMAN!

Chapter Eight

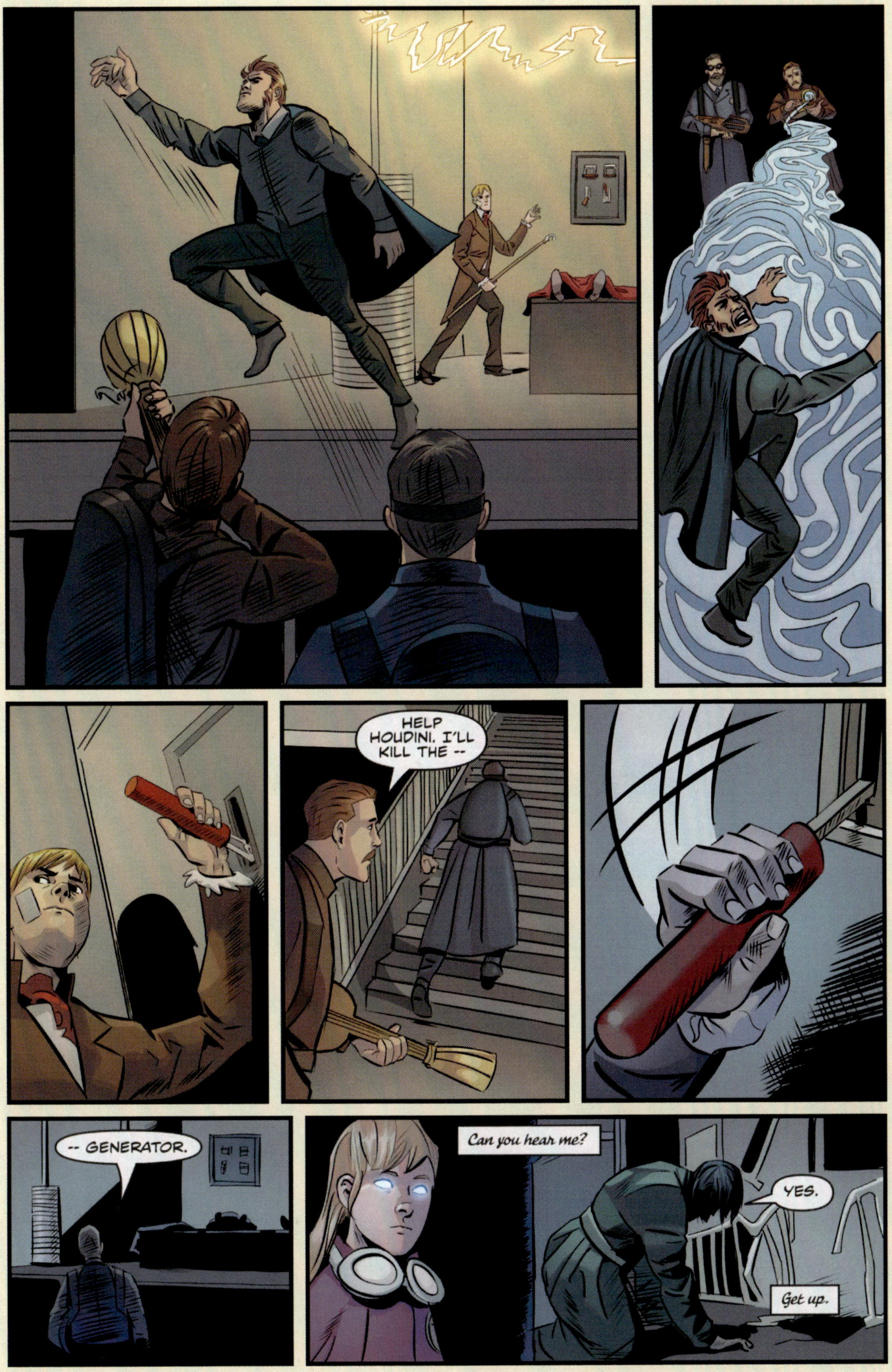
HELP HOUDINI. I'LL KILL THE --
-- GENERATOR.
Can you hear me?
YES.
Get up.

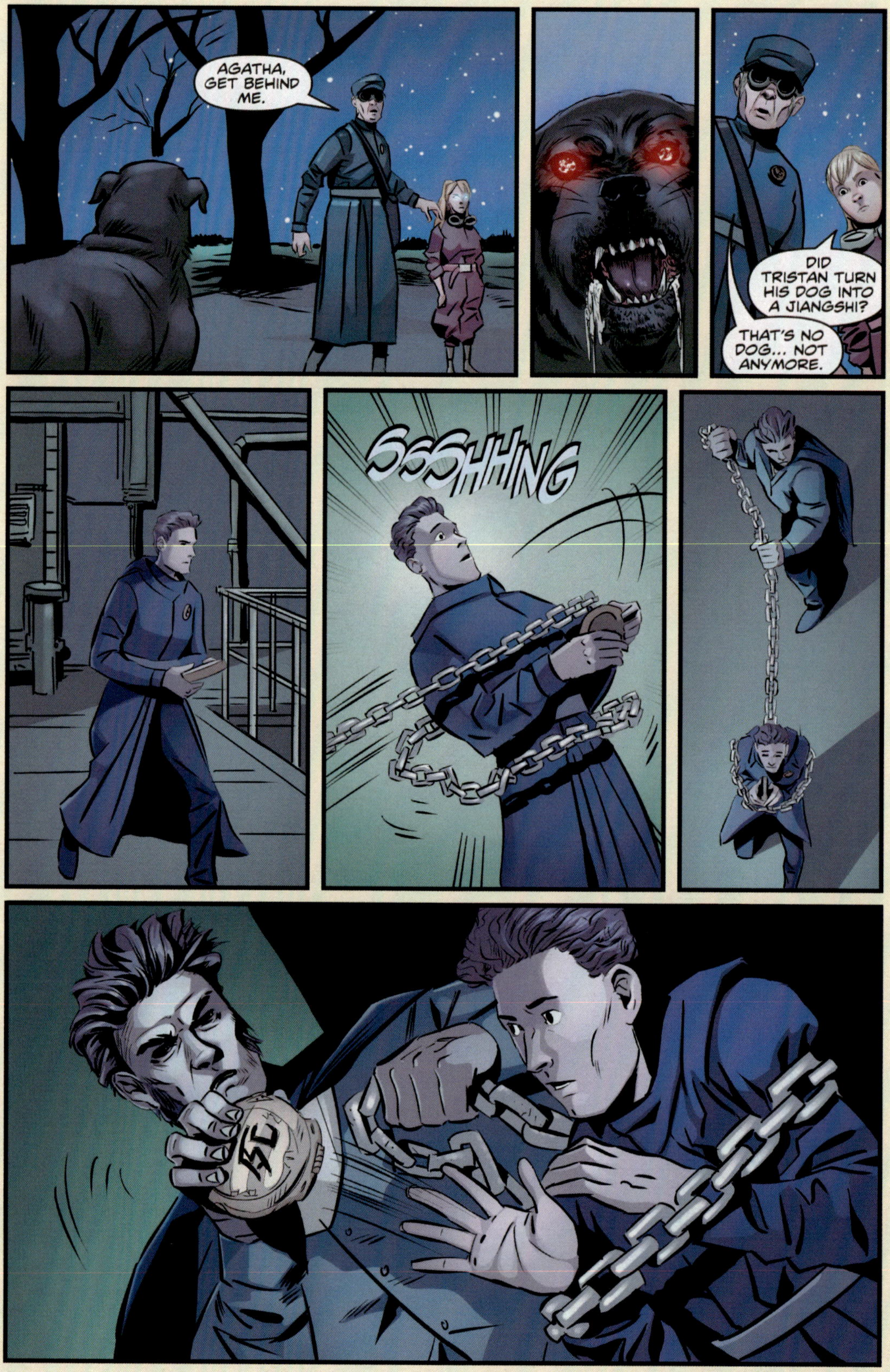
AGATHA, GET BEHIND ME.
DID TRISTAN TURN HIS DOG INTO A JIANGSHI?
THAT'S NO DOG... NOT ANYMORE.
SSSHHING

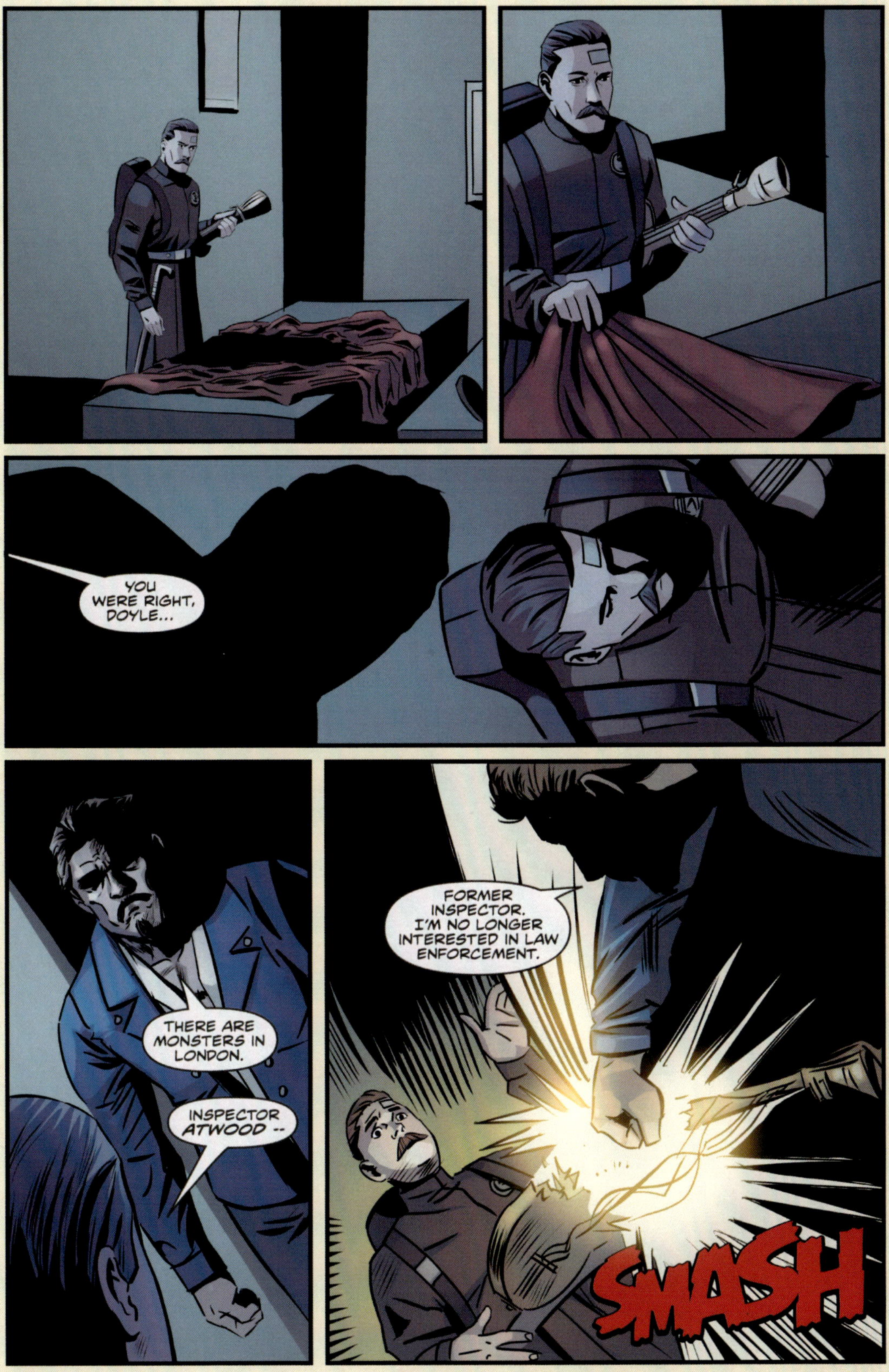
YOU WERE RIGHT, DOYLE...
THERE ARE MONSTERS IN LONDON.
INSPECTOR ATWOOD --
FORMER INSPECTOR. I'M NO LONGER INTERESTED IN LAW ENFORCEMENT.
SMASH

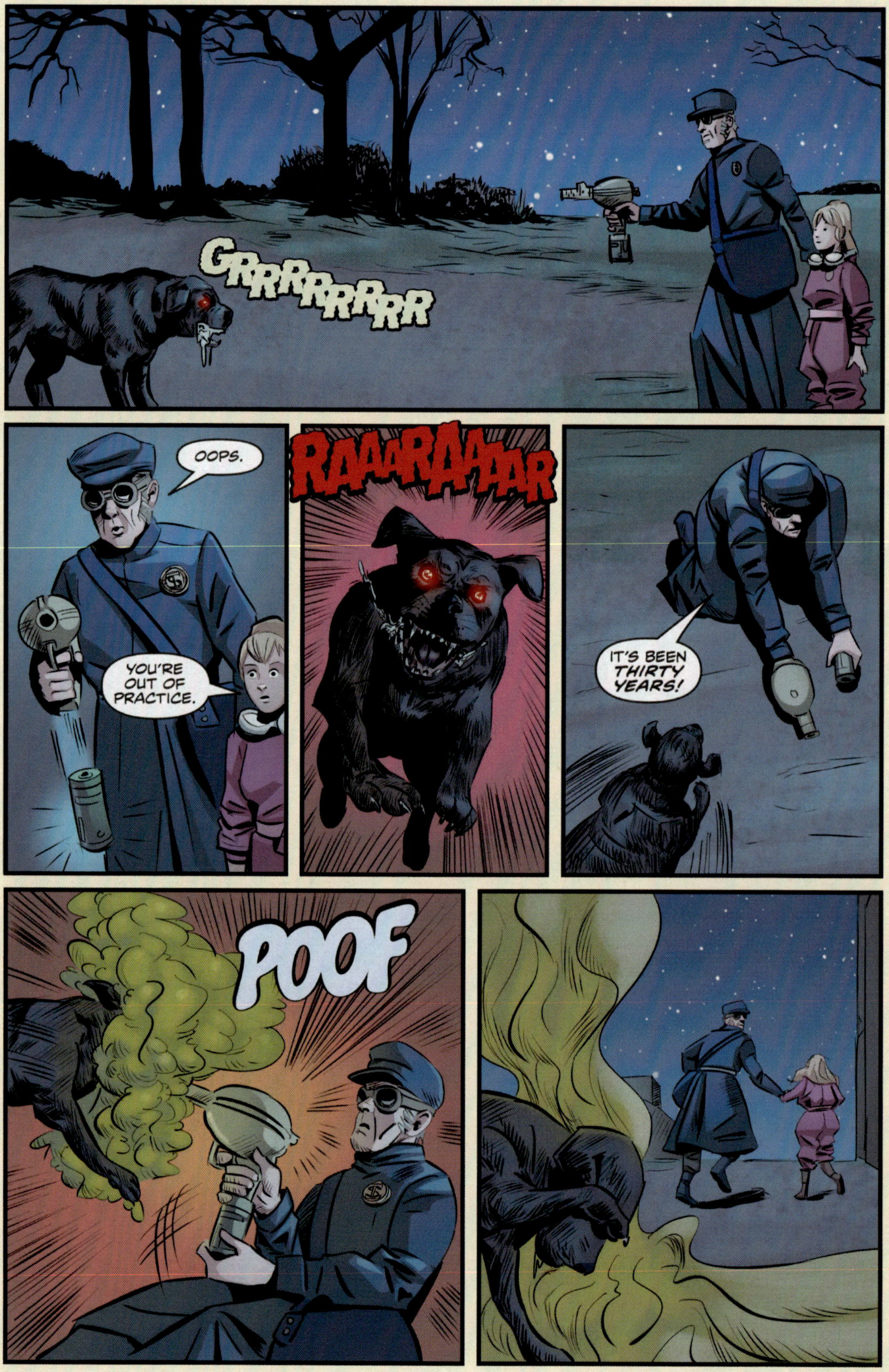
GRRRRRRRR
OOPS.
YOU'RE OUT OF PRACTICE.
RAAARAAAAR
IT'S BEEN THIRTY YEARS!
POOF

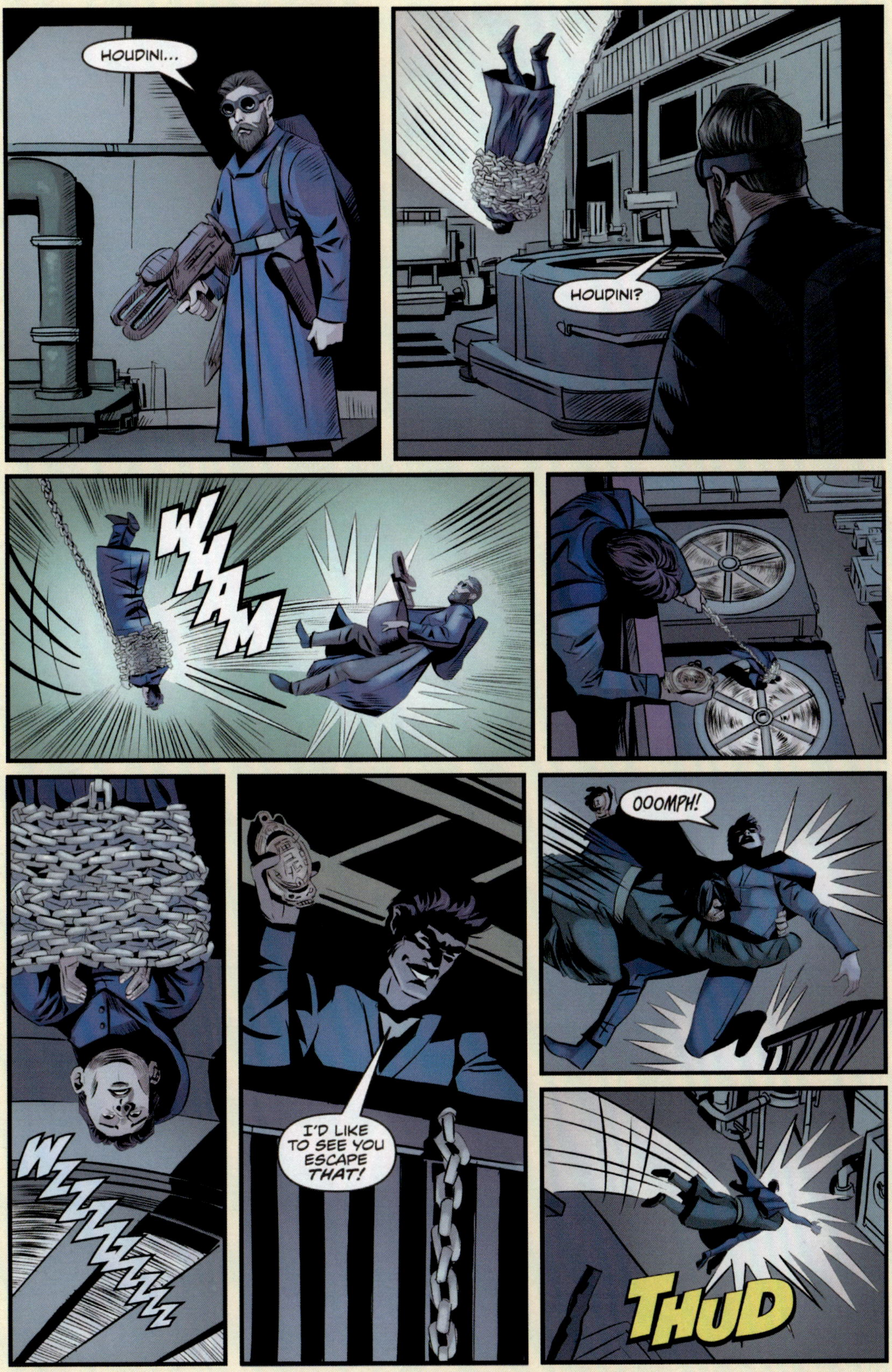
HOUDINI...
HOUDINI?
WHAM
WZZZZZZZZ
I'D LIKE TO SEE YOU ESCAPE THAT!
OOOMPH!
THUD

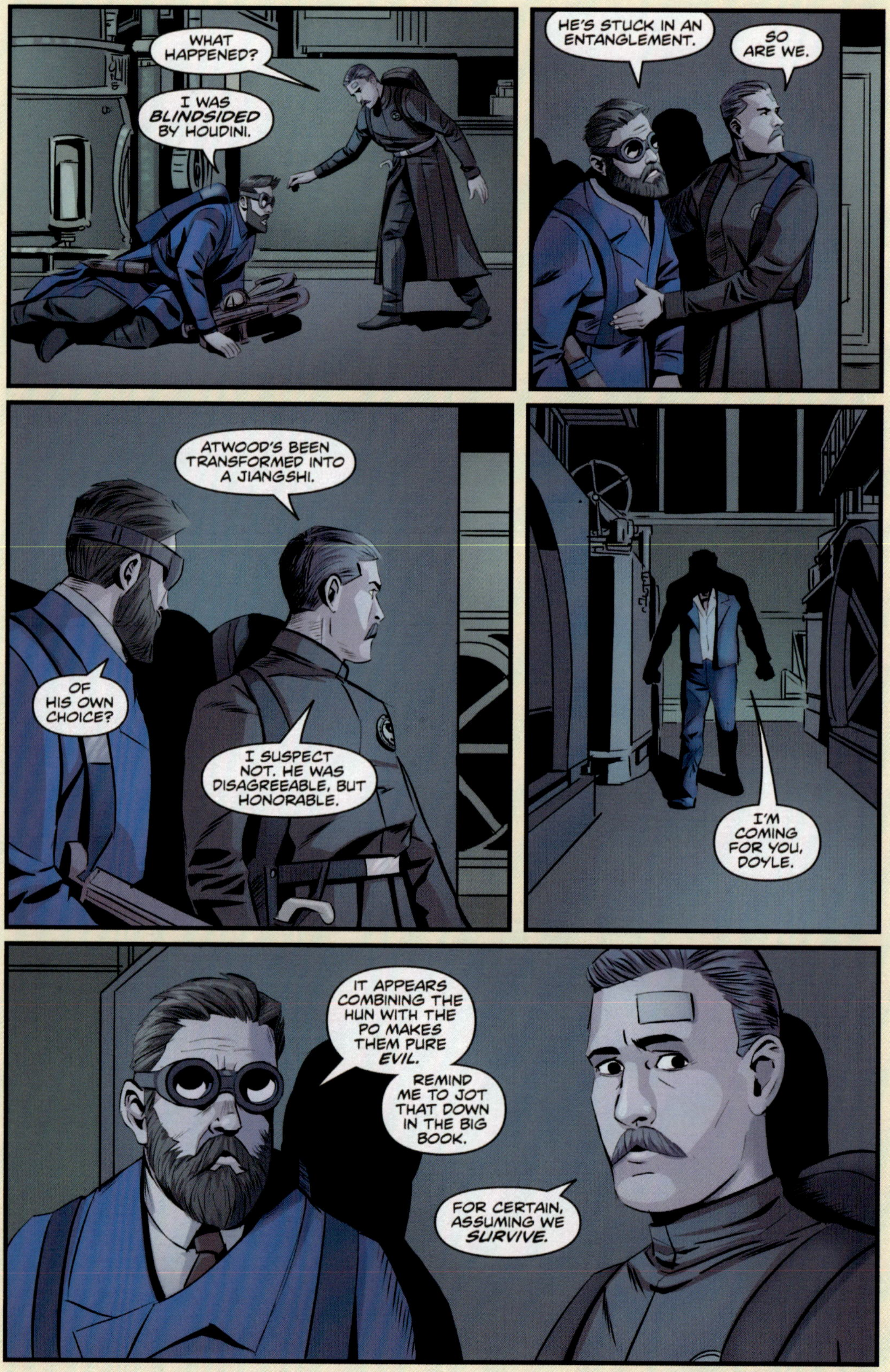
WHAT HAPPENED?
I WAS *BLINDSIDED* BY HOUDINI.
HE'S STUCK IN AN ENTANGLEMENT.
SO ARE WE.
ATWOOD'S BEEN TRANSFORMED INTO A JIANGSHI.
OF HIS OWN CHOICE?
I SUSPECT NOT. HE WAS DISAGREEABLE, BUT HONORABLE.
I'M COMING FOR YOU, DOYLE.
IT APPEARS COMBINING THE HUN WITH THE PO MAKES THEM PURE *EVIL*.
REMIND ME TO JOT THAT DOWN IN THE BIG BOOK.
FOR CERTAIN, ASSUMING WE *SURVIVE*.

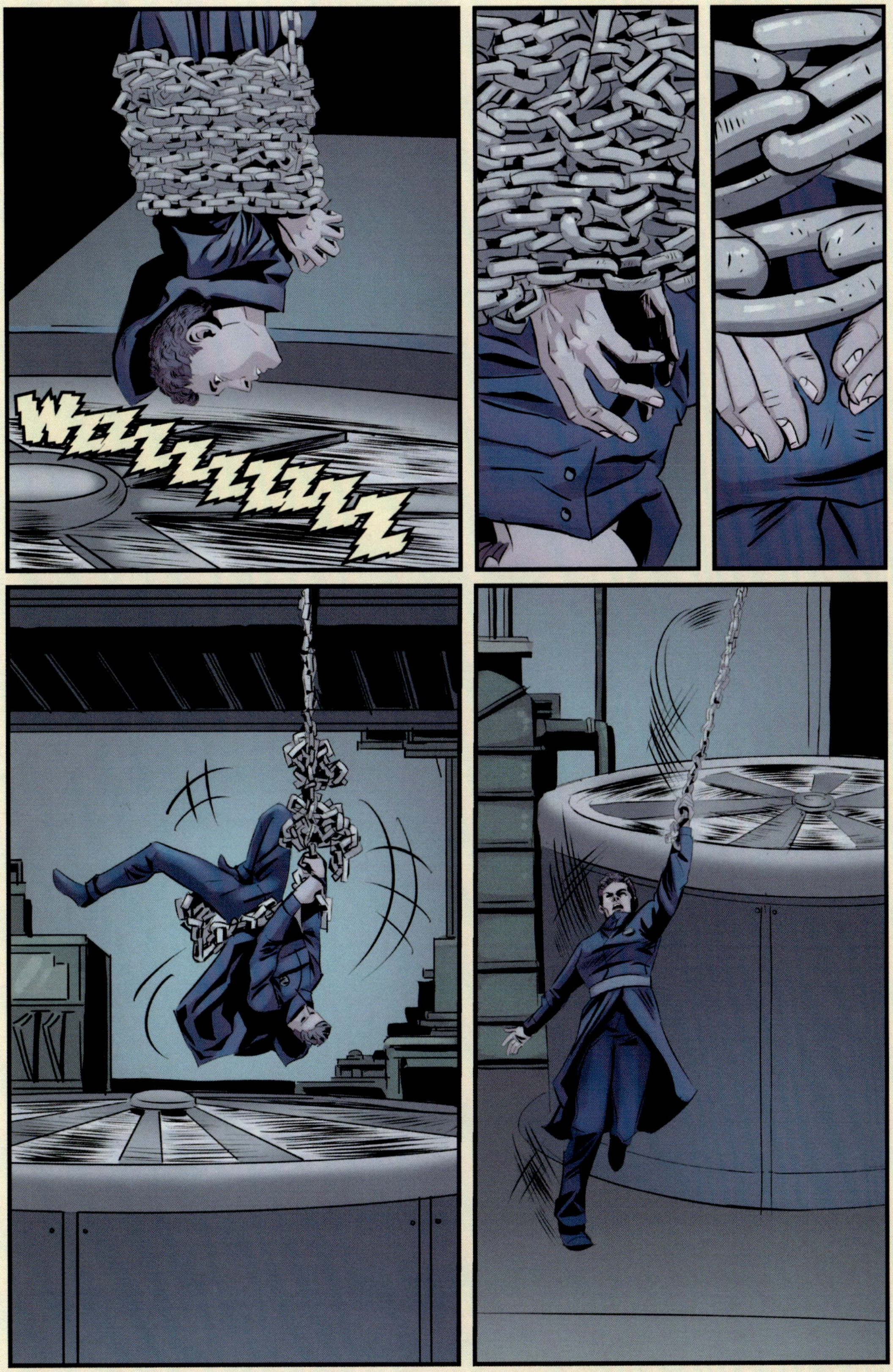
WZZZZZZZZZ

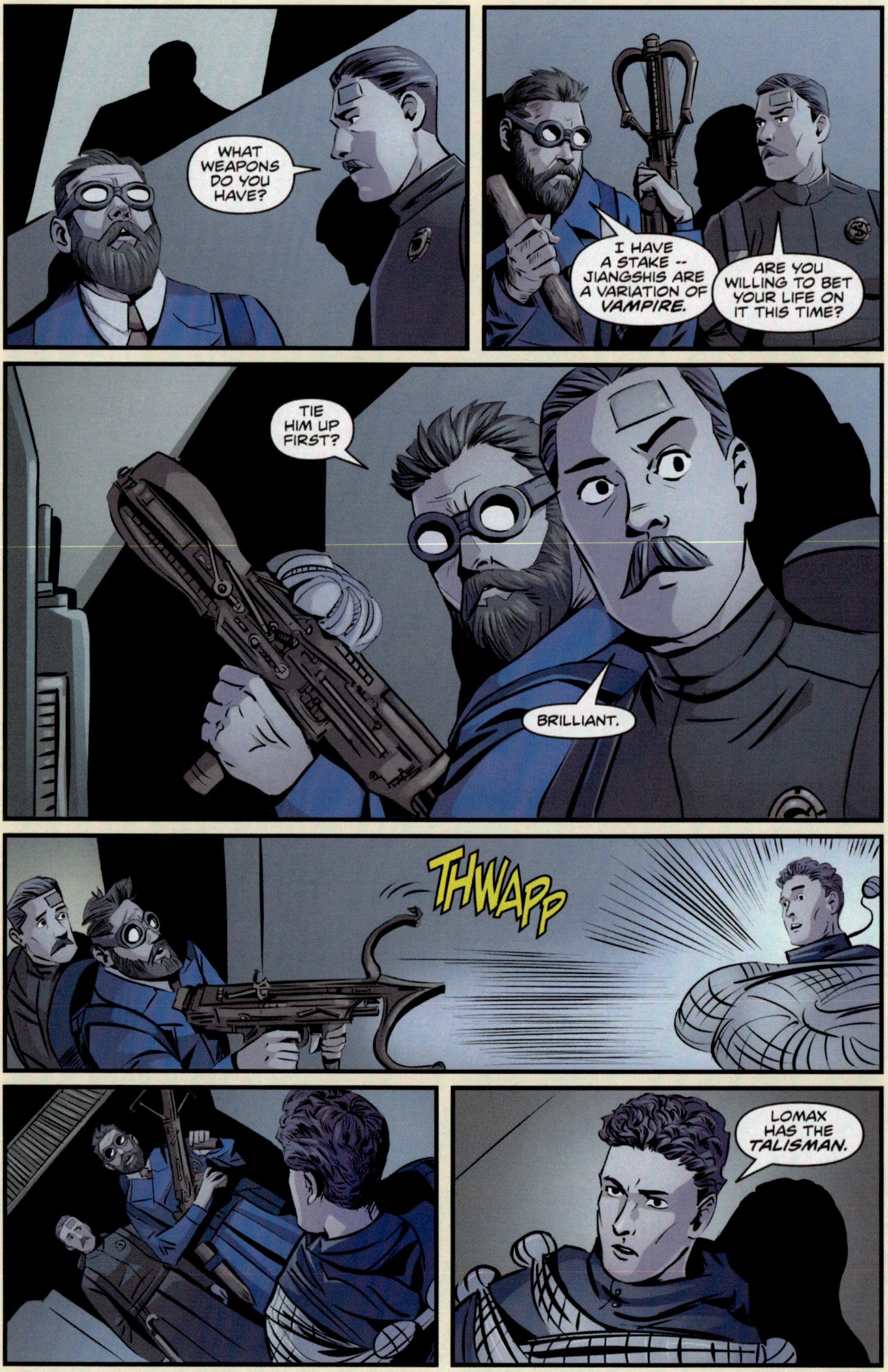
WHAT WEAPONS DO YOU HAVE?
I HAVE A STAKE -- JIANGSHIS ARE A VARIATION OF VAMPIRE.
ARE YOU WILLING TO BET YOUR LIFE ON IT THIS TIME?
TIE HIM UP FIRST?
BRILLIANT.
THWAPP
LOMAX HAS THE TALISMAN.

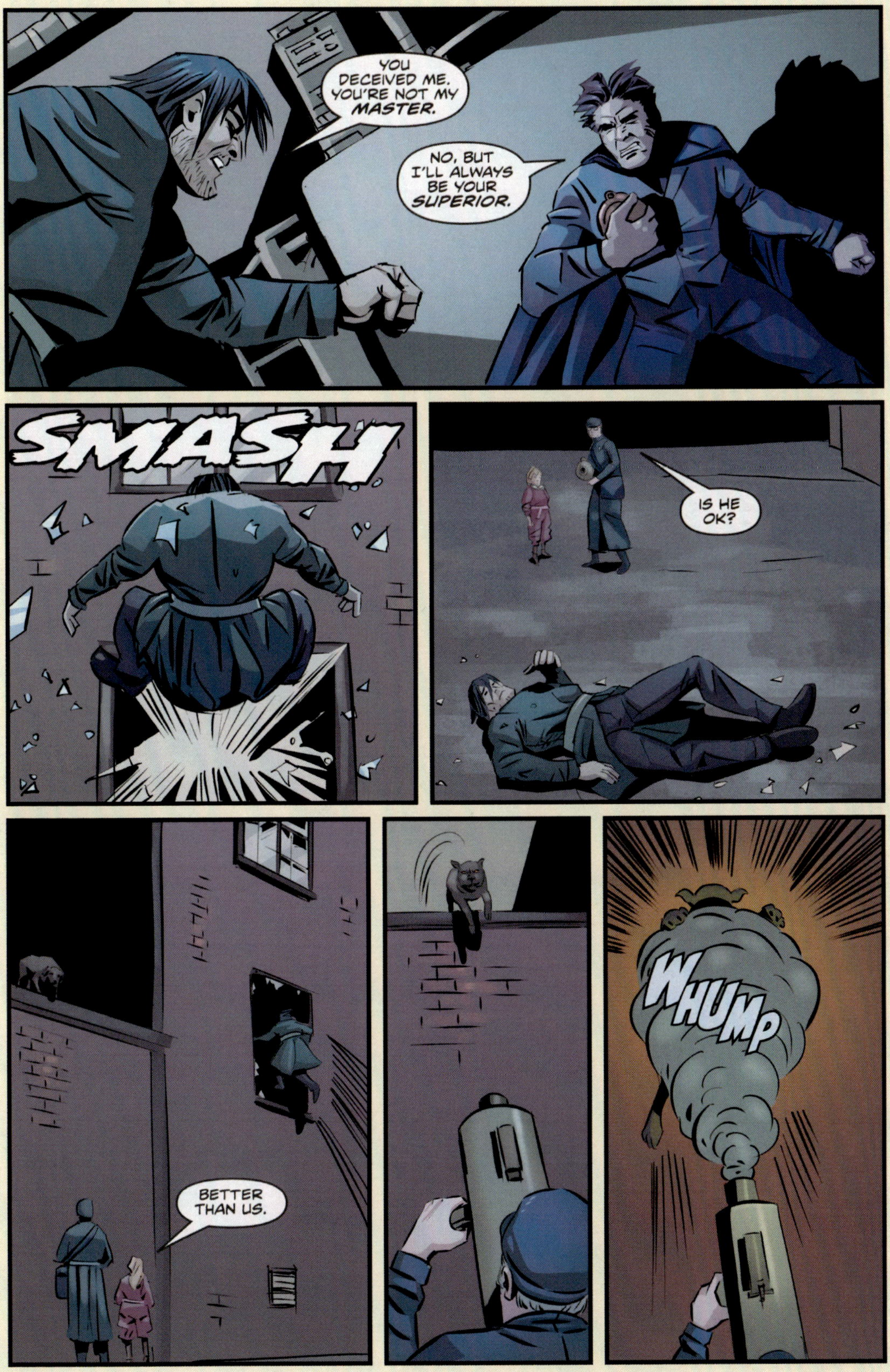
YOU DECEIVED ME. YOU'RE NOT MY MASTER.
NO, BUT I'LL ALWAYS BE YOUR SUPERIOR.
SMASH
IS HE OK?
BETTER THAN US.
WHUMP

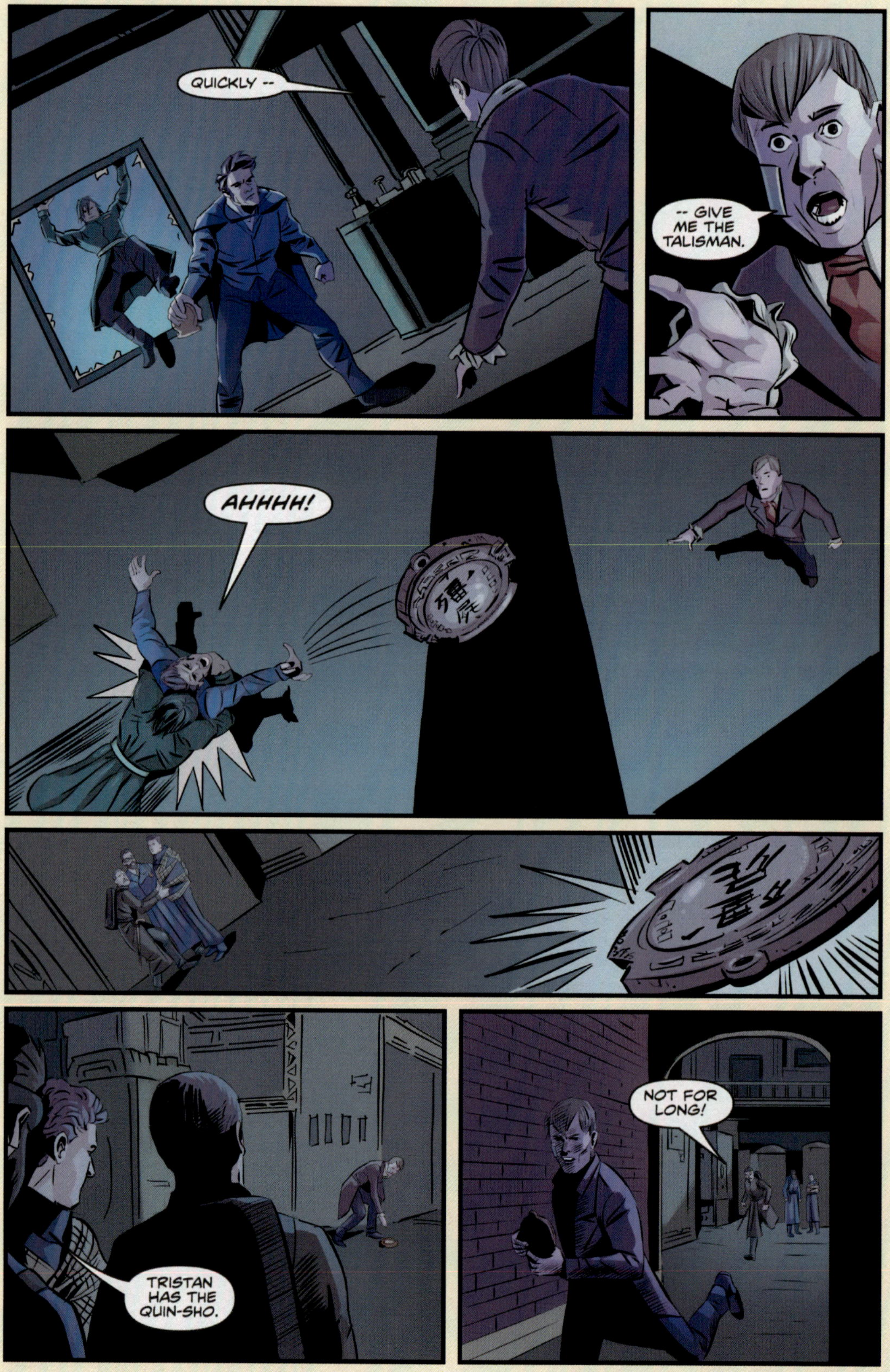
QUICKLY --
-- GIVE ME THE TALISMAN.
AHHHH!
TRISTAN HAS THE QUIN-SHO.
NOT FOR LONG!

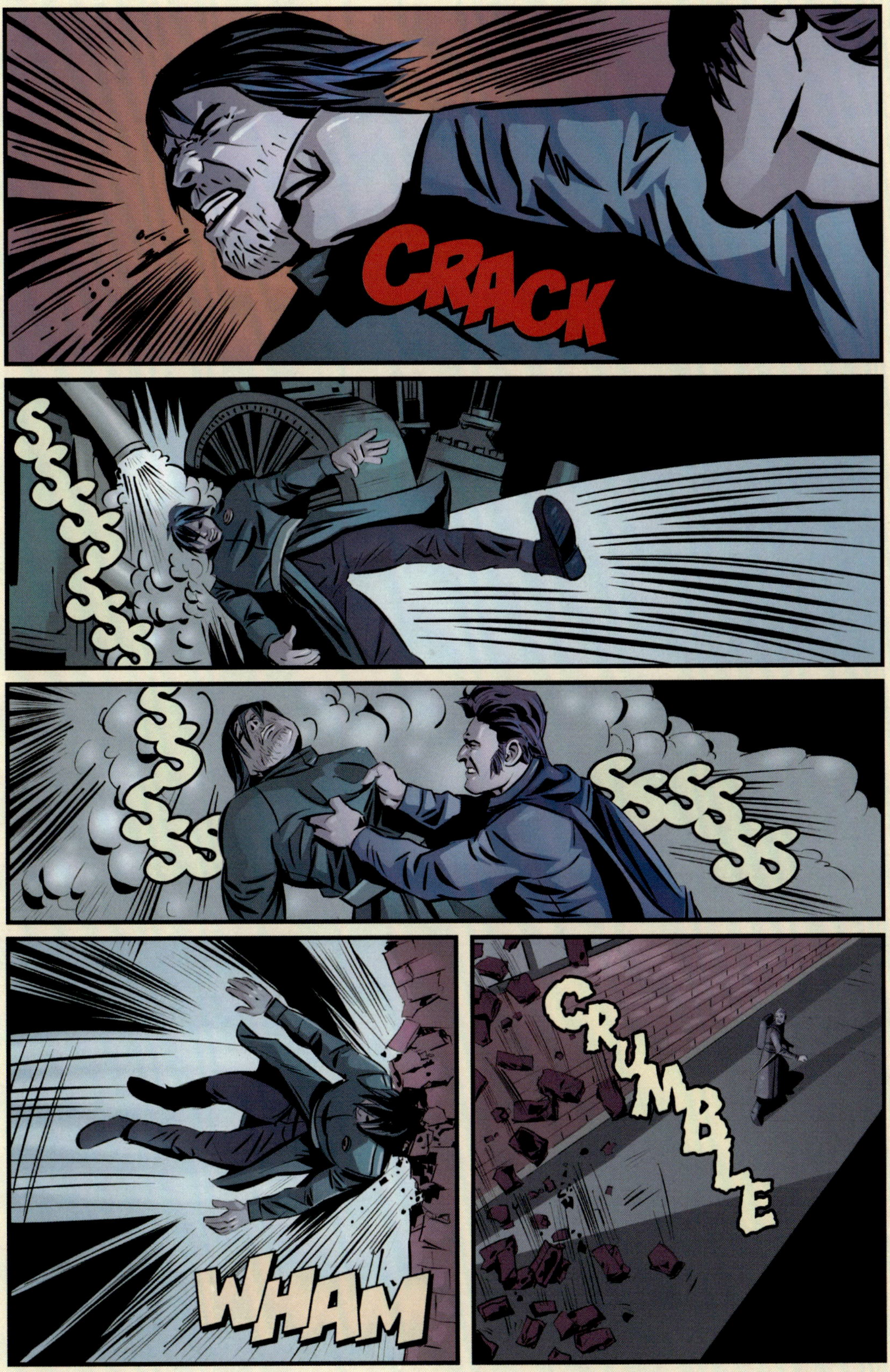
CRACK
SSSSSSS
SSSSSS
SSSSSSS
WHAM
CRUMBLE

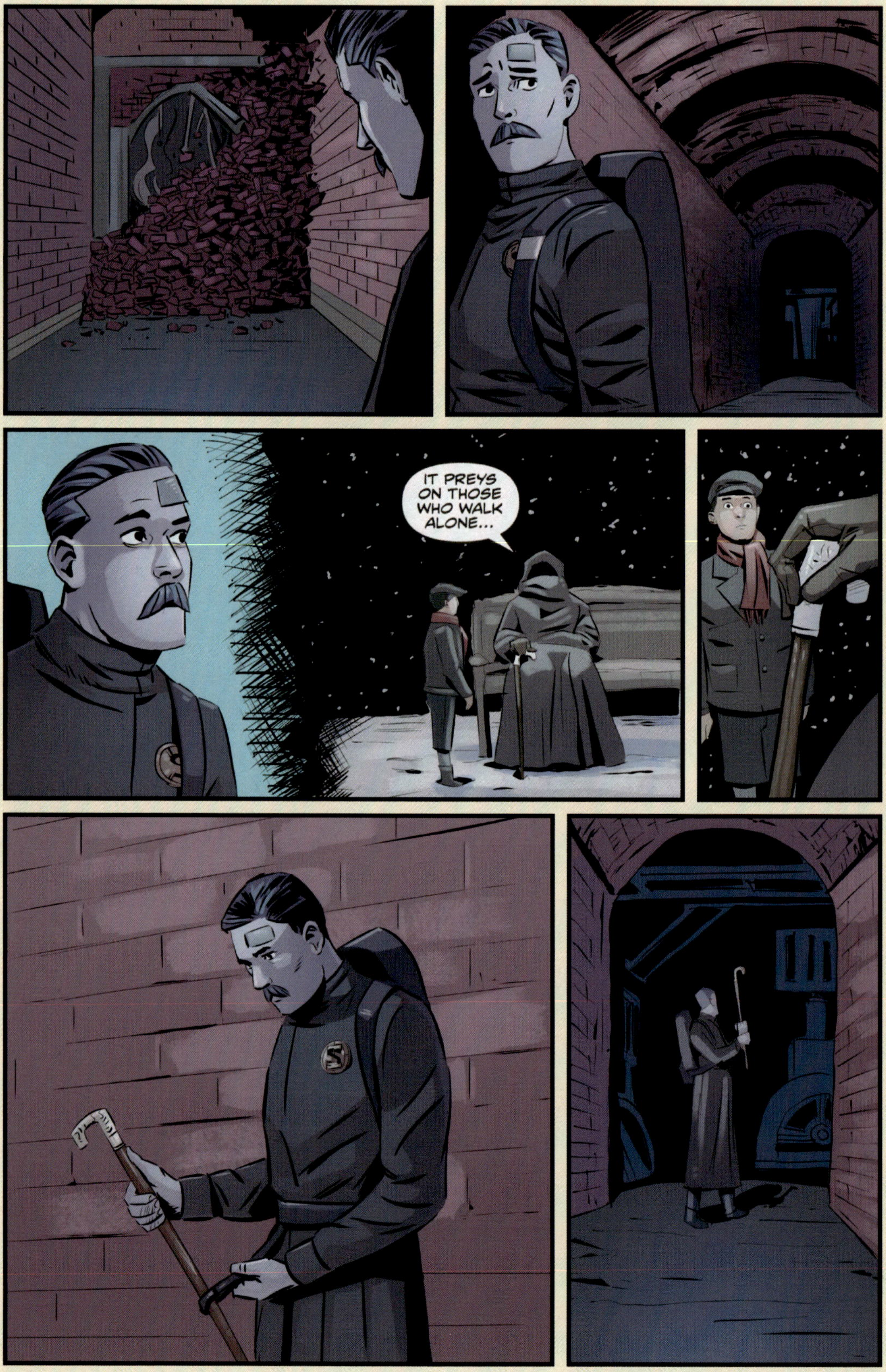
IT PREYS ON THOSE WHO WALK ALONE...

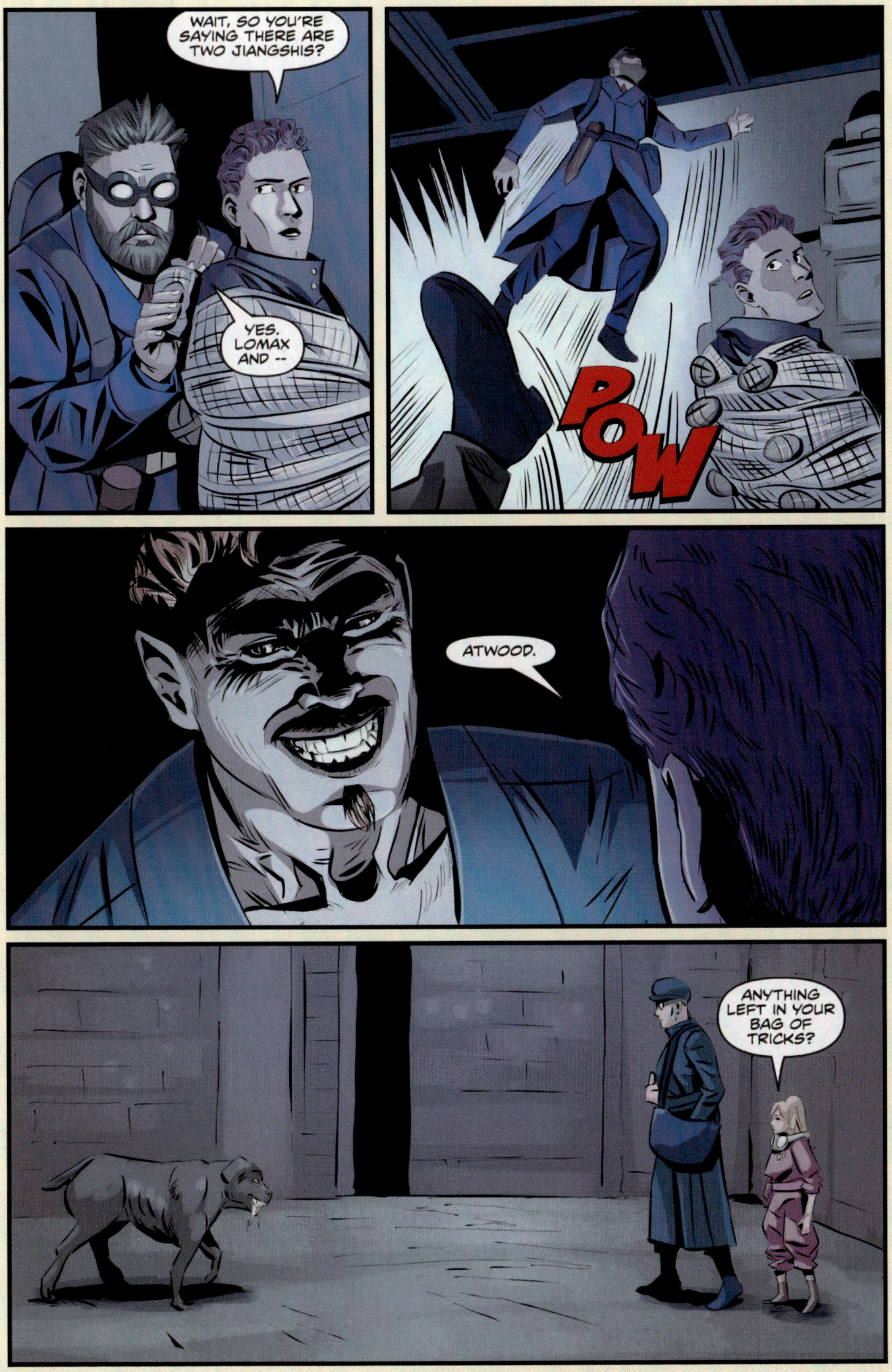
WAIT, SO YOU'RE SAYING THERE ARE TWO JIANGSHIS?
YES. LOMAX AND --
POW
ATWOOD.
ANYTHING LEFT IN YOUR BAG OF TRICKS?

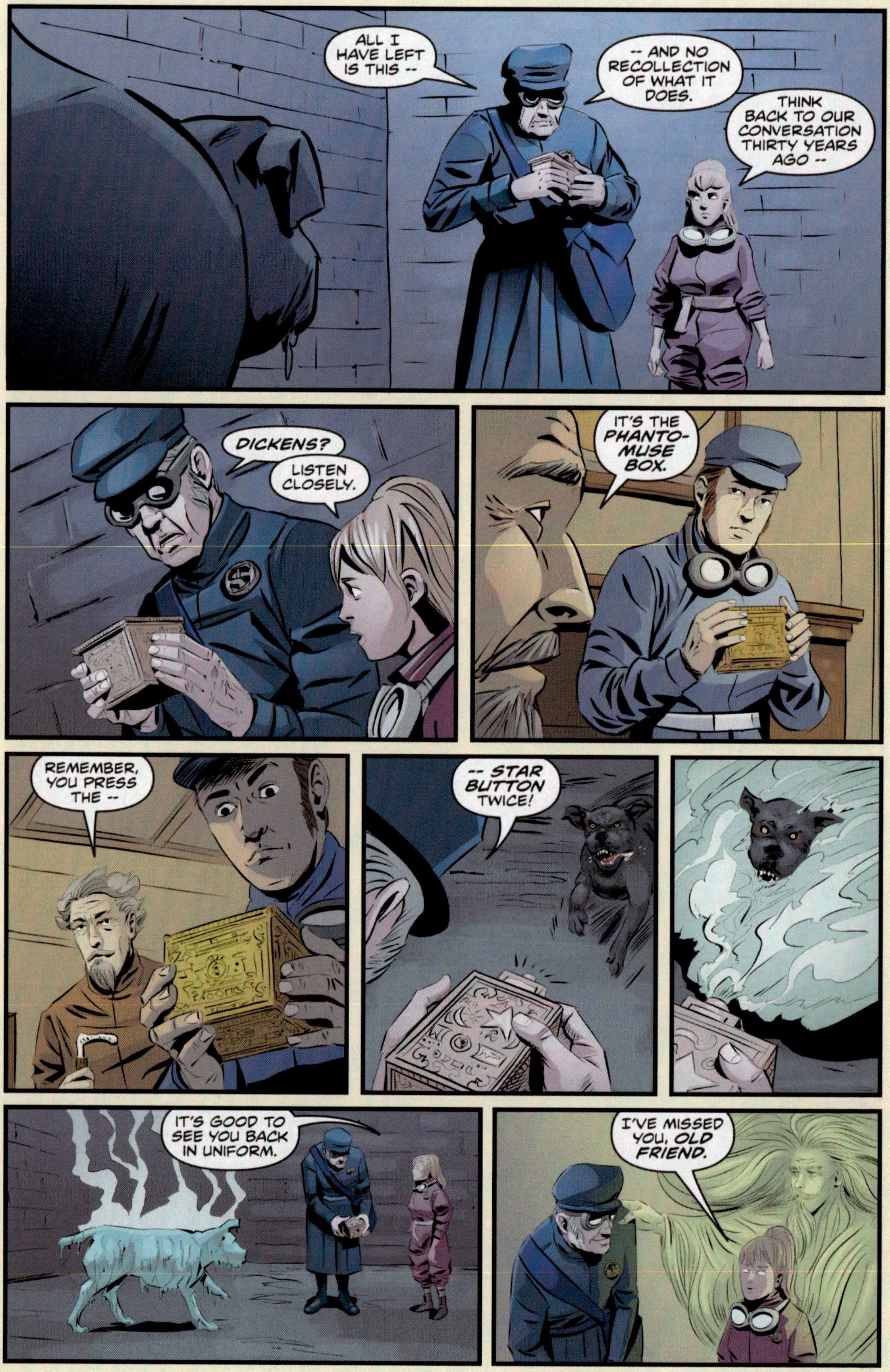
ALL I HAVE LEFT IS THIS --
-- AND NO RECOLLECTION OF WHAT IT DOES.
THINK BACK TO OUR CONVERSATION THIRTY YEARS AGO --
DICKENS?
LISTEN CLOSELY.
IT'S THE PHANTO-MUSE BOX.
REMEMBER, YOU PRESS THE --
-- STAR BUTTON TWICE!
IT'S GOOD TO SEE YOU BACK IN UNIFORM.
I'VE MISSED YOU, OLD FRIEND.

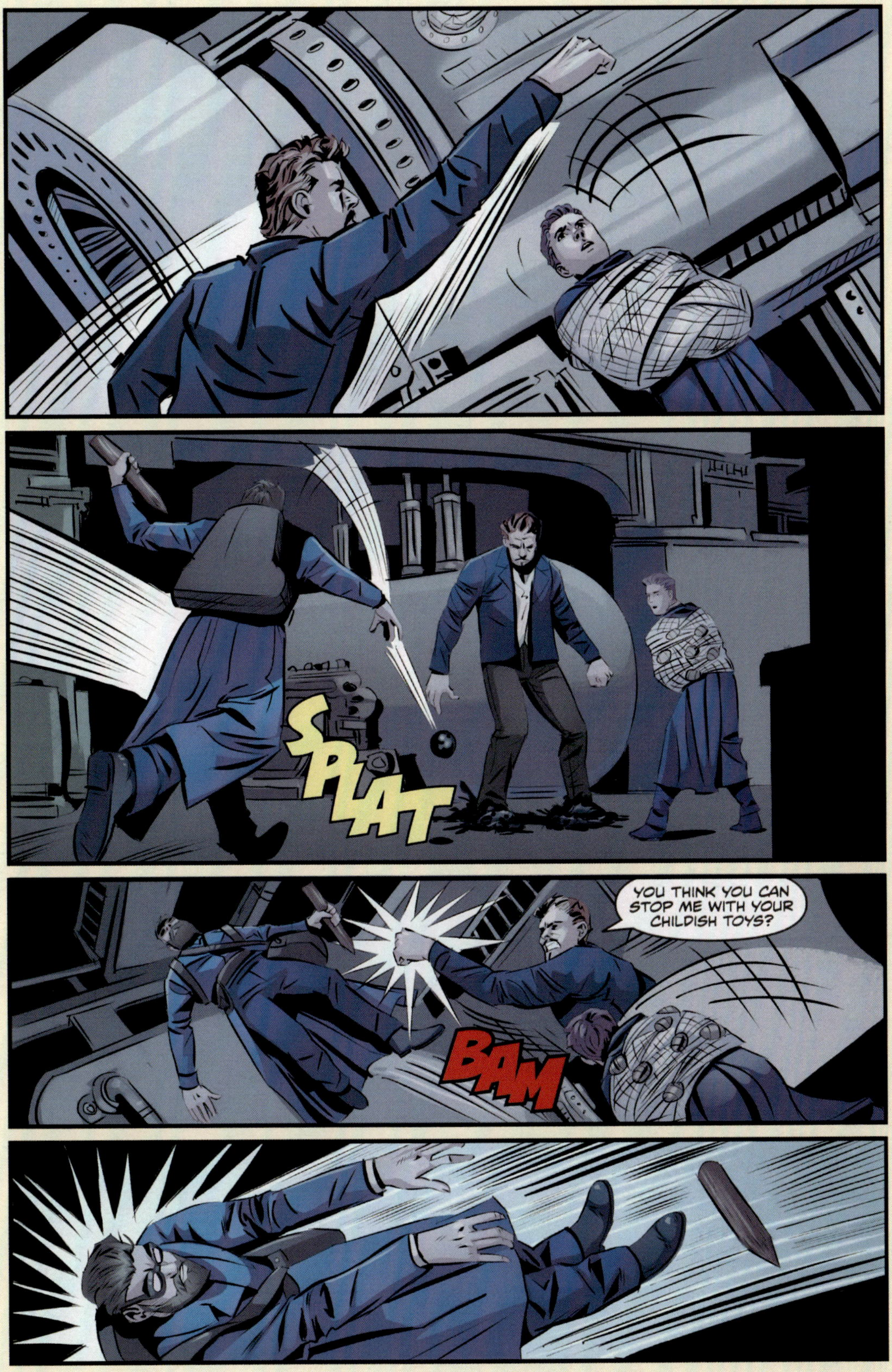
SPLAT
YOU THINK YOU CAN STOP ME WITH YOUR CHILDISH TOYS?
BAM

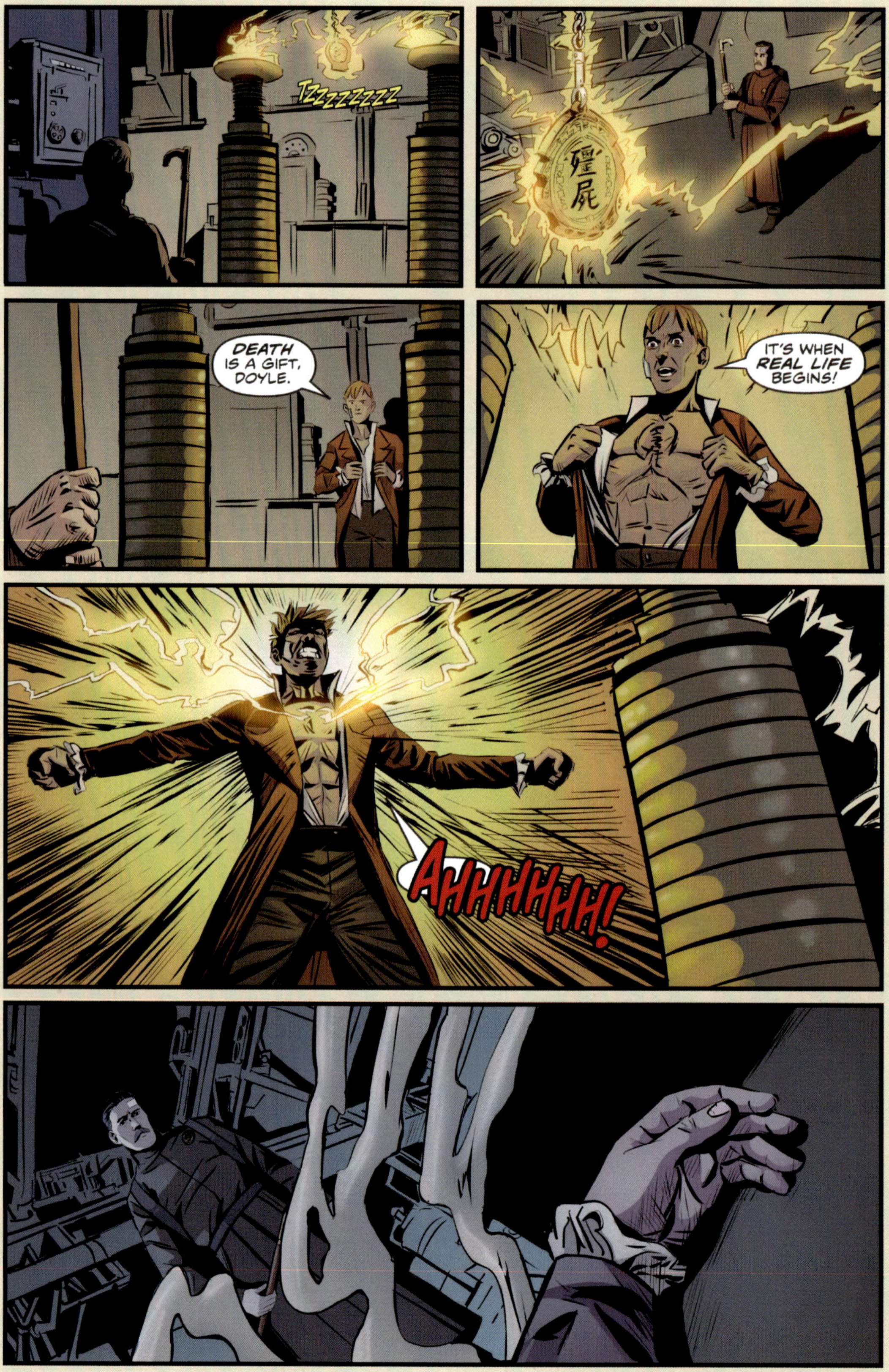
TZZZZZZZZ
殭屍
DEATH IS A GIFT, DOYLE.
IT'S WHEN REAL LIFE BEGINS!
AHHHHHH!

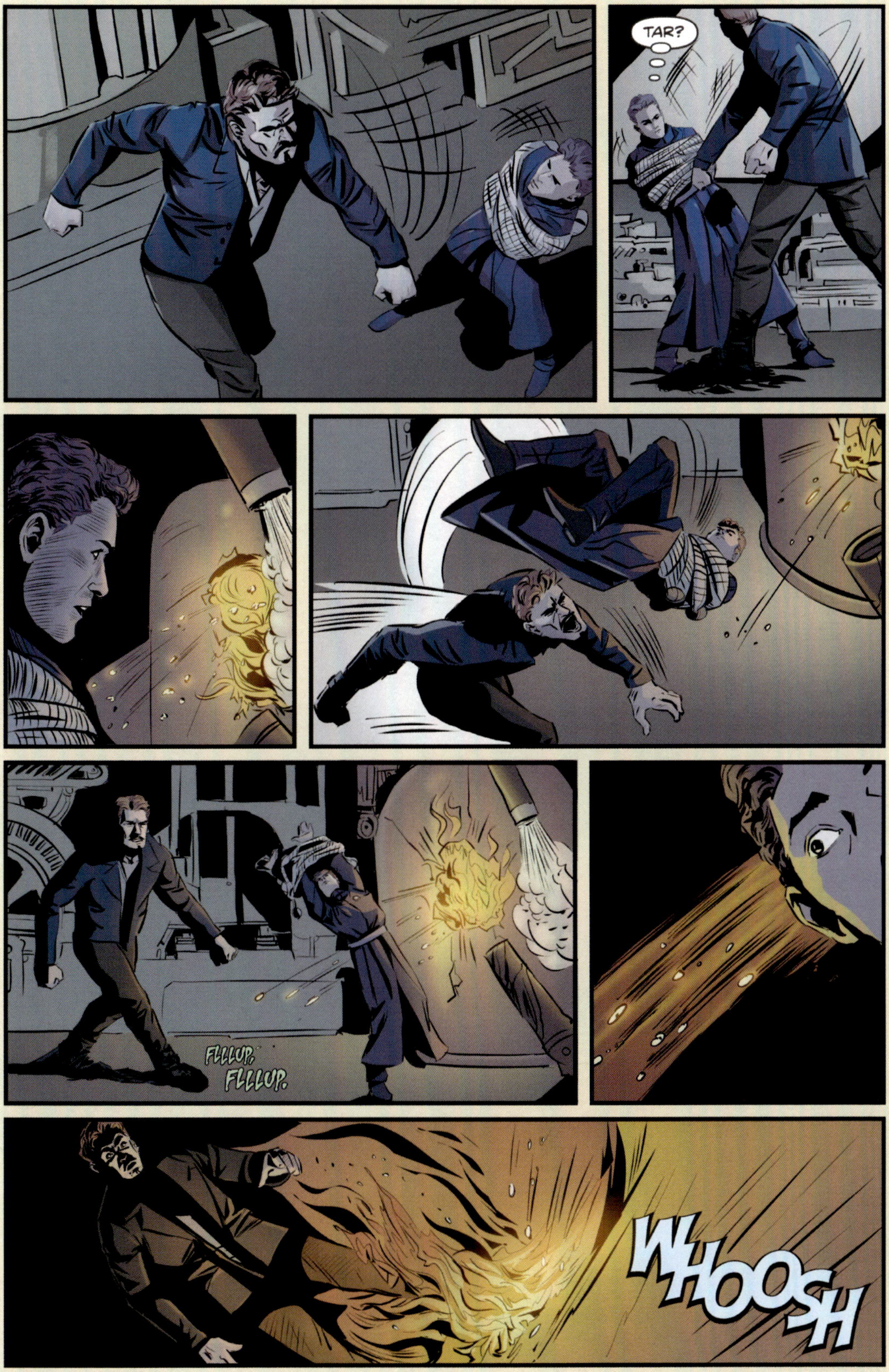
TAR?
FLLLUP,
FLLLUP.
WHOOSH

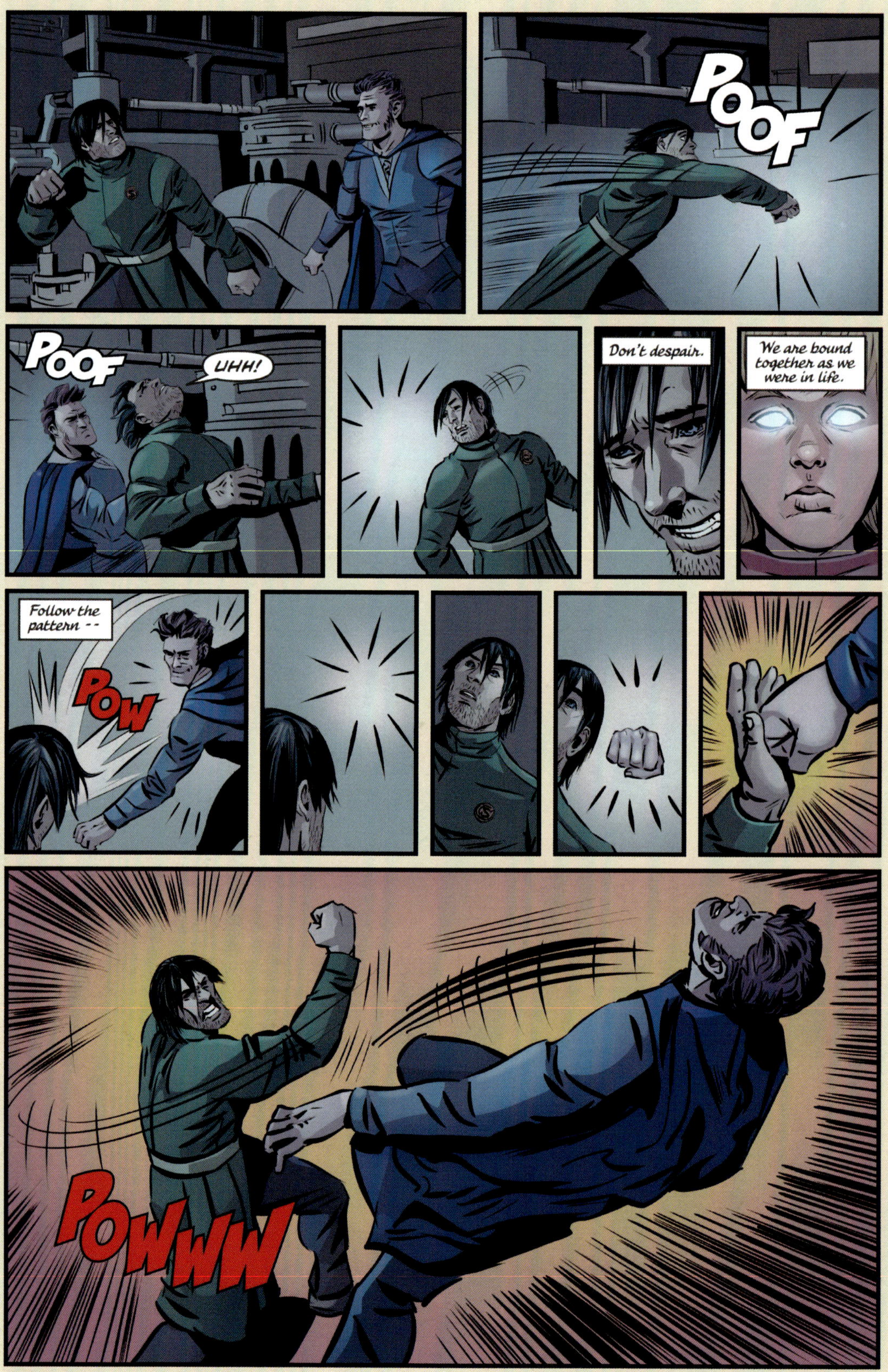
POOF
POOF
UHH!
Don't despair.
We are bound together as we were in life.
Follow the pattern --
POW
POWWW

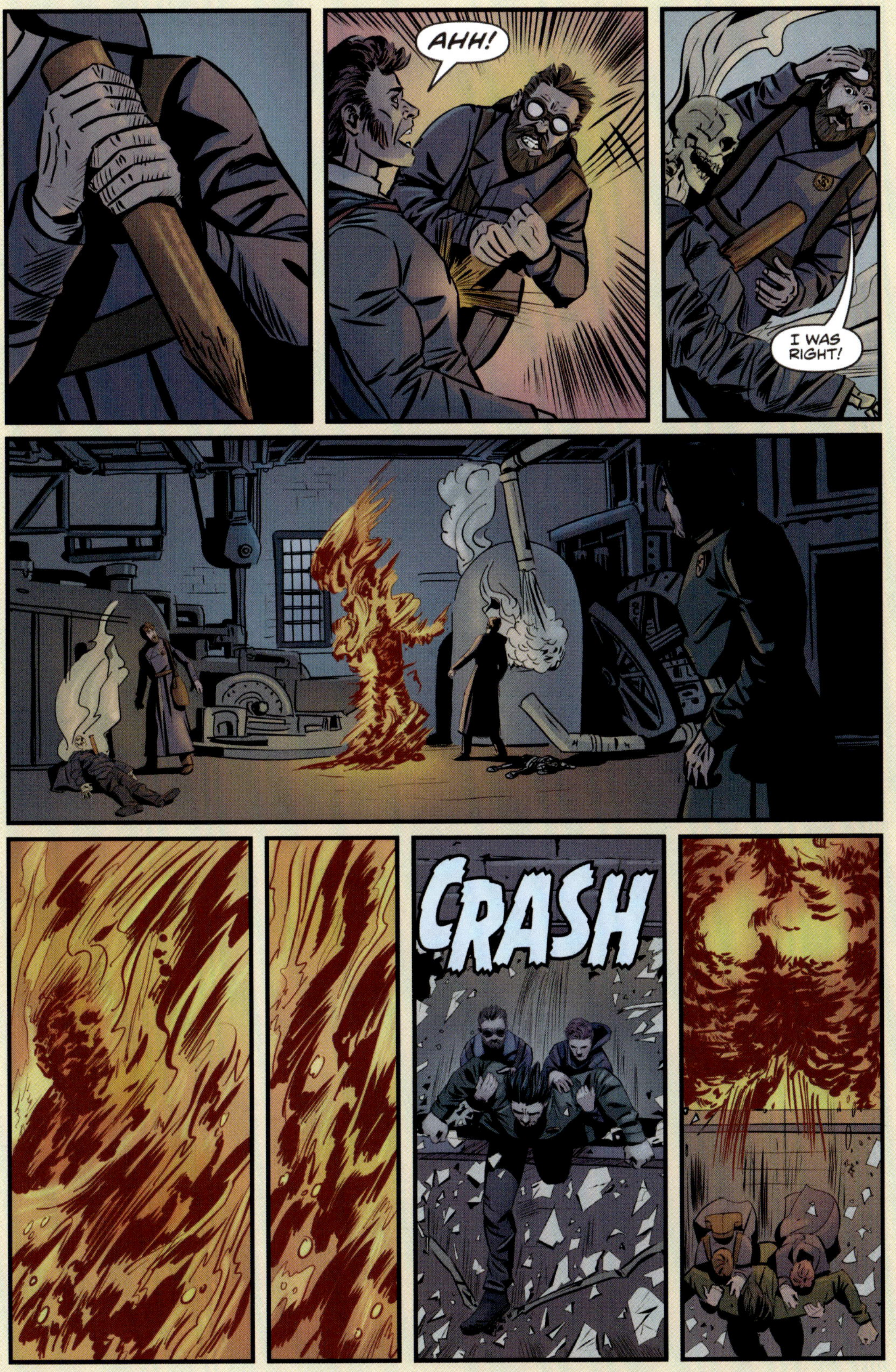
AHH!
I WAS RIGHT!
CRASH

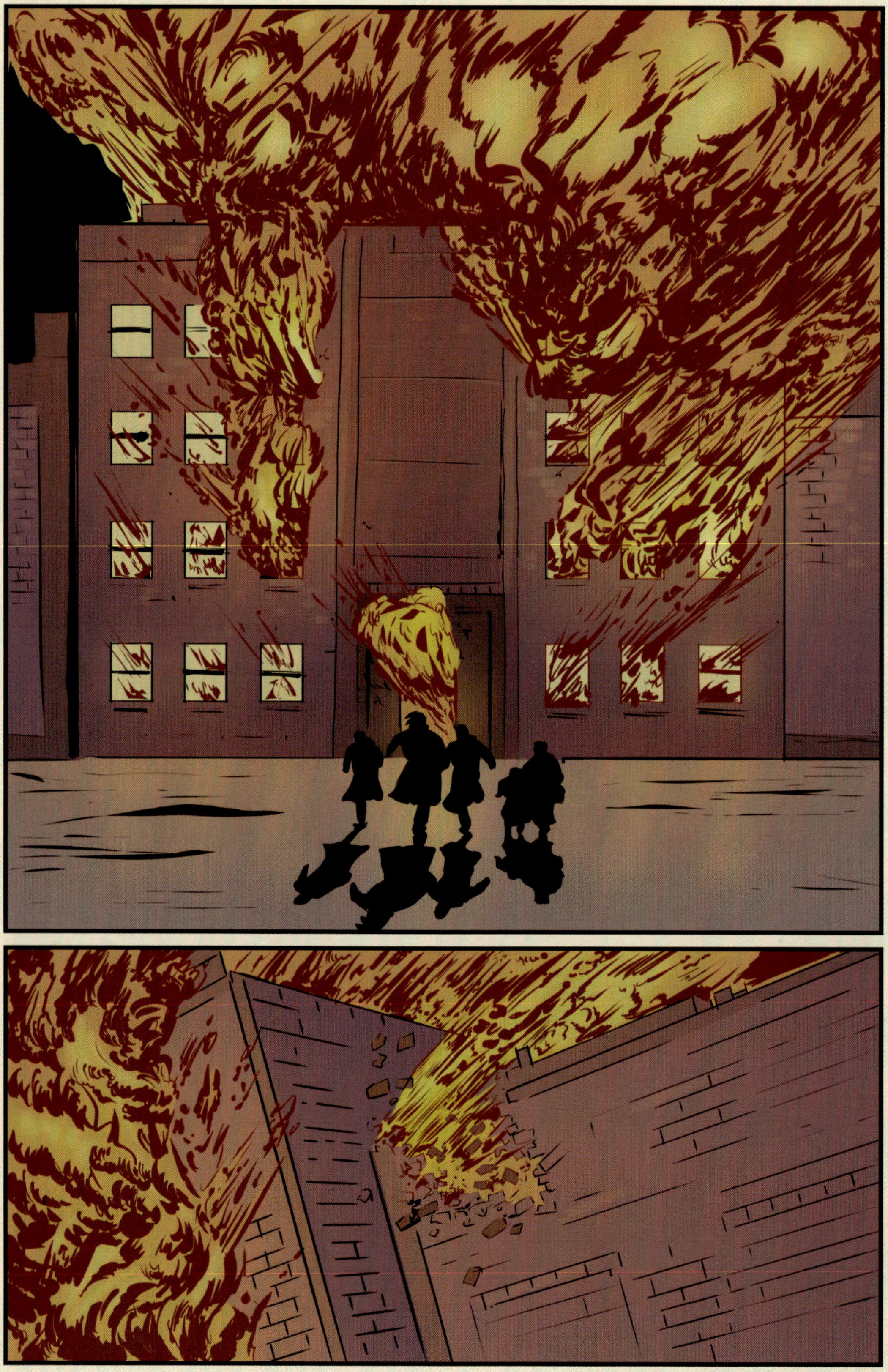

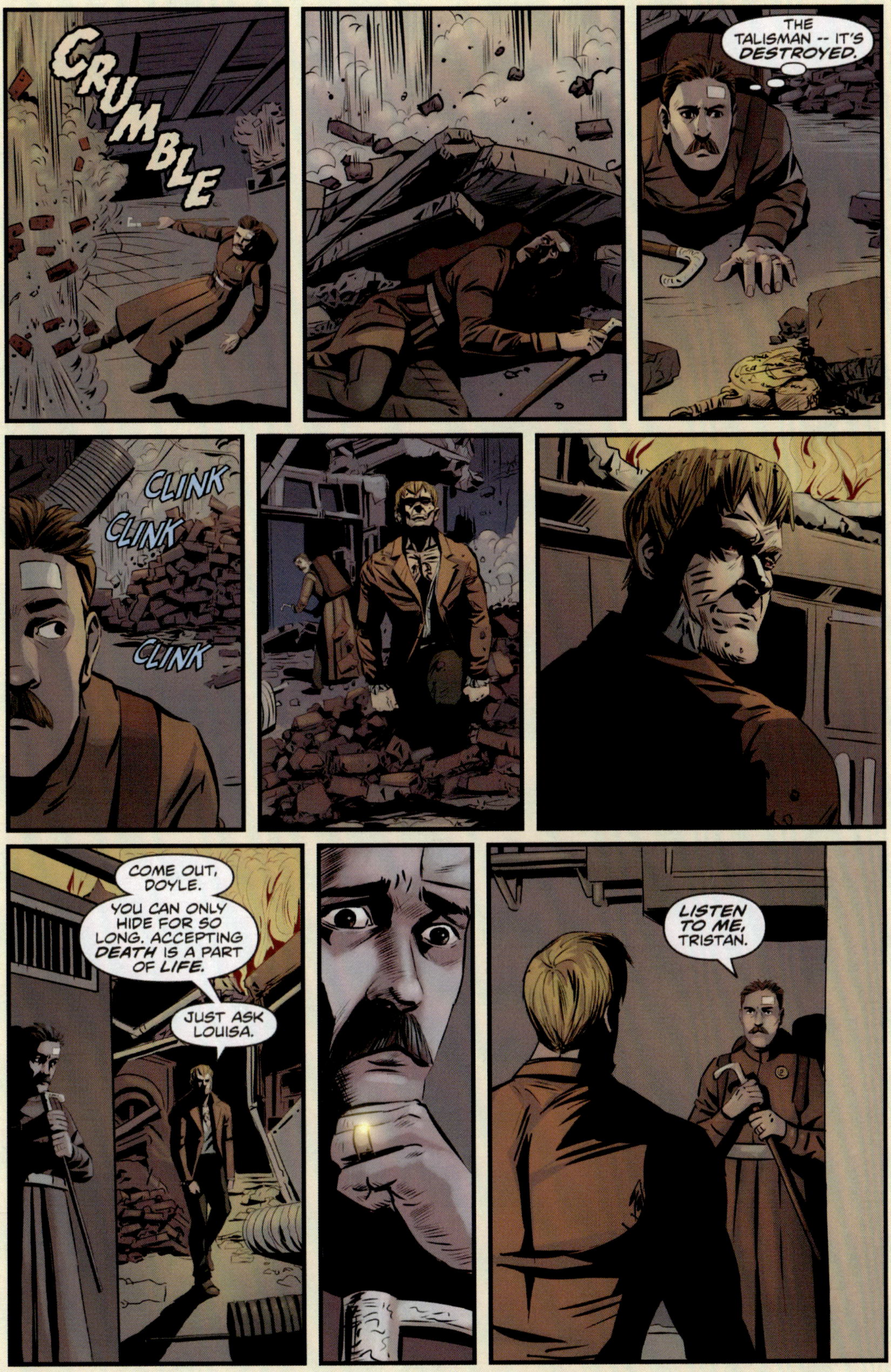

CRUMBLE
THE TALISMAN -- IT'S DESTROYED.
CLINK
CLINK
CLINK
COME OUT, DOYLE.
YOU CAN ONLY HIDE FOR SO LONG. ACCEPTING DEATH IS A PART OF LIFE.
JUST ASK LOUISA.
LISTEN TO ME, TRISTAN.

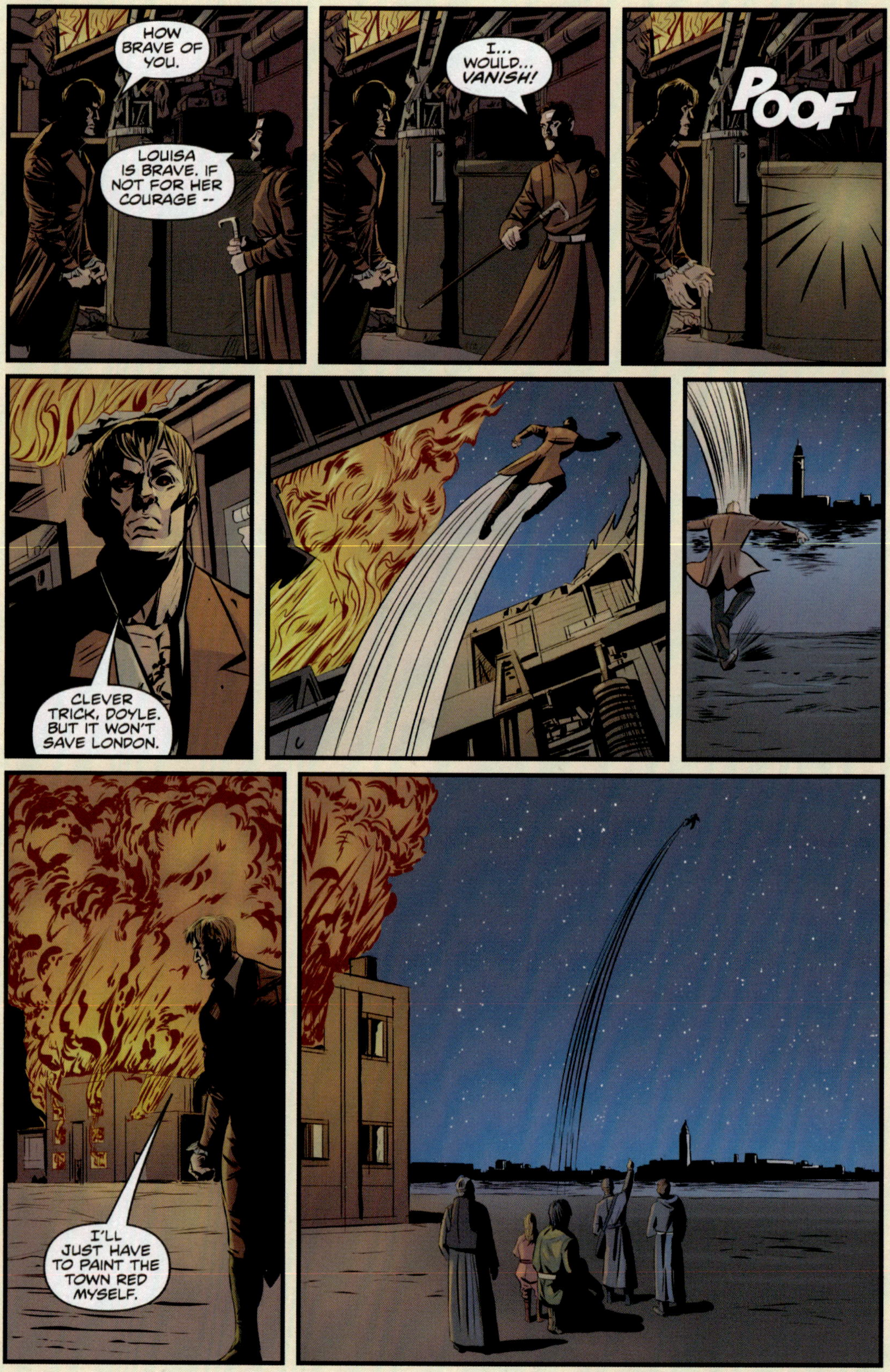
HOW BRAVE OF YOU.
LOUISA IS BRAVE. IF NOT FOR HER COURAGE --
I... WOULD... VANISH!
POOF
CLEVER TRICK, DOYLE. BUT IT WON'T SAVE LONDON.
I'LL JUST HAVE TO PAINT THE TOWN RED MYSELF.

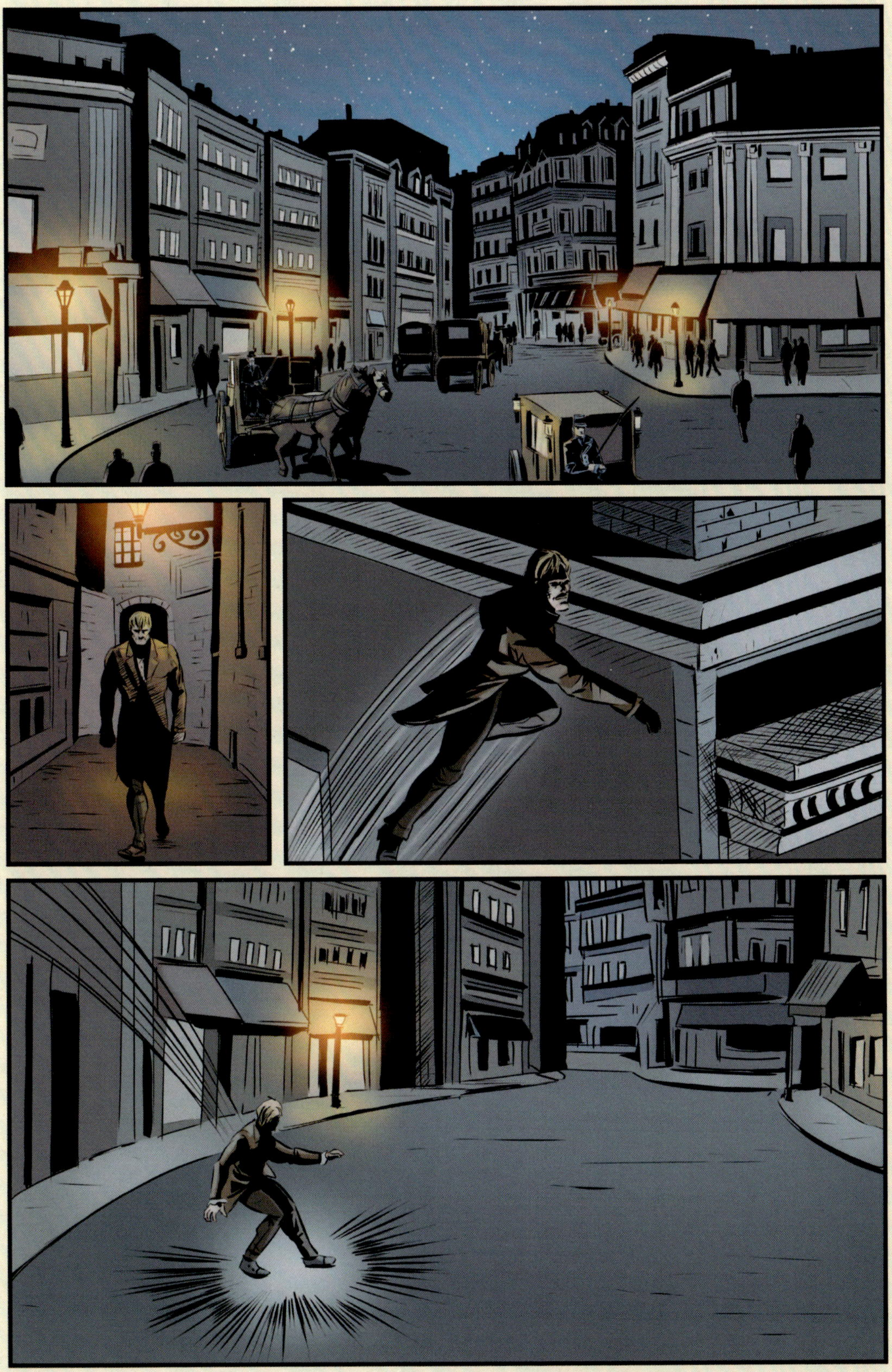

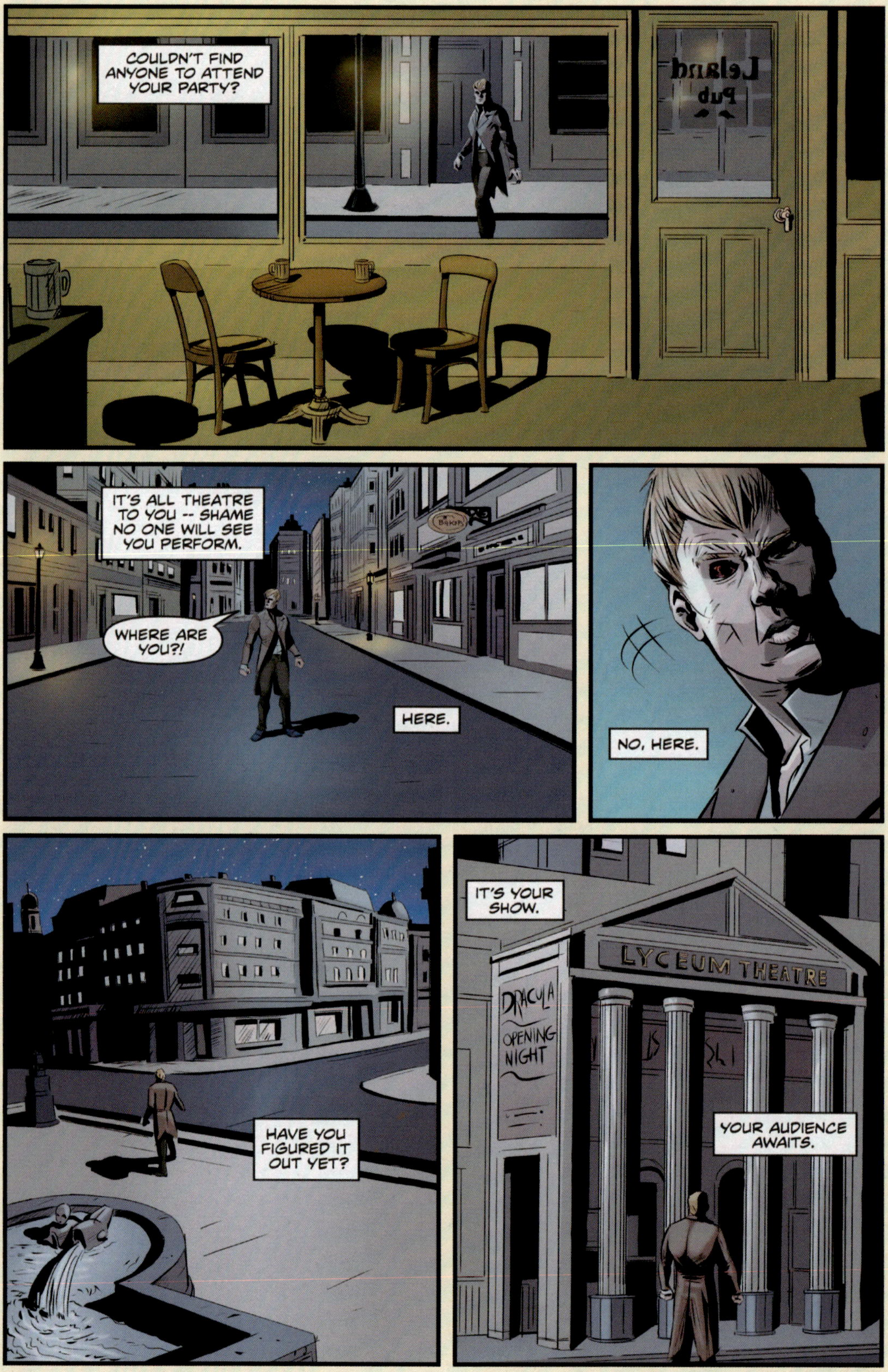
COULDN'T FIND ANYONE TO ATTEND YOUR PARTY?
Leland Pub
IT'S ALL THEATRE TO YOU -- SHAME NO ONE WILL SEE YOU PERFORM.
WHERE ARE YOU?!
HERE.
NO, HERE.
HAVE YOU FIGURED IT OUT YET?
IT'S YOUR SHOW.
LYCEUM THEATRE
DRACULA OPENING NIGHT
YOUR AUDIENCE AWAITS.

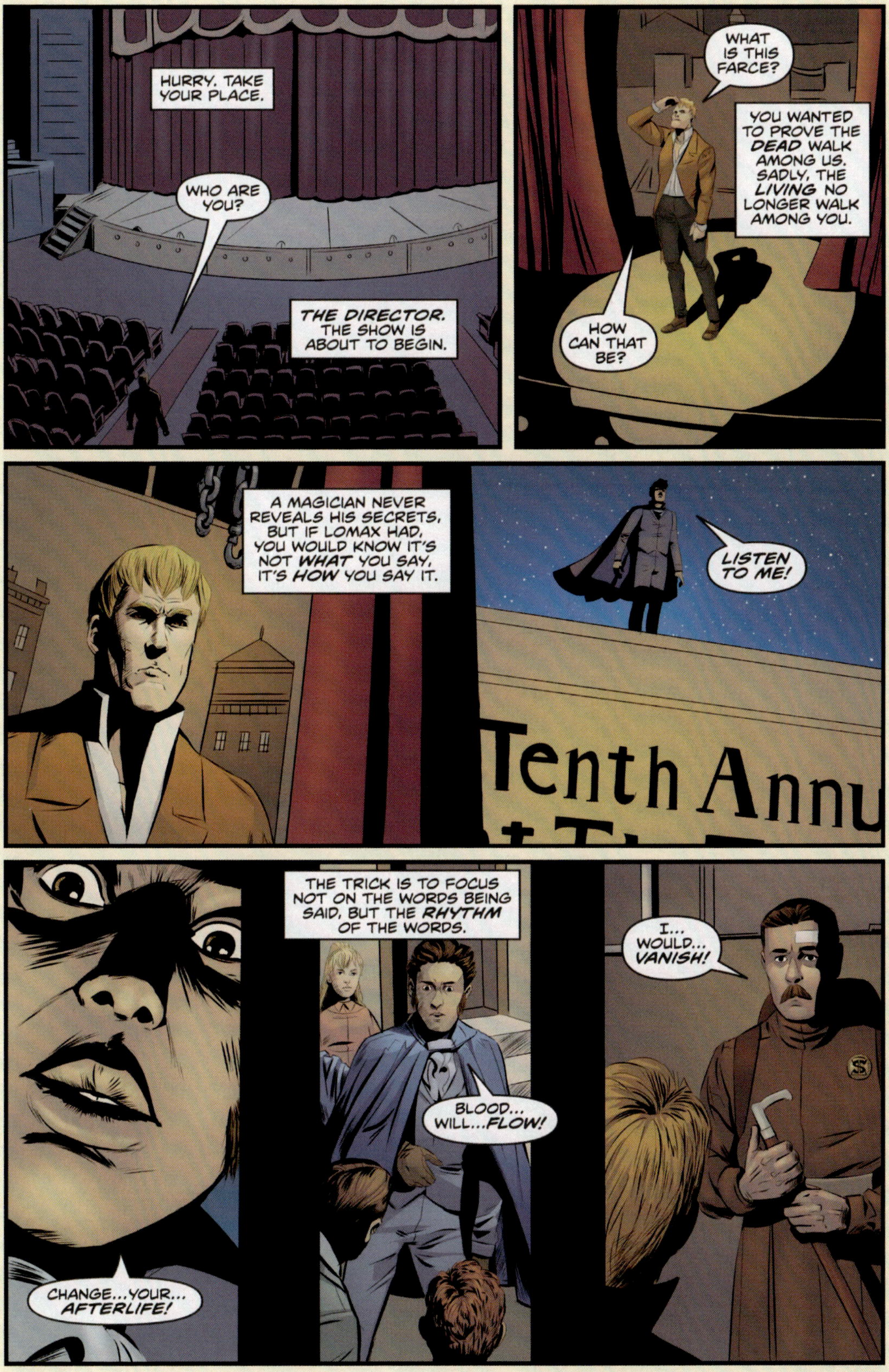
HURRY. TAKE YOUR PLACE.
WHO ARE YOU?
THE DIRECTOR. THE SHOW IS ABOUT TO BEGIN.
WHAT IS THIS FARCE?
YOU WANTED TO PROVE THE DEAD WALK AMONG US. SADLY, THE LIVING NO LONGER WALK AMONG YOU.
HOW CAN THAT BE?
A MAGICIAN NEVER REVEALS HIS SECRETS, BUT IF LOMAX HAD, YOU WOULD KNOW IT'S NOT WHAT YOU SAY, IT'S HOW YOU SAY IT.
LISTEN TO ME!
Tenth Annu
THE TRICK IS TO FOCUS NOT ON THE WORDS BEING SAID, BUT THE RHYTHM OF THE WORDS.
CHANGE...YOUR... AFTERLIFE!
BLOOD... WILL...FLOW!
I... WOULD... VANISH!

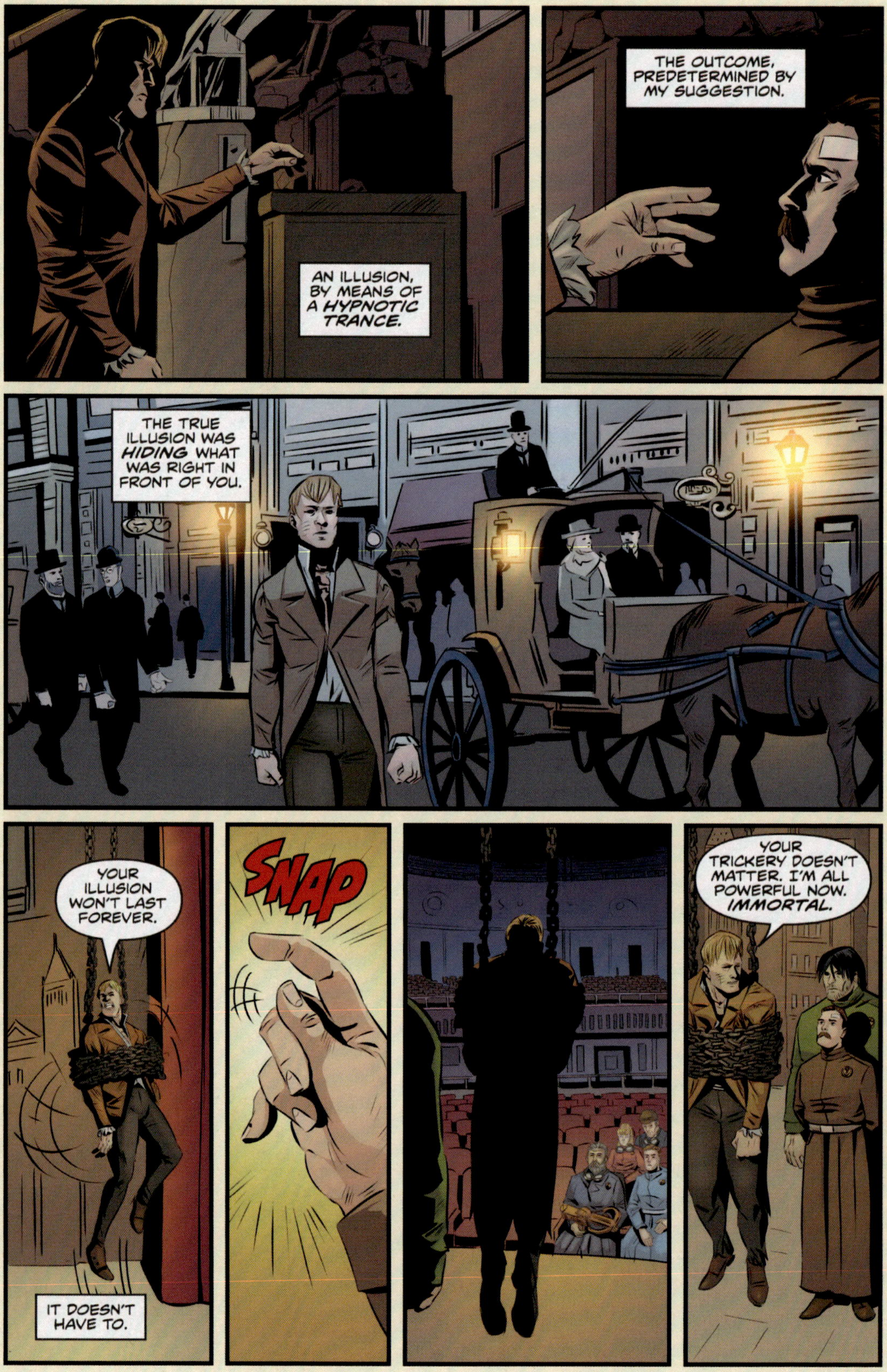
AN ILLUSION, BY MEANS OF A *HYPNOTIC TRANCE.*
THE OUTCOME, PREDETERMINED BY MY SUGGESTION.
THE TRUE ILLUSION WAS *HIDING* WHAT WAS RIGHT IN FRONT OF YOU.
YOUR ILLUSION WON'T LAST FOREVER.
IT DOESN'T HAVE TO.
SNAP
YOUR TRICKERY DOESN'T MATTER. I'M ALL POWERFUL NOW. *IMMORTAL.*

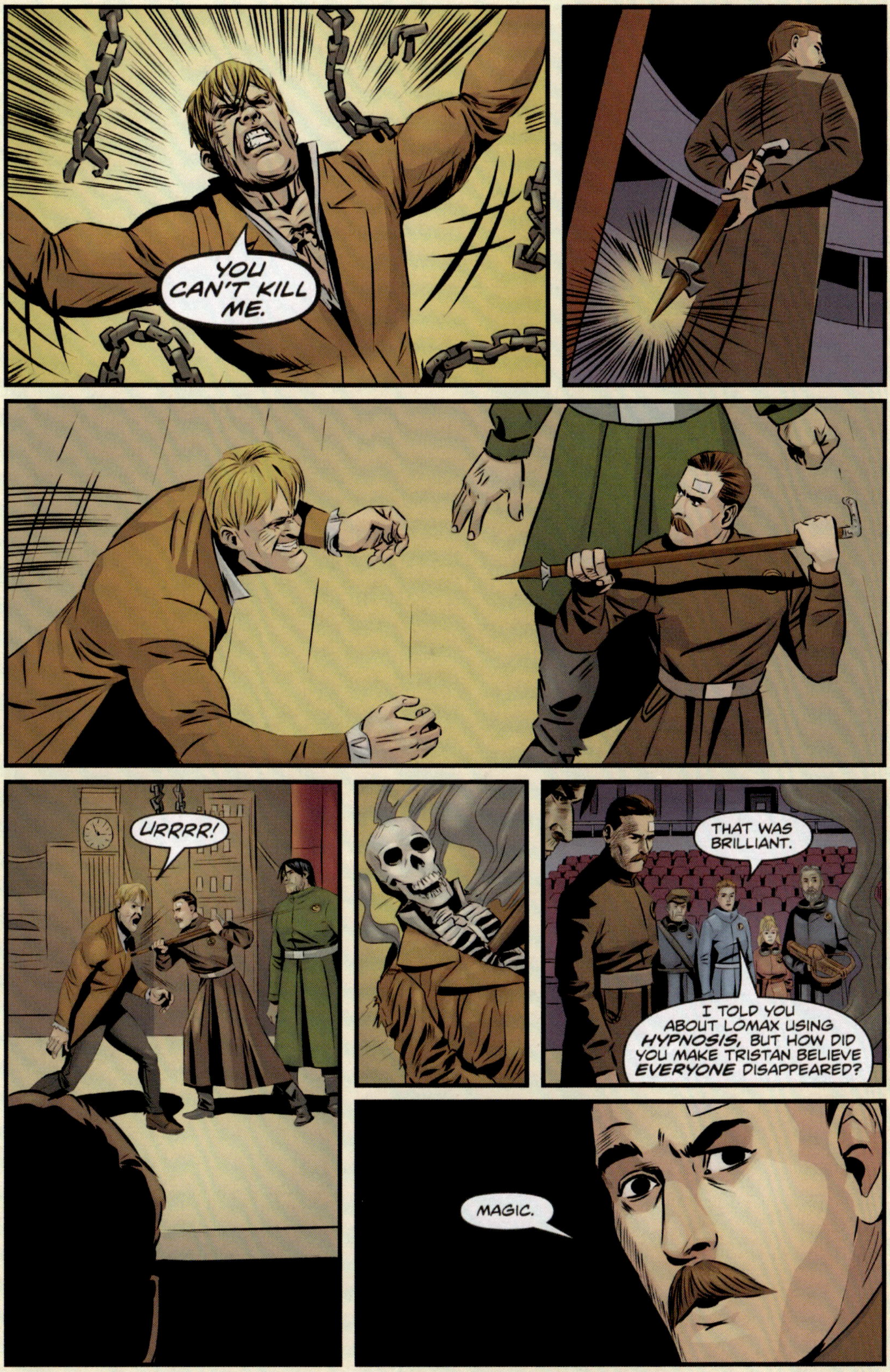
YOU CAN'T KILL ME.
URRRR!
THAT WAS BRILLIANT.
I TOLD YOU ABOUT LOMAX USING HYPNOSIS, BUT HOW DID YOU MAKE TRISTAN BELIEVE EVERYONE DISAPPEARED?
MAGIC.

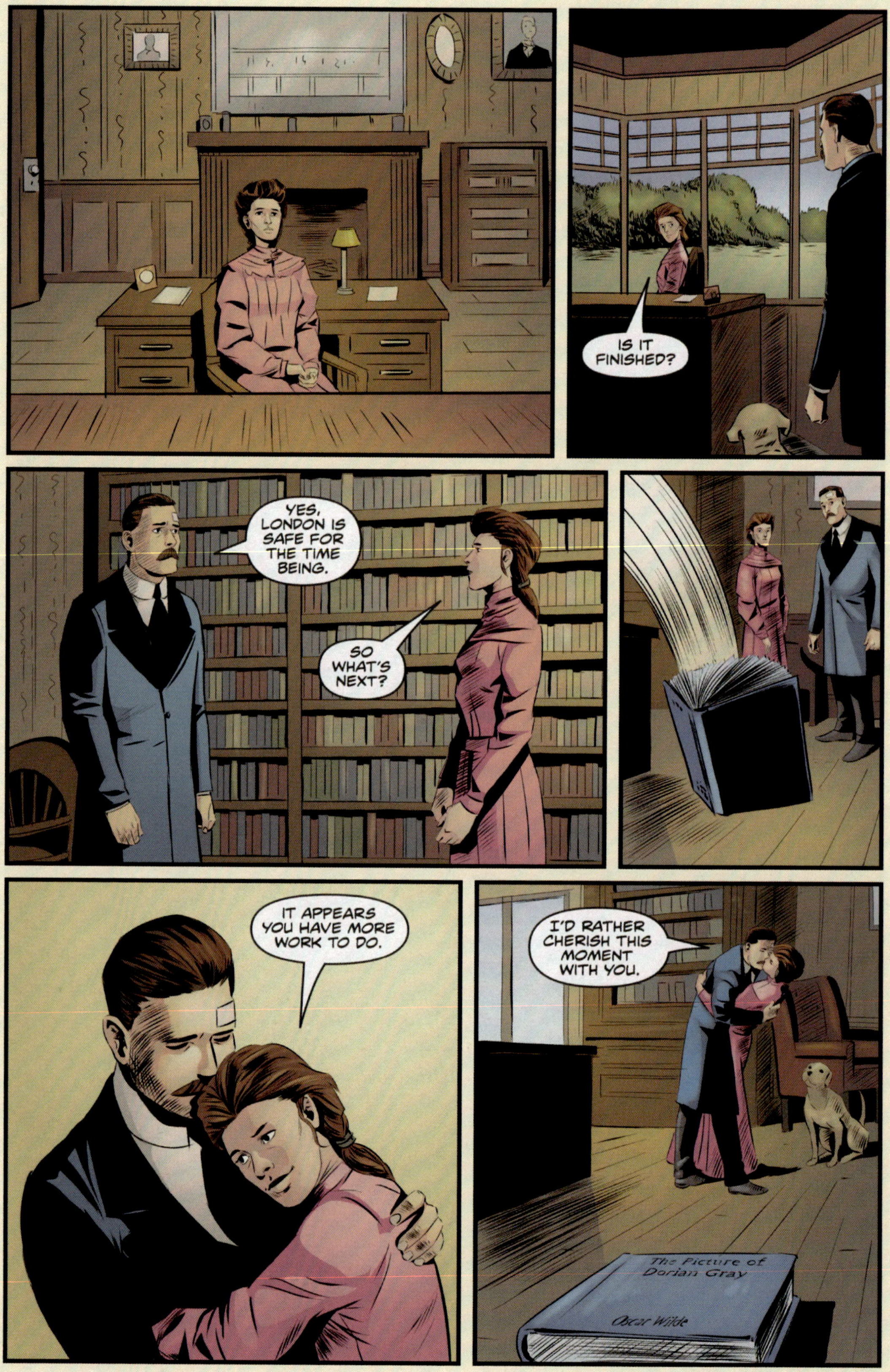
IS IT FINISHED?
YES, LONDON IS SAFE FOR THE TIME BEING.
SO WHAT'S NEXT?
IT APPEARS YOU HAVE MORE WORK TO DO.
I'D RATHER CHERISH THIS MOMENT WITH YOU.
The Picture of Dorian Gray
Oscar Wilde

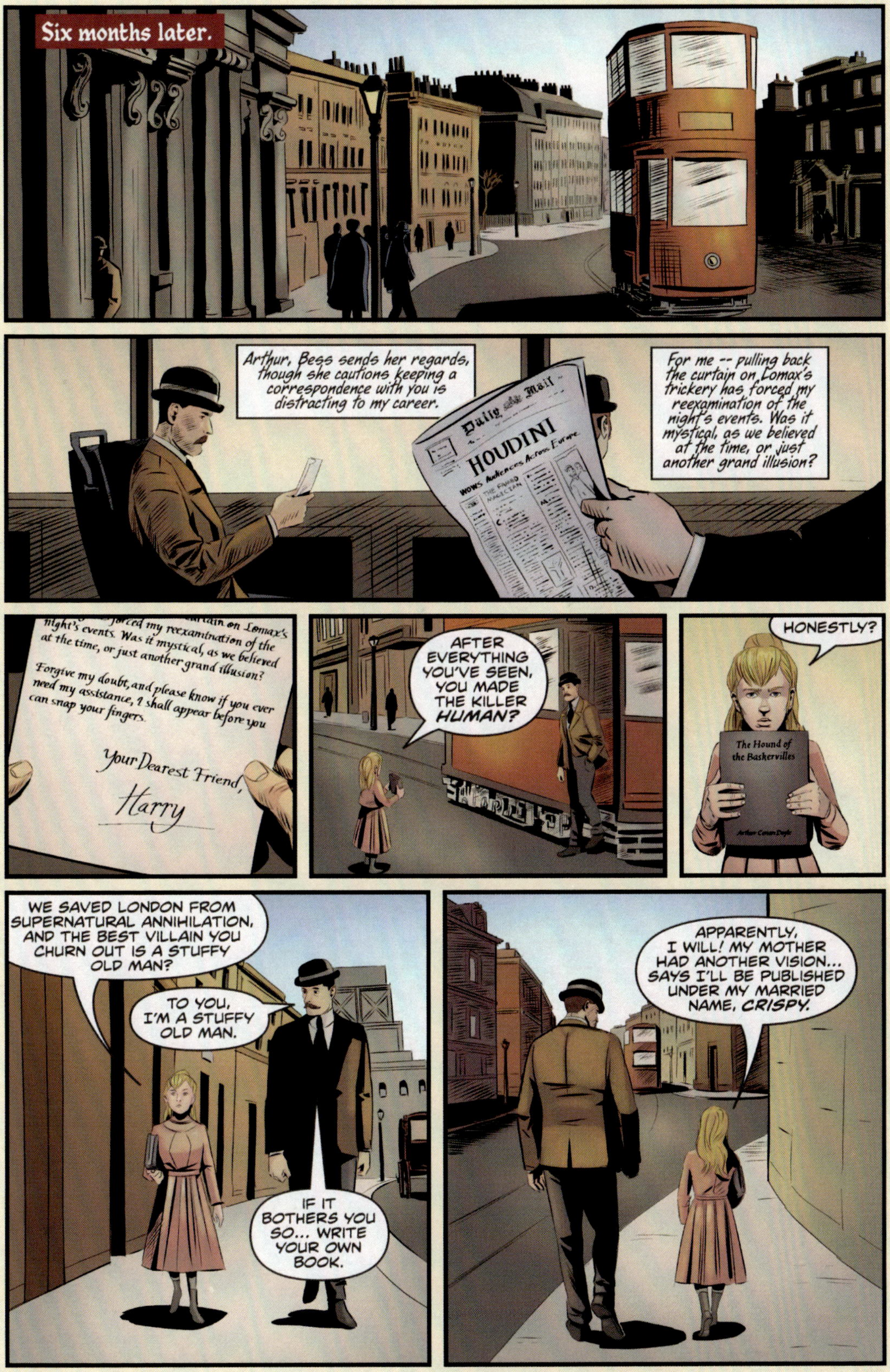
Six months later.
Arthur, Bess sends her regards, though she cautions keeping a correspondence with you is distracting to my career.
Daily Mail
HOUDINI
WOWS Audiences Across Europe
For me -- pulling back the curtain on Lomax's trickery has forced my reexamination of the night's events. Was it mystical, as we believed at the time, or just another grand illusion?
forced my reexamination of the night's events. Was it mystical, as we believed at the time, or just another grand illusion?
Forgive my doubt, and please know if you ever need my assistance, I shall appear before you can snap your fingers.
Your Dearest Friend,
Harry
AFTER EVERYTHING YOU'VE SEEN, YOU MADE THE KILLER HUMAN?
HONESTLY?
The Hound of the Baskervilles
Arthur Conan Doyle
WE SAVED LONDON FROM SUPERNATURAL ANNIHILATION, AND THE BEST VILLAIN YOU CHURN OUT IS A STUFFY OLD MAN?
TO YOU, I'M A STUFFY OLD MAN.
IF IT BOTHERS YOU SO... WRITE YOUR OWN BOOK.
APPARENTLY, I WILL! MY MOTHER HAD ANOTHER VISION... SAYS I'LL BE PUBLISHED UNDER MY MARRIED NAME. CRISPY.

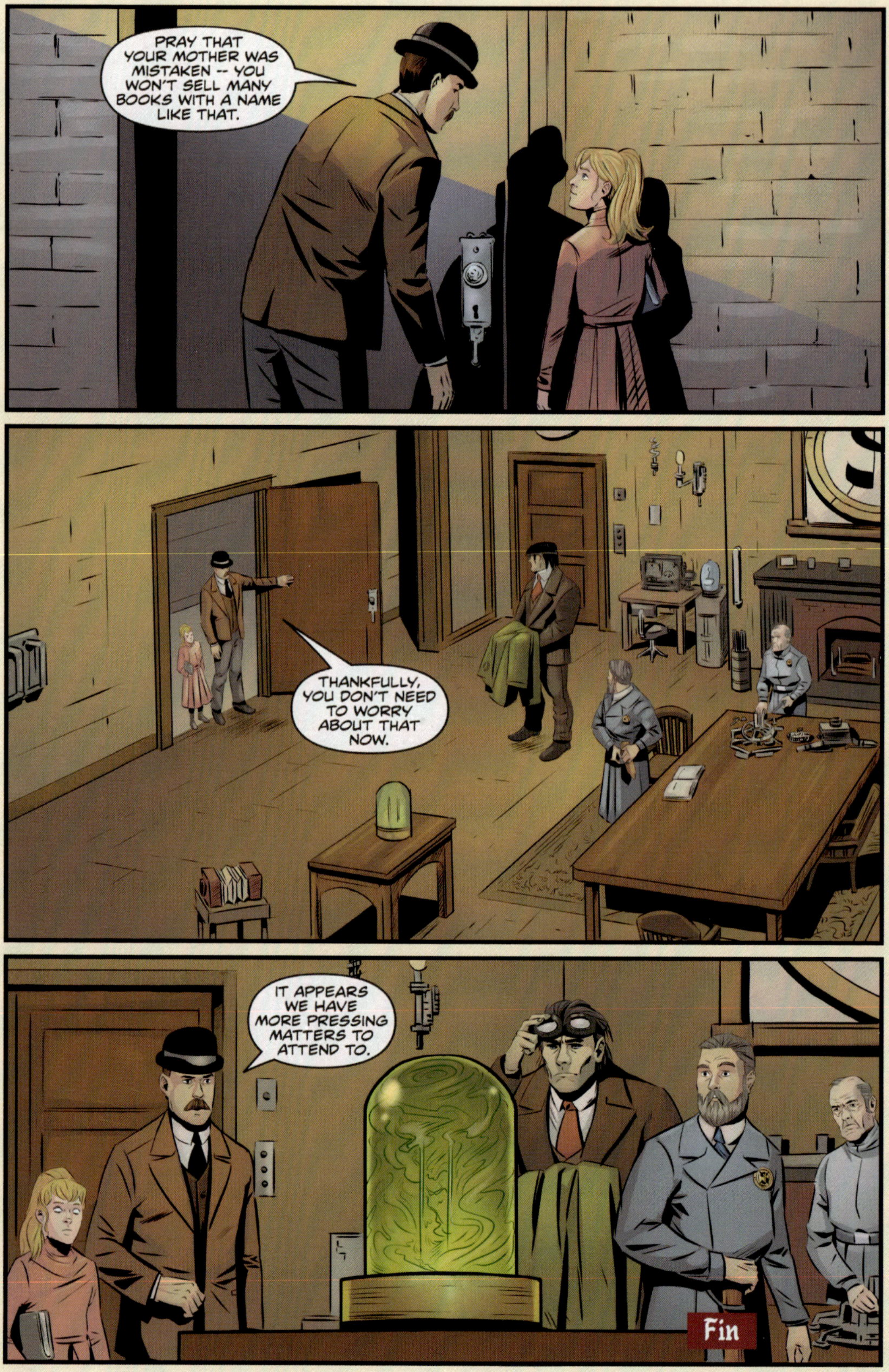
PRAY THAT YOUR MOTHER WAS MISTAKEN -- YOU WON'T SELL MANY BOOKS WITH A NAME LIKE THAT.
THANKFULLY, YOU DON'T NEED TO WORRY ABOUT THAT NOW.
IT APPEARS WE HAVE MORE PRESSING MATTERS TO ATTEND TO.
Fin